BEE STING CAKE

By the same author:

GREENWING & DART
Stargazy Pie
Bee Sting Cake
Whiskeyjack (forthcoming)

TALES FROM THE NINE WORLDS
Till Human Voices Wake Us
The Tower at the Edge of the World
In the Company of Gentlemen
Stone Speaks to Stone

THE SISTERS AVRAMAPUL
The Bride of the Blue Wind
The Warrior of the Third Veil (forthcoming)

The Seven Brides-to-Be of Generalissimo Vlad

BEE STING CAKE

Greenwing & Dart
Book Two

VICTORIA GODDARD

Underhill
Books

Grandview, PEI

2017

ISBN: 978-1-988908-01-4

First published by Underhill Books in 2017.

Underhill Books

4183 Murray Harbour Road

Grandview, PEI C0A 1A0

www.underhillbooks.com

To my family, for all their support.

Thank you.

Chapter One
The Honourable Rag has an Idea

"NO," I SAID, firmly.

"You haven't heard what it is!" Mr. Dart replied, laughing, as he shut the door to Elderflower Books behind him.

"Your mere presence in town on a Friday is sufficient. I'm not recovered from last weekend's disasters."

"Adventures, surely, Mr. Greenwing."

"If you insist, Mr. Dart."

Mr. Dart paused in the act of taking off his greatcoat, an action somewhat hampered by the petrified arm that was a result of last week's *adventures* (along with assorted cuts, scrapes, bruises, revelations, and ruined social reputations), and then nodded decisively. "Why, yes, I believe I do. Insist, that is, on the fact of adventures."

"Have a seat and a gingersnap," I said, and returned to my tallying-up of the day's transactions.

Mr. Dart complied, petting Mrs. Etaris' ginger cat (also named Gingersnap, which I presumed from the evidence was her favourite cookie), which seemed to consider him a particular friend. He stole the newspaper whose crossword I'd been solving earlier and stretched his legs out before the cheerfully burning stove.

I wrote down, A *Guide to the Beginning of a Collection*, by J. Kinross, and wondered whether the J stood for Jullanar or Jakory or Jessamine or even, Emperor help anyone else saddled with it, Jemis. (As a result of a lost bet, I was named after my grandfather's favourite racehorse. This was only the beginning of my life's minor difficulties.) It was probably Jakory or Jessamine; Jullanar, on account of the doings of the infamous heroine of the Red Company, was no longer a common name even in my own duchy, where it originated.

"Hey ho," said Mr. Dart. "They've found the lost heir to the Ironwoods."

I finished writing down three bees, the cost of the book, and dipped my pen into the inkwell again. "Should we be interested?"

"If you want to marry rich—the heir's a 'young gentlewoman of two-and-twenty', according to the *New Salon*. I wonder how they came to lose her in the Fall? Unless she came from a branch line of the family."

"How distressing that the *New Salon* believes only age and wealth are of importance. I suppose if one is considering mercenary marriage, that is what matters. If studying law at Inveragory doesn't work out, perhaps I will be forced to."

"You could put an advertisement in the paper."

"'Item: young man of excellent education and difficult family seeks wealthy bride. Tendency to social disaster mostly counterbalanced by skill at crossword puzzles and cross-country running.'"

"I wonder if the Honourable Rag will take odds on your getting in," Mr. Dart said, chuckling. "Here's another gem that might concern you more nearly: 'Whatever has happened to the fabled honey of the Woods Noirell? Once one of the notable delicacies of the kingdom, the supply has been dwindling at an alarming rate over the past three years and there are rumours there will be none at all for this coming Winterturn. Indeed, the last barrel to be had in Kingsford sold at auction last week for three gold emperors.' Strewth. How big do you reckon the barrel was?"

"I have no idea," I replied shortly. My mother's people were from the Woods, but apart from one visit to my grandmother when I was nine, and one vicious letter in response to mine on the occasion of my mother's death, I had never had anything to do with them. I wiped my pen, re-inked the nib, and returned to my tally.

B. Horpf's *Fauna of the Inner Seas* (of which world? The cover did not indicate) cost a wheatear and had not been bought by anyone despite many protestations of interest. I set it to one side and picked up the receipt for A. Hickton's *The Arts and Artisans of the Wide Sea Islanders of Western Zunidh in Three Volumes*, which was also illustrated, cost nine wheatears, and had been bought by Sir Hamish Lorkin's valet, who must be very well paid indeed. I approved.

That Mrs. Etaris trusted me to close up her store should not have made me so pleased. I ought to have been outraged and indignant at the mere thought that someone might not trust a gentleman such as myself. But I am, to my extended family's voluble regret, a peculiar sort of gentleman, and my late stepfather, a Charese merchant named Mr. Buchance, had always impressed upon me the sacred responsibility of holding the keys of commerce, on which topic alone was he at all poetic.

"Oh, there's a new play coming to Yellton—perhaps we can go after the Fair—*Three Years Gone, the Tragicomedy of the* ..." Mr. Dart's voice trailed off as he read the rest of the subtitle, which was 'the Tragicomedy of the Traitor of Loe'—who was my father.

"I've already seen it," I said, even more shortly.

"Really?"

At his aghast tone I smiled involuntarily. "When I visiting Hal in Fillering Pool, his mother took us. They didn't know the subtitle or the subject, and … well, I hadn't told them my surname. They thought it was just Greene."

"They must have wondered at your reaction."

"I was sick enough from everything else that they took it as a relapse."

Everything else was heartbreak, withdrawal from an unknown addiction to wireweed, and some sort of sensitivity or allergic reaction to magic exacerbated by the fact that my university *amour*, Lark, had not only been giving me the wireweed without my knowledge but also stealing the magic I hadn't known I possessed. Finding out that that was what the spring's illness had been had also been a feature of last week's *adventures*, and I still had no idea what to do with the information, besides endure the lingering effects.

I finished my written account and began to sort through the coins. "Lock the door, would you?" I asked Mr. Dart, but even as he heaved a theatrical sigh and arose to do so, the door opened and the Honourable Roald Ragnor fair blew in.

He caught at his hat, but the draught gusting through the door scattered my papers and flipped it out of his grasp.

I came round from the back of the counter to pick up the papers and, since I was there, the hat. Mr. Dart shut the door, causing a sharp diminishment in noise. I stood up slowly, hat in hand, to find the Honourable Rag staring down at me with an expression of the most vacuous bonhomie.

I handed him his hat. He didn't immediately take it, and for a moment I had a sudden vision of what the three of us might look like to an outside observer: three young gentlemen of the same age, dressed in three iterations of current fashion, still bearing the influences of our respective universities. Tara, Stoneybridge, and Morrowlea: the Three Rivals among the Circle Schools, each of them considered the greatest university in the world, perhaps in all nine worlds.

Tara, the oldest, largest, and most famous, positioned both topographically and metaphysically on the horn of Orio Bay opposite the famous prison, the rich, corrupt, and historic capital of Orio City lying in the crescent between.

Stoneybridge, caring more for excellence than reputation, one of a cluster of schools in and around the small Charese city of the same name, part of a network of scholarship and sports.

And Morrowlea, by far the smallest, with the finest architecture, and from its isolated campus on a hill in the rich bucolic landscape of South Erlingale the heart of radical politics and social revolutions.

Mr. Dart took the hat out of my hand. I returned to the commercial side of the counter. The Honourable Rag blinked amiably around the room. "Mrs. Etaris ain't here?"

"No, I'm closing tonight."

"Good boy," he said, bestowing a knowing smirk on Mr. Dart, who was examining the hat with insincere interest.

Neither of them said anything further, so—in something closer to the revolutionary spirit, the irony of which did not escape me—I tallied the coins as quickly as I could without running into error.

Mr. Buchance had taught me the trick of doing so, measuring a stack of coins against my finger, stacking approximately even amounts before using a level (in this case, a handy copy of *Wines of Northwestern Oriole excluding the Lesser Arcady*) to check the quantities. I had been so dexterous at this that at Morrowlea I had almost always been in charge of money in the little shop the students ran in the summers.

I went through pennies, bees, wheatears, and a few gold emperors in short order, double-checked my count against what I was pleased to determine was the same result in my paper tally, and separated out float from deposit stacks without re-counting individual coins. Closing the till and deposit box, I looked up to see Mr. Dart and the Honourable Rag staring at me in some amazement.

"I wonder if there's a way to bet on that," the Honourable Rag murmured.

"Is that all you think about?" I retorted, gathering together the paraphernalia on the desk. My pen slipped and rolled towards Roald, who took it and proceeded to tap his fingers with it.

"Oh, sometimes it's hunting—or fishing. This time of year, it's all the question of the Fair wagers, o'course. Who're your favourites? Mr. Dart?"

Mr. Dart resettled his sling. "Rigby's got a new chorister for the egg and spoon."

"Chicken stakes," the Honourable Rag said dismissively, throwing himself into the other armchair and nearly squashing the cat. I picked her up and stroked her soothingly.

"Well, then?" Mr. Dart asked challengingly. "Whom do you fancy for the bell-hammer?"

"Roddy Kulfield, surely," I put in.

They both looked at me in surprise. Mr. Dart said, "He's gone to sea."

"I beg your pardon?"

"To be smith and assistant draughtsman on some botanical expedition or other going out West."

"I think I remember reading about it in the spring." I frowned, trying to remember where. "No, not reading—someone was telling me—but I was so damnably ill—"

"Ill?"

If the Honourable Rag had been one of the town gossips, I'd have expanded in the hopes of ameliorating my reputation (which was suffering under the belief that I had missed my stepfather's funeral on purpose), but since gossip was neither a vice nor a virtue of his, I shrugged. "All through the spring and early summer, when I was jauntering around the four duchies."

"Not paying much attention to anything, were you?"

"Apparently not." I decided it was time to change the subject. "Who's sponsoring this expedition, then?"

"The Duke of Fillering Pool. M'father says he's mad about plants, but at least it's not the magical properties of wool, like the last one."

"Poor Hal," I said, laughing.

"D'ye know him, then?"

There was something about the Honourable Rag's habit of slurring some of his words that invariably got my back up, even though I was fairly sure it was something he'd picked up at Tara. Possibly because it was something he'd picked up at Tara. "He was my roommate at Morrowlea."

"Room-mate?" replied the Honourable Rag, as if the concept

was wholly unfamiliar.

Or then again, perhaps he was simply drunk.

"Everyone was assigned rooms to share with another student in their year, as a way of fostering community and egalitarianism. Not though it wasn't obvious that Hal came from a noble background from his speech and manner, but I never guessed it was so high until he told me."

If it had been just Mr. Dart, I would have told the story of how Hal had stood there that first evening, unsure of how to take off his boots without assistance. He'd been embarrassed by his helplessness, and I, who had never graduated to a valet (something Mr. Buchance decried as a 'poncy northern custom' and accordingly refused to pay for), was heartened by being able to teach such an obviously grand aristocrat something useful.

"Anyway," I said, realizing the silence had gone somewhat over-long, "he must have mentioned it while I was staying with him at Fillering Pool this summer. Very likely I paid no attention. I'm sure he's unutterably proud of the whole thing and wishes he were the botanist instead of the patron."

The Honourable Rag chuckled. There was an infinitesimal warming in his attitude, to which I was about to respond when his next words demonstrated why.

"That could be very useful indeed."

I turned to fuss with the pile of *New Salons* to avoid showing my disdain quite so obviously, cat squirming in my grasp. "That I know a duke?"

"That you know an imperial duke, no less," he replied with unimpaired vacuous bonhomie. "There aren't so very many imperial titles floating around, and most of the Northwest Oriolese ones stand empty."

I smiled wryly. "They've just found the Ironwoods'—an heir-ess."

"A gentlewoman of twenty-two years of age," Mr. Dart put in. "Just in case you need to remedy your fortune at some point, Master Roald. She sounds quite in your style."

"She must be quite the antidote if she's not called a beauty, with all that fortune behind her."

The cat took exception to my involuntary squeeze, and jumped out of my hands with an affronted meow. The Honourable Rag nudged her out of his way with one of his shining black boots (which he undoubtedly required the assistance of his valet to don and doff), to which the cat responded with a purr and a beatific rub against the sole.

I wished with a sudden fury that I was working at the book-store out of pure political idealism and not brute practical necessity.

"I hear you've been out, ah, running, Greenwing," the Honourable Rag said, tapping my pen on his teeth with a deeply irritating noise. "Practicing for one of the Fair races, are you?"

Mr. Dart raised his eyebrows at me in polite wonder—for the footraces were invariably the province of the lower classes of Ragnor society—and all my good intentions to be keep my head down, avoid giving the gossips any further ammunition, make it safely to the Winterturn Assizes, &cetera and &cetera, went out the window.

"Why, yes, actually," I said, firmly. "The three-mile circuit."

"Ah," said the Honourable Rag, winking at Mr. Dart. "Good boy."

Chapter Two
Mrs. Henny has an Idea

"HAVE YOU WRITTEN to your friend Hal since you came back?" Mr. Dart demanded.

I turned back from latching the door behind the Honourable Rag, who had finally left after eating all the gingersnaps. "No, I haven't written anyone." I tried to think back through the summer, which felt enormously long ago, and half-fogged in my memory. My heart sank. "I don't think I've written since I left Kingsbury. I saw a book and thought he'd like it. And then I went along the coast to Ghilousette and just felt so ... down ... I didn't write."

"Kingsbury was when you last wrote to me, too. You went to a museum of naval architecture and sent me that funny booklet about ships' figureheads. With no return address or hint of where you planned on going, except for a certain suggestion that you wanted to go away and not see anyone ever again."

"Did I say that?" I frowned, trying to remember. I'd been having recurring bouts of tremors, nausea, and vicious headaches combined with a devastating lassitude and total disinclination for company, all salted with occasional unnerving blanks of memory.

Quite the opposite of how I'd been for the three years before, when I had delighted in company and activity and merriment and wit. Though there had been tremors and headaches before the winter illness, and feverish energy, and perhaps all of that was due to the wireweed and the ensorcellments, and the real Jemis Greenwing was disaster-prone and dull.

"You were so poorly that you don't remember your friend talking about an expedition across the Western Sea he was sponsoring—"

"I do," I protested. "I remember him mentioning it, now that I'm thinking about it. When we were looking at his estate he told me where he was going to put the arboretum. I thought he was joking but he must have been serious. I kept going in and out of things."

"He must be worried sick," Mr. Dart said bluntly.

I sat down in the other armchair. "I beg your pardon."

He tugged at the knot on his sling until it sat better. "I was afraid your last letter had a—a melancholic tinge to it. But I thought you were still writing to your stepfather, so I tried not to worry. It was only when Mrs. Buchance asked me if I had any idea where you were, after your stepfather died, that I learned no one had heard from you all summer. By then it was too late to find you easily. You *must* write to Hal. Immediately."

"What? Why?"

He tore a page out of my notebook and handed it to me. "Write. Now. We can still make the last post if you hurry."

"What am I to say in such a hurry?"

"That you're alive and sane and are sorry you haven't written since *June*, but as you learned last week you were recovering from

Lark drugging and bespelling you."

"I can't just leave a letter there."

"You said he doesn't know your surname—nor more than you're from Fiellan, either, I wager? Come now, Mr. Greenwing. He has no way to find out what happened to you."

I squirmed. The quarter chime came through the window faintly, and he made a hurry-up gesture to me. "Go to. There's no post after this till Monday."

"Dammit, Roald stole my pen."

He pushed me the pen-stand from the other side of the desk, and I relented and wrote a brief and totally ridiculous missive that would probably worry Hal more than my silence. "There," I said resentfully, and under Mr. Dart's watchful eye got up to take an envelope from the box under the counter.

"We have five minutes till the posting coach comes."

I smiled insincerely and made a show of writing

His Grace the Honourable Halioren Lord Leaveringham

Duke of Fillering Pool

Leaveringham Castle

Fillering Pool

Ronderell

"It's pronounced 'Lingham'," I informed him, picking up the deposit box, which I had to deliver to the post office as well.

"More haste, less waste."

"I don't believe that is how the proverb usually goes." But I moved quickly to lock the door and we proceeded through town towards Small Square, where the Ragnor Arms and the post office faced each other.

Mr. Dart stayed outside, to bodily prevent the coach—which

didn't appear to have arrived yet—from leaving without my letter, I supposed. I went inside in a fit of irritation and guilt that I had alarmed him that much, as I must have done to make him so alert to Hal's likely distress. I was more anxious than I wished to show about whether Hal thought I might have done myself a mischief, and nothing to do about it except wonder and look for 'Mr. Greene.' And worry. Hal was something of a worry-wart. He would be biting his nails over his ship's adventures.

Perhaps I could find an expedition to sail off on, and not bother about rectifying my father's inheritance—*my* inheritance—from my uncle, and instead of being the son of the infamous Jakory Greenwing I could be—

I'd always be my father's son, I thought ruefully as it came to my turn at the counter, and old Mrs. Henny the postmistress said, "Welladay and Emperor bless, young Mr. Greenwing, I thought you'd forgotten the use of a post office this summer."

"I was unwell," I said, and set the deposit box on the counter with my letter on top. "Trying to remedy the matter now, Mrs. Henny. How are you?"

She made no move to take the money, instead giving me a piercing once-over. I felt absurdly naked under the scrutiny, aware that at least I did look as if I'd been ill, if my skinniness and what I had been assured by numerous people was not so very peaky a look as all that, truly, were any indication. I sighed. "I'd like to get this letter on today's post if I can, Mrs. Henny."

Mrs. Henny started as if she'd fallen asleep staring. She was somewhere on the north side of seventy, with twinkling eyes and round red cheeks like a Winterturn doll, but I had always eyed her a bit askance because I distinctly remembered my father warning me that she was the best player of Poacher he'd ever met.

I had been too young to wonder then, as I did now, when on earth my father had ever played Poacher with Mrs. Henny. At the time I had very earnestly promised never ever to attempt cheating her. "For you will surely pay for it if you do," my father had said in an awful voice, while my mother laughed and told him not to put ideas into my head.

Looking at Mrs. Henny, who was like a plump dove in her proportions, I was inclined to think the warning more of social regret than physical ruin.

Though, as I was coming to learn, in Ragnor Bella you never knew.

"You're enjoying working for Mrs. Etaris, are you?"

It sounded more an order than a question. "Yes, ma'am."

"You and Mr. Dart had an eventful time of it last weekend, I hear."

"Yes, ma'am."

"Any plans for the Fair?"

And the part of me that could not truckle to the Honourable Rag raised its stubborn head once more, and I said, "Yes, ma'am, I am going to enter the three-mile race."

"Are you now?"

It might have been my imagination but I fancied I saw sharp calculations running behind those twinkling blue eyes. If she were a superb Poacher player, she would be very good indeed at making calculations of character and odds and tall tales.

"I hear you've been out … training? Planning ahead, were you?"

The running I'd been doing the past week had been light conditioning, nothing like the speed or endurance I was still more than capable of despite the spring's illness. I smiled lopsidedly, wondering what my father would have thought of my choosing to run in the poor man's steeplechase. He'd been an officer through and through.

I had not realized before my return home how much adulthood was like a huge and endless game of Poacher. Well, my father might not have approved of the poor man's steeplechase, but he *had* taught me how to play *that* game.

I smiled, winked, did not say I had trained for three years on Morrowlea's cross-country team.

"Oh, I merely dawdle, Mrs. Henny. I've Mrs. Etaris' deposit box here."

"Hmm? Oh yes, Mr. Greenwing. Emperor bless, I must be getting old. Here is the slip and here is the stamp on your letter—to a duke, now? High friends you made at Morrowlea, Mr. Greenwing—over in Ronderell, so that will be two wheatears, please, and you tell Mrs. Etaris I'll not be at the meeting, a'cause my granddaughter's confinement, so she'll have to make certain the recipes are true herself."

True was an odd choice of word—but Mrs. Henny was old, and perhaps that was what they used to say, once upon a time. "I'll tell her," I promised, giving her the money. "This is for the Embroidery Circle, I take it?"

Mrs. Henny chuckled and actually tapped her nose at me. "What else would it be? Emperor bless. There's the coach at last. The bag's tied up so give the man your letter yourself, now."

I went out, letter in hand, to find Mr. Dart laughing at something said by one of the passengers alighting from the coach. They all looked as if they were in the process of being jollied out of what was probably justified disgruntlement, helped by Mr. Dart, who could be effortlessly cheerful to any passing stranger.

And then one of the last passengers disembarked, turning as he did to help a stout woman out of the carriage behind him, and as he smiled up at her I realized I knew him.

Chapter Three
Mr. Dart has an Idea

"HAL," I SAID, holding out my letter. Mr. Dart turned from the coachman with a quizzical frown, then followed my progress over, whereupon his eyebrows lifted in astonishment.

I looked at Hal, who was dressed like a journeyman Scholar at best, and frowned quizzically myself. Hal had not heard me, being still preoccupied with the stout woman, so I cleared my throat and tried more loudly. "Hal. Hal!"

"I believe that young gentleman is calling you, my dear," said the stout woman.

Hal opened his mouth in some shock. And, I saw, blatant relief. "Jemis?"

"The very same." I considered his expression. "I take it you weren't expecting me to meet you?"

"No, your letters must have gone astray."

I held up the one in my hand. "Sorry."

"Oh, is that for me?" He smiled at the woman. "Madam Lezré, are you certain you will not need any further escort?"

"Young man, you have already gone *far* out of your way. I'll settle myself in the inn here, where I've stayed before, and will get all my things ready for the expedition into the Fair. You see your friend and don't you fret about me. There's more than honey in my sights, let me tell you." She patted him once more on the shoulder and stumped away towards the Arms.

Hal regarded me narrowly. "Is that truly a letter for me? I am entirely astonished. Also relieved to find you at last. I was worried you might have—" He made a face. "Anyhow, glad to be wrong there."

Mr. Dart did not say anything, but then he didn't have to.

I cleared my throat, but before I could formulate either apology or question a cat ran out in front of the horses. I stepped back out of the coachman's way as he made to soothe them, and trod on someone's foot behind me.

"Oh, I am dreadfully sorry," I began, turning, only to find that I had stumbled into my aunt. She was evidently preparing to be polite in return when she saw it was me, and instead of either smiling or speaking went a pinched white and jerked back her skirts.

Here came the next hand at Poacher, I thought. I bowed. With a heel-click *and* a curlicue hand gesture with my hat. "I do beg your pardon, Lady Flora." My uncle was staring down his nose at me from her other side, so for good measure I bowed to him as well. "Good evening, Sir Vorel."

"Good evening!" Mr. Dart chimed in, sketching a bow. My aunt and uncle looked frigidly at us both.

"Mr. Dart," Sir Vorel said curtly at last, nodded at me with the barest possible minimum of courtesy, then swivelled his wife on his arm to lead her to the inn.

I sighed and turned back to Hal, who was watching this mortification with interest. "Charming people," he said, grinning.

"Oh, entirely."

Mr. Dart looked at me and then at Hal. I moved out of the coachman's way again as he lifted down trunks, valises, sacks, and a few wicker baskets smelling incongruously like smoke. I sneezed reflexively and reached for a handkerchief. "Hal, this is Mr. Dart— Mr. Dart, this is—"

"Hal Leaveringham," said Hal firmly. It was the name he'd given when we were ambling around Erlingale, before the somewhat awkward conversation when Marcan, met by servants sent by his father, confessed he was the Count of Westmoor and Hal, after a robust evening spent teasing Marcan, eventually admitted that yes, it was spelled Leaveringham like the castle and he was actually the Imperial Duke of Fillering Pool.

"Aha!" said Mr. Dart, shaking the hand Hal had held out in eastern fashion. "It is indeed pronounced Lingham, is it? We were talking about you just now."

"Were you?" Hal said doubtfully. "Seems a frightful coincidence."

"Nevertheless true," Mr. Dart assured him.

"Do you live here, Jemis? I mean, if you are being disdained by the local gentry I presume you've been here longer than a week."

"Barely," I replied, laughing along with Mr. Dart. "Whatever are you doing here, Hal?"

"Oh, looking for my great-uncle, who's gone walkabout, and investigating a business opportunity or two. Yes, my good man?"

This was the coachman, who had one of the crates in hand. I sneezed again and looked doubtfully from the crate to the golden ring I had acquired last week and which generally served to suppress my sneezing. The coachman nodded deferentially at Mr. Dart before addressing Hal. "Staying on again, sir? Or do you want your luggage down?"

"I thought this was the end of your route?"

The coachman smiled and touched his cap. "I go back north from here, aye, but up through Yellem before I get back on the king's highway through Middle Fiellan."

"Perhaps I shall explore Yellem one day, but it will not be today nor even tomorrow. Thank you." The coachman pulled down the last item from the roof of the coach, a battered leather and canvas knapsack I recognized from our walking tour. Hal exchanged this for a coin of some sort, ostentatiously rejected the crate (to the coachman's mirth, this evidently being in the way of a running joke), and then turned expectantly to me.

"So! I am looking for my great-uncle, you have been here barely longer than a week but this is enough to raise hackles. What next?"

"We could go to the Ragglebridge for a drink," I suggested.

"Not the—what is it? Ah yes, the Ragnor Arms?" Hal laughed, reading the sign and then waving at the stout woman as she emerged to collect the crates. "But yes, let us. Riding coach is thirsty work."

"You said that about walking."

"It was. We are not all so sober and respectable as you this summer, Jemis."

Mr. Dart laughed. "I think we will get along—Mr. Leaveringham. As I was about to say earlier, why don't we go to Dartington? You're not working this weekend, are you, Jemis?"

"No, only on market Saturdays."

Hal gave me a curious glance, no doubt wondering what the

'work' was when I was still dressed as a young gentleman—but I had not, during those teasing conversations, mentioned anything of my family, and he and Marcan had probably assumed (and quite correctly) that it was neither so titled nor so grand as theirs.

There would be a lot of explanations about my family tonight.

"Perfect," Mr. Dart was saying. "You'll be very welcome to stay, both of you. Have you any other baggage, Mr. Leaveringham?"

"Do call me Hal. No, the rest ended up in the river at Otterburn, and my valet's taken it back to Fillering Pool."

"I smell a story," Mr. Dart said, and took Hal's arm to lead him towards the north gate. I picked up Hal's dropped knapsack, which was heavy, and trailed on after until Mr. Dart suddenly interrupted his merry account of the various charms of Ragnor Bella to ask if I wanted to go home for anything.

"I suspect I shall need at least a change of clothes," I said dryly, and we turned turned down the side street towards technically-my-stepmother Mrs. Buchance's house. When we reached it, the door was ajar and the sound of much commotion spilled forth, along with the smell of baking.

"Mmm," said Mr. Dart. "Is it tea-time yet, do you think?"

I frowned at him and pushed open the door. Mrs. Buchance was standing in the front hall, bouncing a wailing Lamissa in her hands while trying to finish a conversation with her sister-in-law Mrs. Inglesides, a pretty plump woman who appeared to be increasing. Ricocheting around them, up and down the stairs, in and out of the dining room, and chasing a mysterious barking dog were my sisters and a handful of small boys I supposed were Mrs. Inglesides's children.

Sela, the younger of my two half-sisters, came barrelling around the hall corner, saw us, squealed, and launched herself at me. As I caught her, she cried, "Jemis is home!" in piercing tones.

There was a moment's pause as everyone turned to stare, and then Lamissa started to wail again and all the mobile children, accompanied by the dog, clamoured up to us. "Did you bring us anything?" Sela asked, squirming in my arms so she could bat her eyes at me.

"Not tonight," I said apologetically.

"What about a story?" Lauren began, interrupted first by Sela saying, "You have to say *please*," and then by several boys who all began shouting out suggestions for what story, except for the smallest boy, who poked me in the leg. I set Sela back on the ground and leaned over the boy, who whispered, "Toby ate a *whole* cake," and then buried his head in my breeches, overcome apparently at this revelation.

Not having any idea whether Toby was a step-cousin or the dog, I opted not to say anything. Lauren and Sela started dancing, the dog reappeared, barking, and Mrs. Inglesides' voice went louder and louder as she tried to make herself heard. She was saying something about baking and the Dartington Harvest Fair. I tried to extricate myself from Zangora, who was swinging off my arm, and glanced at my friends.

They both looked utterly stunned.

I grinned at Mrs. Buchance. We'd more or less progressed, over the past week, to calling each other 'Jemis' and 'Ellie', at least in the house, when we didn't forget and go more formal. It made me feel less of a lodger, for which I was grateful.

"Now, children," she said, "leave Jemis alone—oh, and Mr. Dart! How wonderful, we were just trialling some recipes for the

Fair. You'll have to help us eat them." She nodded at her sister-in-law, who nodded back decisively, as one with a secret, and then began to gather up coats and hats and wooden toys from where they lay strewn about the hall.

"I should be delighted, ma'am," replied Mr. Dart gravely.

I managed to disentangle myself from the overwrought boy so that I could let my friends across the threshold. Mrs. Buchance handed me Lamissa, who had, incredibly, fallen asleep, and turned to greet Mr. Dart properly, whereupon she saw Hal. "Oh!" she said again, this time more uncertainly. "You've brought another friend?"

Despite his outfit, Hal stood like a duke, and, being dark-skinned and long-nosed, looked like one, too. He bowed politely to Mrs. Buchance. "Hal," I said, flustered as Lamissa fussed slightly, "Mrs. Buchance and Mrs. Inglesides. Ellie, this is Hal Leavering-ham, a very good friend of mine from Morrowlea. He came on the mail coach."

She curtsied, her expression welcoming if confused. "Will you be staying with us, Mr. Lingham?"

He cast me an equally bemused glance, then bowed again. "Wouldn't want to put you out of countenance, ma'am, on such short notice. I got off the coach to stretch my legs, and there was Jemis. He promptly suggested a drink, Mr. Dart here invited us to—Dartington, was it?—for the weekend, and Jemis decided he needed a few things."

"Come and have cake, at least," Mrs. Buchance said, smiling more brightly. "Nora, will you come?"

"I've eaten enough cake for a week," Mrs. Inglesides said, "and I must take advantage of the evening to myself. Good evening, gentlemen. Now, you be good," she added firmly to miscellaneous children, deposited her pile of coats on the bottom of the stair rail, and departed.

"*Will* you read us a story, Jemis?" Sela asked, trying to look winsome.

"Later," Mrs. Buchance said. "Take your cousins outside to play for now."

Sela pouted, but the dog chose that moment to start barking hysterically at something out the back, and all the children still in the hall ran off to see what he had found. In the sudden silence my ears rang.

"I had hoped you might go out with Mr. Dart again this evening," Mrs. Buchance said, taking Lamissa back from me. "My sister-in-law's brother is coming to visit for the fair, and she very much wanted to get the house ready, so I said I would take my nephews for the weekend. It does make for a noisy household, I am afraid. Come back to the kitchen. You will find we are not very formal, Mr. Leaveringham."

Hal and Mr. Dart were both still looking stunned, but increasingly amused. I grinned at their astonishment and led the way down the hall.

I made coffee while Mrs. Buchance cut the cakes. She set Lamissa on Mr. Dart's lap, despite his protests that he had never held a baby before.

"Don't you visit your tenants, Mr. Dart?" I tried, but he made a face and said he left that to his brother and Hamish. Hal said, "I do," and took Lamissa with a better grip, though as she was nearly walking she could sit up for herself just fine.

Mrs. Buchance gave each of the three of us three slices of cake—a blackberry cream, a chocolate hazelnut, and some sort of layered pear and apple confection—and then poured the coffee and smiled warmly. "What brings you to Ragnor Bella, Mr. Leaveringham? Visiting Jemis? Or are you here for the Dartington Fair?"

"*Am* I here for the Fair? I have been hearing nothing but the wildest speculation about the Dartington Fair since we left Yrchester."

"What's the gossip on the mail coach?" Mr. Dart asked. Mrs. Buchance also looked keenly intrigued.

"Gossip is that the baking competition is likely to be fierce—and if this is the quality of the offerings, ma'am, I can well see why—shall you enter your name in, Jemis, for a cake?"

"You're the better baker, Hal."

"No one else creams butter and honey as well as you."

"Why, thank you," I replied, before catching the expression on Mrs. Buchance's face and subsiding in embarrassment.

"Perhaps you can enter together," Mr. Dart said, with obvious calculation—no doubt as to potential bets on the topic.

"If it's permitted, I'd be delighted. We have nothing so exciting in Fillering Pool, let me tell you. No one gossips about *our* summer fair across three baronies. As we came south the more serious-minded kept trying to get on topic of the current crop of legislation or the dangers of highwaymen or the strange lack of Noirell honey, but everyone else wanted to gossip about how Mad Jack Greenwing's son is back from university and the bets are accordingly *wide* open. I am delighted to find you're a local, Jemis, I desire greatly to meet the man."

"Indeed," I said weakly.

Mrs. Buchance said, "I think I had better see what the children are up to," and hastened off before we could do more than half-stand.

Mr. Dart caught my eye. "Perhaps I had best use the privy." He disappeared almost as quickly.

Hal frowned. "Is something wrong? Your sister and Mr. Dart—"

"She's not my sister. My stepfather's second wife."

"... I see."

I sighed. "Probably you don't. I didn't tell you before, but—"

"Jemis!" cried Mr. Dart, running back in, his expression so shocked we both stood up in alarm. "You *must* come!"

Hal and I followed him out to the back garden, where seven little boys and girls and one woman stood with their heads tilted back and their mouths open as they stared at the sky.

I tilted my head back. My mouth opened of its own accord when I saw what they were looking at.

It was a dragon.

Chapter Four
Theories on Dragons

DRAGONS, ACCORDING TO the natural philosophers of Astandalas, are the material embodiment of the chaos to be found outside the Pax Astandalatis. As the borders of the Empire were pushed outwards, so too were the dragons, until all that was left were legends and a few place names.

Astandalas fell a dozen (or so) years ago, so I supposed it made sense that the dragons were coming back. Looking at this one, dancing in the sky like a vision of the beauty of violence, I was glad that we'd had six months of 'how to fight legendary creatures' in Self-Defence at Morrowlea.

I am not much of a romantic.

It was somewhere over the fields north of town, and as I watched a huge flock of starlings suddenly swirled around it. In a final twist of wings and tail it disappeared behind the trees.

There was a prolonged moment of silence, and then all the dogs of town started barking madly, the starlings began screeching, and someone began ringing the alarm bells. Sela proclaimed, "That is the most beautiful thing I have ever seen!" and all the other children started talking at once.

"It's headed towards Dartington," Mr. Dart said suddenly, and took off for the garden gate. Hal and I made hasty adieus to Mrs. Buchance and set off after him. I paused to pick up Hal's dropped knapsack and then half-tripped over the dog, falling behind in my efforts to make it stay within the yard, though I caught up quickly once I had room to run. We found Mr. Dart halfway to the river path, half-running as he tried to get to the north gate bridge.

Other people had the same idea, for the side roads were busy and people were standing on their steps gawping and gossiping, but they all seemed to stop at the town walls, where they stood chattering like the outraged starlings.

"A dragon!" Hal said. "Can you believe it, Jemis? Where could it possibly have *come* from?"

"Arguty Forest?" said Mr. Dart as we caught up. He grinned at me when I frowned at him.

"That's highwaymen—there are always rumours," I added to Hal. "I expect from the Farry March."

"Or the Woods Noirell. People say there are unicorns in there."

"It's a fair leap from unicorns to dragons," Hal objected. "Unicorns are very rare but they're the symbol of the Lady for a reason. Dragons, though."

"The Kingdom can be reached through the Woods Noirell, or so they say," said Mr. Dart.

"The King—Fairyland, do you mean?"

I shivered and twirled the ring on my finger. My mother had always warned me about loose talk when magic was afoot. "Better not to name them aloud. We don't want to draw their attention, if the Good Neighbours are out-and-about."

Hal laughed. "That's an old wives' tale, surely."

"A *dragon* just flew by," I said.

"And our Mr. Greenwing is most particular about his family legends," Mr. Dart said, causing Hal to trip and fall over.

He sat for an instant on the ground staring up at us. "I *beg* your pardon?"

"My surname is not Greene but Greenwing," I said, and then, when Hal continued gaping, added defiantly, "My father was Jakory Greenwing."

Hal accepted the hand I held out and stood up slowly. "No. You never said."

"I know."

"Not when Lark did her piece. Not after, when we were walking. Not when my mother took us to see that damned play—by the Emperor, Jemis, you didn't say *anything*."

I fiddled with the strap on Hal's knapsack. Mr. Dart walked a few paces off, looking at the sky as if after dragons, but not so far that I didn't think he wasn't listening. Hal shook his head.

"Your father saved my great-uncle's life *twice*. Didn't you think we'd be pleased—*overjoyed*—to know?"

I started at a movement in the hedgerow as a small bird flew off. I'd liked Hal's mother, the dowager duchess. Hal was my closest friend bar Mr. Dart. And yet I had not been able to confess the shame, nor the pride, I felt at being my father's son, not after the mortification of Lark's paper—not even though Hal had stood beside me—nor after the horrible evening at the theatre. The dowager duchess hadn't known the subtitle nor the subject, she'd said at the intermission, when the audience had been laughing hysterically and the ducal party were sitting in shock and I had pretended to another attack of the mysterious illness.

"I'm sorry," I said again.

"Jemis—you know *me*. You could hardly think I'd be anything but honoured to know your story?"

I seemed to be spending the afternoon in a state of excruciating embarrassment. I forced myself to meet Hal's puzzled, unhappy expression. I swallowed dryly. "You stood up when no one else would. You helped me through a terrible time this spring. I know I should have told you earlier. I'm sorry. I'm *sorry*."

"But why didn't you?" he asked, as honestly puzzled as I'd ever seen him. "Once we were out of Morrowlea, why didn't you tell us then?"

"Why didn't you tell us you were a duke till Marcan was found out by the outriders his father sent?"

"It would have changed things," he said after a pause. "It did change things, even though you mostly just laughed, when you were feeling up to it."

Mr. Dart came back, evidently deciding to participate in the conversation. I felt a flash of commingled relief and irritation that he did so. "You must have been perilously ill, Jemis."

"It would be nice to say that was the reason, but it wasn't."

Hal frowned. I smiled painfully at him. "It's not that I had … blanks," I added earnestly to Mr. Dart, who was suddenly looking appalled. "But there were a number of things, conversations especially, that I was present for but paid no attention to. As it seems."

"And you went off by *yourself*?" Mr. Dart said. "You *let* him go off by himself?"

"I couldn't keep him a prisoner at Leaveringham Castle," Hal pointed out reasonably. "And he didn't exactly mention that he was losing track of conversations. He just seemed excessively quiet. By June he'd seemed in much better nick. Until the letters didn't come."

"He stopped writing here, too. But we didn't know about the illness, or the situation at Morrowlea."

"You seem recovered now," Hal said, giving me a penetrating stare as he suddenly swung around. I tried not to squirm. At least they were speaking directly to me. "Or are you pretending to be well? But you haven't sneezed *once* since the posting yard! I can't believe I hadn't noticed until now."

I smiled reluctantly and decided that while I was admitting to gross negligences of friendship I might as well continue with the rest. "I found out what it was."

"Oh? Is that what you were doing after Kingsbury, visiting physickers?"

"No, just wandering around through north Fiellan and Ghilousette. Recuperating from a broken heart, what I thought was a failed degree, and—" I took a breath. Mr. Dart nodded encouragingly. "And from what turned out to be withdrawal from a serious addiction to wireweed and the effects of being ensorcelled for nearly three years."

Hal stared. "Who could possibly—" And then, as I had, he knew. His expression hardened instantly. "Lark." He spat several curses. "What did she get out of it?"

"Besides my abject devotion? It appears I have an untrained gift at magic, which she was stealing. The sneezing is by way of an allergy."

Hal started to march down the road. Mr. Dart and I followed. Mr. Dart said quietly, "You'd better tell him the rest of it."

Hal swung his arms. "The rest of *what*? How did you figure this out, anyway? Are Fiellanese physickers so accustomed to wireweed addiction they recognize its effects?"

"No, but ... Violet is."

Hal nearly went down again. "These boots went into the Otterburn, too," he muttered as he caught his balance. "Damned leather's all stretched. What do you mean, Violet knows all about wireweed addiction? How? Why? How do you know that she knows?"

I pinched my nose. My head was starting to pound. "She came here last week. She's—I think Lark is one of the Indrillines, and Violet is their agent."

"Lark is one of the ... Bloody hell, Jemis! are you even listening to yourself?"

"Not far from here is a country house that last week was attacked by a group of cultists being used as cover for a wireweed growing concern. Violet was here for I know not what nefarious purpose—"

"She was here to *warn you*, Mr. Greenwing. Because you had no idea Lark was an Indrilline, and you humiliated her."

"And did a good job of it, too," Hal growled, and then seemed to realize, as I had been trying not to, that thoroughly and publicly humiliating a member of the most powerful and feared criminal family on the continent, no matter how much she deserved it, was not perhaps a very good idea.

"Perhaps she's not an important Indrilline," Mr. Dart said unconvincingly.

Hal and I looked soberly at each other. Hal had learned surprisingly quickly how to behave as a "plain gentleman" (the standard of conduct to which Morrowlea students were held), but Lark had never comported herself as anything much less than a queen. She had been so glittering and magnificent and *charming* that no one had ever minded.

"Violet—did she know you're Jemis Greenwing, then?"

"She says she didn't, but … Lark did."

"Through her nefarious connections, I suppose?"

I shuddered at the thought of Lark having *nefarious connections*, ones she might send after me.

—No, I thought. She was barely twenty-one. She had spent three years at Morrowlea not being in the criminal courts of Orio. She surely couldn't have gone straight back and become—

I looked at Hal pacing along beside me, and swallowed hard. Hal had. We'd walked up to the front door of Leaveringham Castle, he and I, looking much as we did now, and from the moment the butler had answered the ring he had been His Grace the Duke, come home at last.

"No," I said belatedly. "I told her."

"Oh, Jemis. It wasn't just coincidence about her final paper, then?"

I looked at him and shook my head slowly, then turned my attention forward as we crested a gentle rise and saw stretching out before us the long gentle valley of the river Rag. Dartington village was visible to the northeast, the lady-tower of its church a lovely spire of punctuation, surrounded by a pleasant patchwork of harvest-ready fields and woodlots just starting to colour for autumn.

"No sign of the dragon," Mr. Dart said, sounding disappointed.

"There's smoke over there." Hal pointed.

"That's Magistra Bellamy's cottage. She was away earlier—do you mind if we stop? She said she might have something for my arm today."

"Of course," Hal said politely, in what I thought a rather ducal manner, at least until he added to me in a low voice, "His arm? Is it not simply broken? Is she a physicker-wizard? *Here?*"

I reflected that I didn't know what Magistra Bellamy was, exactly, and that the unfashionableness of magic extended to Fillering Pool. "No, Mr. Dart ended up with a stone arm last weekend. It was rather eventful. I'll explain later."

Hal gave me a crooked grin. "There seem to be a lot of things you need to explain later, Master Jemis."

"It's *Mr. Greenwing,*" I said, much more vehemently than I meant, and his smile faded into puzzlement again.

Mr. Dart opened the latch of the witch's gate. Magistra Bellamy had a pretty cottage, timber-and-plaster as was usual for the upper vale of the Rag, and an even prettier garden full of herbs and flowers, many of which were still blooming.

"She has a passionflower!" Hal cried, and plunged off the path to examine a vine clambering up the wall. "And, oh, look, Jemis, the crimson glory vine—and isn't it a beauty." He touched wide crimson-purple leaves with gentle hands, murmuring names as he went from wall to bed to pot.

"I think we've lost him," Mr. Dart said, amused. He entered the gate and strode directly to the cottage. "I can well believe Roddy Kulfield writing to say his ducal patron was mad about plants. Shall we call him?"

"No true gardener would be offended, surely."

"Verily." Mr. Dart lifted the knocker, which was shaped like a unicorn.

"Rare, but not unknown," I murmured, though only Mr. Dart

was there to smile, Hal himself by this time having his face deep into a patch of what I just about guessed was mint.

Footsteps sounded, the door flew open, and Mrs. Etaris said, "*There* you are at last!"

★★★

Ten minutes of utter confusion later, I abruptly remembered that Hal was still investigating Magistra Bellamy's garden. There was no sign of the witch herself. Mrs. Etaris had put me immediately to work scrubbing what seemed a remarkable quantity of copper and iron pots. Mr. Dart's arm meant he was spared scouring, so he had been sent off with an amiable shaggy dog. Mrs. Etaris herself had disappeared somewhere to make mysterious thumping noises.

I finished the first pot, a cauldron that had been caked with noxious grey-brown sludge I hoped very much was old pease porridge. It was when turning to the next that I recalled Hal, and also that duke or no duke, we'd been on kitchen duty a fair number of days together, and so rather than starting on the second I wiped off my hands and went in search of him.

He was kneeling before some sort of bush, humming. I watched him for a moment as he carefully bent a branch down so he could examine the leaves better. Examining their shape and situation, I guessed, something he'd said about plant identification swimming to mind. He looked quite absurdly happy.

He really would have been far happier as a second son, I thought with a pang, the one who could go off on the expeditions to hunt for plants in the mysterious regions of the world. Instead he was stuck being the sponsor of said expeditions and planning an arboretum that his people would probably not let him plant himself, either.

We were who we were. Duke and hero-traitor's son, our lives shaped by fate and accidents of birth.

"You look very solemn, Jemis," Hal said, and I jumped at finding him grinning up at me.

"I was thinking about fate and families and how wonderful it was to ignore them at Morrowlea."

He scrambled to his feet and took in my coatless and rolled-sleeve state. "You look as if you've been put to work."

"I have. Come help me scrub cauldrons?"

"Witch's cauldrons? Assuredly! Where's your Mr. Dart?"

"Taken the dog. Hard to wash with a petrified arm."

"This is the most unusual place," Hal said as we went back inside. It was a bright and cheerful cottage within, with white-washed walls and brightly coloured fabric curtains and cushions, the floor dark stone tiles or wood. I felt immediately comfortable on entering: it reminded me very much of the snug little cottage in a corner of the Arguty estates where my mother and I had lived while my father was off at war.

Thumps were still coming from upstairs. Hal shook his head at a corn broom hung on the wall. "What on earth is the magistra doing?"

"I have no idea, I've not actually met her." I opened the kitchen door with a flourish and discovered in doing so that there were aprons hung behind it. I gave Hal the first one, which was a plain blue and white striped cotton and which he accepted in bemusement, and then looked at the second. It was a very feminine floral print, and matched the curtains we'd just passed.

I considered the stack of pots and the fact that Mrs. Etaris and

Mr. Dart had seen me in pink satin last week, and that Hal had been witness to the second-most unpleasant experience of my life, and that I had not actually brought a change of clothes with me, and so I put on the apron.

Hal wordlessly went to the sink while I built up the fire in the range to heat up more water. When I turned he had the scouring pad in one hand, and said: "I take precedence."

I preferred drying, as he well knew, so I bowed as low as I could without hitting the table or stove. "As you wish, your grace."

He rolled his eyes and set in to washing. We fell quickly into the old familiar routine. After a few minutes he said, "I never thought I'd be doing this again. I rather miss working with my hands."

"Mm," I replied, not sure what else to say, and then without intending to I went on: "My father was reported shot running away from a court-martial for high treason about a week after my tenth birthday. They said he'd opened the gates of Loe to the enemy and caused the worst single loss to an Imperial army ever recorded. About two months later we received another letter, this one commending my father for his extreme bravery and reporting him presumed dead across the Border on a scouting mission."

Hal passed me a pot to dry and set an iron cauldron in the sink to soak. "Your mother must have written to the command staff."

"She did. No answer ever came."

"It must have gone astray. There were a lot of letters after Loe. Did she try again? Go to the Seventh Army's headquarters at Eil, even?"

"My father had been gone seven months when the first letter came. She'd been with child, but lost the baby after the news. I don't think she wrote again." I frowned at the rag in my hands, which was getting damp. When I spread it on the rail next to the stove my hands were trembling. I tried hard not to dwell on that period.

"What about your father's people? Did they not write?"

"He had two brothers and a sister. The sister had passed away a few years before. My older uncle was called Rinald. He and my father got on best, I think, of the four. He would have written or even gone, if—if he hadn't died before the second letter came. Broke his neck out hunting. He was so angry," I said in a lower voice, a memory stirring. People shouting, sneering, *commenting*, my mother crying, my uncle Rinald ferocious in his protection of us.

His lifeless body brought back to Arguty Hall in a sad procession, my mother gripping my hand so hard I thought she'd break a bone. "He couldn't believe my father would have done such a thing. And he died thinking that he had."

Hal turned as if to offer some comfort. I couldn't look at him, plunged my hands into the sink and started to scrub vigorously. He moved over, picked up the dry cloth, and waited until I had scoured the pot clean. Then he said tentatively, "And your other uncle?"

"You met my other uncle. Saw him, anyway. He was the one disdaining me outside the Ragnor Arms. He was quite happy to inherit the Greenwing estate after Uncle Rinald died, on the grounds that a traitor forfeits his patrimony."

"Oh," he said quietly.

"My mother and I lived in a cottage on the estates. Not too different from this one, really. My uncle didn't try to *evict* us, precisely, but he made things very uncomfortable. We stayed, though.

There wasn't much money—my mother had a small independence, but it didn't go far without my father's income. No pension, of course, for a traitor's widow. My mother started being courted by this Charese merchant who kept making excuses for why he was coming to Ragnor Bella all the time. Though in those days the Imperial highway to Astandalas went by, so we weren't quite such a backwater. Then came the Fall, which was … hard. Here as everywhere, though we didn't have nearly as many problems as most places."

I thought about the stories we'd heard about Ghilousette and shuddered. Hal didn't say anything; he didn't need to, though I didn't really know what had happened in Ronderell. I swallowed. "Mr. Buchance, the Charese merchant, came back eventually. He was about the first one to make it through the Arguty Forest after the Fall. When he proposed that time my mother accepted."

I scrubbed at another cauldron, this one caked with grease and burned bits. Neither my mother nor the second Mrs. Buchance was ever so lax in the kitchen, not even in those dark days during the early Interim when it was just my mother and me in the cottage and a half-day expedition to cross the grounds to Arguty Hall. Not that we'd gone very often begging to my uncle's door; for it was begging, with Sir Vorel.

"Mr. Buchance thought we should move to Chare, where no one would know us and we could be just the Buchances, but it was a long and dangerous journey, and my mother was desperate to make amends with my grandmother."

"Did she disapprove of her daughter marrying a foreign merchant?"

"I believe so."

"Did she ever make up with your mother?"

I shook my head, remembering again the only note I had ever received from my grandmother, after I had written to inform her of my mother's passing. No salutations or words of comfort or consolation or acknowledgement. Just: *My daughter has been dead these five years since.*

"There were some indications my grandmother was thawing—she sent me a birthday gift that year, when I turned thirteen, I remember, and my mother hoped she would come around. Especially when it turned out my mother was expecting another child."

I frowned at the sink. At this rate I was going to have a line permanently drawn between my brows, like one of the old fields ploughed so many years the same way the lines were etched into the ground five hundred years after they'd been turned to pasture.

The kettle started to boil and Hal went to take it off the hob. I spoke to the sink. "My mother had just had Lauren when—when the doorbell rang and I answered. And there was my father."

I felt a burning in my eyes and my throat. People—Lark—teased me for crying too easily: a poem or a song or even a nice painting could make me well up. I frowned even harder, but I was thinking of that moment, of seeing the ghost on the doorstep. He was so thin, gaunt even, but clean-shaven and smiling that familiar lop-sided grin, the smile that my mother always said was the only way I resembled him physically.

I couldn't bear to describe the ensuing scenes. His face when my mother came out with a new baby in her arms. Her face when she saw him. Mr. Buchance coming up behind her, furious at her upset. Me trying … I tried not to think about them at all. I cleared my throat. "I think I was the only one unequivocally glad to see him. I believed him, you see, when he said he was no traitor, that he had been stranded on the far side of the Border when the Empire fell. Everyone else ..."

I lost the rag under the water and spent some time fishing it out before deciding the water was too filthy to bother and un-plugging the sink. Hal was standing beside the stove, drying cloth motionless in his hands.

"Three weeks later they found him hanging in the forest. I found the note. But they wouldn't let me see him." I watched the water gurgling down the drain. "Or go to the funeral. Not that there was one. As a suicide and a traitor they buried him at a cross-roads at midnight."

There was an appalling silence. I cast about desperately for some way to break it, to lighten it, to push back my emotions. I needed to be the detached ironic young gentleman of fashion or else I would start sobbing. I smiled crookedly. "No flowers."

"But your father wasn't a traitor."

"The suicide was taken as admission of guilt." I was proud of how dry my voice was.

"Did you move to Chare after that?"

I laughed wearily. "No. You'd think we would have at that point, wouldn't you? My mother a bigamist, the doubts about my father laid to rest on the lurid side, my future looking bleak. Mr. Buchance offered to formally adopt me, but ... no. We stayed. My mother was not a strong woman physically, and she never really recovered from the shock. She died a year later when a bad in-fluenza swept through. My stepfather married the nurse he hired, Miss Inglesides that was, and they had three more children—Elinor, Zangora, and Lamissa—while I was at Morrowlea. Then—"

"You can come live with me."

I turned to look directly at him at last. He was holding the dishtowel with a death grip, his eyes wide with astonishment. He looked so stunned and dismayed and altogether discomfited that I started to laugh.

I reached for the plug and the ring slid off my soapy finger and landed in the sink.

Hal was used to my endless sneezing and at first, I'm sure, thought nothing of the fact that I started. I felt my nose and throat close up, and even as I fumbled for handkerchiefs I scrabbled at the sink with hands gone clumsy.

"Ring—" I wheezed.

Hal stared at me. "I beg your pardon?"

"Ring—sink—" I keeled against the wood stove and recoiled from the hot metal. The sneezes weren't stopping, they were building force. I tried to breathe through my mouth, count slowly, think of something else—all the old devices—but I could hardly draw breath before it exploded forth. I could see stars.

"Jemis!"

I buried my face in my handkerchief, trying desperately to catch my breath, sparks filling my vision and roaring my ears. I felt my knees start to give way and then someone was shouting and tugging and after a moment's resistance I followed blindly where I was led, until I sank down on the ground, head aching, drawing in long shuddering breaths until I no longer felt as if I were suffocating.

When I opened my eyes and raised my head, I saw I was sitting on the grass some distance from the cottage. Magistra Bellamy's dog was sitting beside me, licking my ear. I petted it warily; it thumped its tail.

"Are you all right?" Mr. Dart said.

I took another few shaky breaths. "Yes. Think so." I wiped my eyes on the back of my hand, unable to reach a clean handkerchief while sitting. I smiled awkwardly at Mr. Dart and then at Hal, who stood behind him still holding the dishtowel. "Sorry." I felt I should say more but my throat was raw. "Water?"

"I'll get you some," Hal promised, and went at a half-run to the cottage, the dog gambolling beside him.

Mr. Dart pondered for a moment, then sat down beside me heedless of his velvet coat. "I saw the dragon again," he ventured.

I had entirely forgotten about the dragon. "Mm?" I managed by way of encouragement.

"It was drinking from Taylor's cow pond. It must be bigger than a cart horse. The dog started barking and it flew off north again."

"Mm."

"Any idea at all why Mrs. Etaris is here making us do Magistra Bellamy's chores?"

I smiled. "No."

"She's coming back with Hal. His grace. Not very high-and-mighty, is he? I'm glad to meet him. I liked the sound of him in your letters."

Had I ever written about Lark? Or even Violet? Probably not very much. Lark had often insisted on reading my letters home, another thing that in retrospect should have raised suspicions, and sometimes she dictated parts, to make sure the stories were told properly, she'd told me. She had not wanted me to describe her in anything but the most glowing terms, and even then only rarely, as if she were a distant and unattainable object of my affections instead of the woman I spent nearly every waking hour and half the nights with.

"Stop looking morose, Mr. Greenwing. It doesn't suit you."

I used Mr. Dart's shoulder for support and hauled myself to my feet. He bounced up next to me, grinning. Hal was carrying a water glass with exaggerated care, looking baffled by the apparently perfectly ordinary and perfectly respectable middle-class middle-aged woman beside him. It was a sentiment Mrs. Etaris prompted in me quite frequently.

"Thank you," I rasped, taking the water. "Hal, this is—" My voice gave out and I coughed.

Mr. Dart shook his head at me. "Hal, this is Mrs. Etaris, the local bookmistress. Mrs. Etaris, this is Hal Leaveringham, Mr. Greenwing's friend from Morrowlea."

"The one who stood beside you in your contretemps this spring? Of course. I am delighted to meet you, your grace. Oh, are you here incognito? Mr. Lingham, then."

"It's spelled 'Leaveringham'," Mr. Dart said helpfully.

"Did you tell everyone?" Hal demanded.

I lowered my glass. "I didn't think it a secret that you were a duke. As for the spring, certainly not." I rubbed my throat. "I don't see why my throat feels so raw. It never used to."

Mrs. Etaris looked at me as if I were being slow. "Quite apart from the fact that you're not continuing to take wireweed, there was the fire."

"Fire?" Hal looked back at the thin column of smoke rising from the cottage chimney.

"Mr. Greenwing and Miss Redshank rescued someone from a

burning house last week."

"Violet," I supplied.

"Why was Violet in a burning building?"

"No, she's Miss—"

"Violet *Redshank?*"

"Mm."

"What in hell is going on around here?" Hal demanded, then flushed and presented a very courtly half-bow to Mrs. Etaris. "My apologies, ma'am. I had never expected anything from Ragnor Bella."

"No one does," she agreed placidly.

"What *is* going on here, Mrs. Etaris?" Mr. Dart asked. "Why are you here, and where is Magistra Bellamy?"

"And why are we doing her dishes?" I added.

Mrs. Etaris stared at us for a moment and then burst out laughing. "Oh my dears, did I not tell you? I thought Mrs. Buchance had sent you to help."

"We were on our way to Dartington to see where the dragon had gone."

Mrs. Etaris went very still. "I do beg your pardon?"

"A dragon flew over," Mr. Dart said. "Saw it again drinking from Taylor's pond."

"A *dragon*," Mrs. Etaris breathed. She did not looked alarmed; she looked delighted. She'd looked delighted when we'd had to storm the Talgarths' house last week, too. Then her voice turned brisk and businesslike. "Are you certain it was a dragon, Mr. Dart?"

"They don't exactly look like anything else," he replied, obviously exasperated.

"Could be a wyvern," Hal said solemnly.

"Or a fire salamander," I suggested.

"Or an illusion created by an overexcited student wizard," Mrs. Etaris added firmly, and frowned at me.

"I haven't had any lessons," I protested. "Magistra Bellamy wasn't in when I came by, and I am *not* going to Dominus Gleason."

"And otherwise? I am glad to know it is mere lack of skill preventing you from tearing up the countryside, Mr. Greenwing."

I bowed elaborately to her, making my head swim dizzily. "What is going on, Mrs. Etaris? Mrs. Buchance didn't mention anything about you needing help—though she was perhaps somewhat distracted by the arrival of her nephews for the evening, and we left in haste once we saw the dragon."

"Magistra Bellamy said to call today," Mr. Dart interjected, "as she thought she might have a remedy for my arm. She wasn't in when I knocked on my way to town. Nor obviously now, neither."

"Either," Mrs. Etaris corrected absently. She bit her lip, a surprisingly girlish gesture, then seemed to come to some decision. "Do come within, gentlemen. There has been a complication and I would value your assistance."

"We shall most certainly be delighted," Hal said, with a florid courtly bow. No heel-clicks, but there were elaborate curlicues. I smiled, thinking he'd well got the measure of Mrs. Etaris.

Mrs. Etaris paused, head tilted slightly to one side. "Delight may enter into it, but then again—" She paused again, then smiled with a disquieting pleasure. "No, I think delight may indeed be involved. There is danger and derring-do and deviltry afoot, after all." I stumbled slightly on a tussock of grass. She took my arm. "Fetching apron, Mr. Greenwing."

Chapter Five
Theories on Sneezing

WHEN I CROSSED the garden threshold I began immediately to sneeze. Not quite so violently as before, but enough to make me stagger back from the gate. I pulled out another handkerchief from my clean handkerchief pocket. A week without sneezing more than normal people had not broken me of the multiple-handkerchief habit. Fortunately, I supposed.

Mrs. Etaris stopped and frowned back at me. "This will be a difficult conversation if you cannot participate, Mr. Greenwing."

"The ring went into the sink," I explained, lifting my right hand to show her its absence.

"I'll go look for it," Mr. Dart said, resettling his sling

"Thank you," I replied meekly, then laughed at Hal's expression. "I acquired a ring last week that has the property of suppressing magic—and therefore my sneezes—when I wear it."

Hal frowned. "You can't be *allergic* to magic, in that case; the ring would still set you off."

"Indeed," said Mrs. Etaris, gazing at him thoughtfully. "Are you a practitioner, ah, Mr. Lingham?"

He shrugged. "A minor one. I was taught the basics before the Fall, of course, and afterwards my mother felt that even if it were dreadfully unfashionable it behoved me to know what can, or at least could, be done."

"A wise woman," Mrs. Etaris said. She then looked arrested at the way that Hal laughed in response. I wanted to ask why she looked so surprised, but before I could gather breath the moment passed, and Hal went on.

"She is. She's also a fair practitioner herself and doesn't much like having to refrain in polite company. She's not the only one of her circle, either. I don't think it'll be too many years before the fashion comes around. Certainly by the time Wulf is king; he's been making lights since he was an infant."

Wulf must be Prince Wulfric, King Roald's grandson.

"That may be for the best," Mrs. Etaris was saying.

I rallied myself away from the daunting thought that Hal knew the future king by his nickname. They were probably related. "Mr. Dart and I will be at the vanguard, then," I said lightly, "if only by necessity."

"Never admit to fashion being a result of necessity," Mrs. Etaris admonished with mock severity.

"Where did you acquire a magic ring, anyway? They are not exactly common."

I swallowed. "I won it in a game of Poacher from a Tarvenol duellist while waiting for Violet at the Green Dragon. That's a tavern on the other side of town."

"Oh, of course."

"Mr. Dart is returning," Mrs. Etaris murmured.

"I can see the ring but can't reach it," Mr. Dart reported, and after a small discussion I went to sit on the bank again while they went in together.

After a while I began to feel restless. I had gotten into the habit of long cross-country runs while at university, when—in retrospect—the wireweed and ensorcellments and Lady knew what else Lark had been doing got too much. I had not been able to go either as often or for as long I liked since I returned. Running was not something anyone else did for pleasure, and my capacity to take sidelong glances and outright comments occasionally faltered.

I had gone running yesterday for an hour before breakfast, but even that was going to have to stop, as the year was well into autumn and soon there would not be enough light, and people were certainly beginning to talk about this new eccentricity of Jemis Greenwing's.

I hugged my knees and frowned at the stretch of road visible between the cottage and a clump of tall bushes.

Violet had been the one to suggest I join the cross-country team.

It had been in the library one day. I was on cataloguing duty, which I'd loved, until that afternoon when suddenly I could no longer focus on the words before me. Violet had been looking for a book, she'd said, and asked if I were feverish.

I'd felt as if I were jumping out of my skin with excess energy.

(My unknown and uncontrolled magic flaring up under the catalyst of wireweed? The drug overstimulating me? There was so much I didn't know.)

She'd said I must have been spending too much time indoors and that she'd heard the games master was putting together a cross-country running team, and I had the right build for it. It was a sport they did at home, she'd said; though not, of course, where that was.

I had been desperate for some outlet to the energy, and went to the try-outs. And even though initially Lark had disapproved of the amount of time I shortly began spending running, after a few days she'd stopped pouting and started encouraging.

I'd run nearly as much as I'd studied; more, in the last few months of my degree. What Lark had been doing when I was out for my three- and four-hour loops I did not know.

Perhaps I could guess, though that additional betrayal hurt more than I would have thought, after all the rest. Lark behaved like a queen, and there were always many courtiers willing to usurp my place at her side.

I frowned hard at the road again and made myself think of Violet. Violet had been full of helpful little suggestions that had gone much further towards mitigating my illness than anything the university physickers prescribed. Not really a surprise, now that I knew she'd known what it was.

But what, I wondered suddenly, watching a crow hopping along the road pecking at things, had Violet gotten out of it? Was it merely that she didn't like what Lark was doing, and though she dared not or could not stop it, she did her best to make sure I didn't end up ... well, however wireweed addicts usually ended up.

The crow tilted its head to one side, staring intently at some spot before it. I had never heard much about wireweed beyond the barest rumours until I was travelling in Ghilousette. There had been what I thought a disturbing number of incapacitated beggars on the streets of Newbury, treated by the hale citizens

with terrifying disregard. When I'd been able to bestir myself
out of my own despondency I'd asked a few people, who looked
surprised and perturbed that I mentioned them. They were not
citizens, I was told; they *used magic*.

Magic was illegal in Ghilousette, and at the time I had taken
it at face value. But there was one incident that I had tried hard
to suppress in my memory, when a drunkard in a tavern I'd gone
to (needing, at last, company, even of the worst sort) had started
railing against the duke and the infamous treatment of those
born to magic and the epidemic of addiction as people tried to
cope.

He had not belaboured *wireweed*, and at the time I had not
thought of it except as one of an arsenal of possible drugs and liquor. He was drunk, and although the others in the tavern were
ignoring his raving, they stopped him once he got to a certain
point. Not before he'd said that the gibbet cage held the future
of Ghilousette if the duke kept ignoring magic and the claims
of his people.

I'd gone past the gibbet cage on my way to the Hall of Marvels. The Hall of Marvels had the best of Ghilousette, the glorious mechanical contrivances, all the unmagical devices that
people invented to make up for the Fall and the dreadful results
of the Interim in that duchy. A terrible stench had been the first
thing to catch my attention, and when I had ceased sneezing in
reaction there had been something else calling to me, making
me look.

Inside the gibbet cage was a huddle of rags surrounded by rotting fruit and bones. It was a hot summer's day and the stench and
flies were almost unbearable. The good citizens of Newbury were

walking past as if the thing wasn't there. Even the two guards at the gate of the Hall of Marvels were paying no attention. I was drawn by horrified curiosity to step closer.

There was a man inside the huddle of rags, or what had been a man. He looked whole on the outside, despite the filth. He raised his head when I came between him and the sun, and looked at me.

I had been reading about wireweed this week, few though were the books Mrs. Etaris had on the subject. Wireweed gave its users such a pure and piercing intensity of connection and exaltation that it was nearly always immediately addicting. A few hits of wireweed and you felt as if the world was gilded and your source was the sun: as if, in fact, you were in love.

Even without an immoral wizard to augment the effect, wireweed burned up one's natural magic. When that was gone the fortunate died.

The less fortunate became addicted to worse drugs, for wireweed was useless once there was nothing for it to burn. The truly unfortunate—

I had a lot to thank Violet for, I thought.

The guards had come up to me and poked the man, or what had been a man, with a spear, and laughed roughly and said that that was what trafficking in magic brought you. But I had looked at the man and he had looked at me and I had seen hell and hunger and what happened when all the magic left a person.

If Hal had seen even an inkling of that in *me*—

Magistra Bellamy's dog suddenly barked. I jumped up in agitation, whirling to look for it, and something grazed my shoulder and thudded loudly into the ground where I had been sitting.

I whirled back and stopped dead. It was an arrow.

Chapter Six
Mrs. Etaris has an Idea

THE ARROW HAD sunk a good six inches into the ground. I stared at it. If the dog hadn't barked—

Even as I thought that, the dog bolted past me, growling deep in her throat. At the same moment I realized that it was no bird arrow. It was a yardlong from a longbow.

I traced the angle of the arrow, spun around to follow the arc it must have taken. The arrow flight and the dog's charge met at— two men.

One held a longbow. He was unhurriedly raising it again, one arm reaching behind to his quiver for a second arrow. He was thirty yards away across open ground. They were in the shadow of a clump of trees along the river footpath. I was in plain sight.

I tensed. No sense standing like an idiot while someone *shot* me.

The second man made a sharp movement, something glinting in sunlight, the dog barked and lunged forward. The archer raised his bow with an evil grin I could see from here—

—And I *snapped*.

I had only ever fought once in earnest, when Violet had attacked me last weekend. I hadn't known it was her, and I responded as if my life were in real danger. Which—in retrospect—it may well have been. I still wasn't at all certain why Violet had come, or what I was to her. Or she to me.

I had not spoken to anyone about what it had felt like. Events had far outpaced it last week. As I re-entered that space of mortal danger, I felt a shock—not of fear but—

—*delight*.

It was a place of pure thought married to physical exertion. I had come close to it when studying the structure of a poem and discovering the key of its composition, but this was the inverse— the key was to the composition of life, the world itself snapping into sense around me.

The dog scared up a flock of pigeons feeding on the grass.

I grabbed the arrow with one hand and *ran*.

Not towards the cottage or the road, either of which would probably have been the sensible thing to do. I was far beyond common sense. It felt as if time had stopped around me, though I could hear shouting and barking and the stuttering wings of the pigeons, and see ahead of me the archer unhurriedly bringing down his arm with the second arrow.

The cross-country games master had insisted we practice sprinting as well as long distance running. You never know when that will make all the difference in a race, she'd said, and most people can only do one or the other because the muscles are different.

I had been good at it then.

I was still good at it now.

I covered the distance in something rather better than my usual six seconds, arriving before the dog had jumped on the first man or the pigeons had risen above the trees.

Two men. One with the now-useless longbow, which he was bringing down to try to fend off the dog.

The other man had a drawn knife and a short sword. He grinned at me, not so much evilly as cockily.

I'd never liked cockiness.

I feinted left with the arrow. As the cocky man raised his knife arm to block it, sword moving forward to my opening, I stepped left and sideways into the space created by his movement, inside his sword arm, and as he moved his sword back and out I brought up my right knee and right hand together, kneecap to groin and stiff fingers to throat, and as he crumpled I used the final energy of the motion to take the sword from his suddenly limp fingers. As I continued to swivel into his motion my left hand reversed its direction and brought the butt of the arrow down into his temple.

I landed in a guard position, ready to throw my weight behind the arrow at the archer, but he saw me and kicked the dog at me. While I tried not to stab it he turned and ran.

I tumbled over the dog and rolled upright to be sure no one else was there, and discovered I had an audience.

Mr. Dart, Hal, and Mrs. Etaris stood in a staggered line some ten yards away. Mrs. Etaris held a poker, Hal a plant pot, and Mr. Dart some sort of line. They were all staring at me in total consternation.

Mrs. Etaris recovered her poise first. "Mr. Greenwing, you are a man of many unexpected talents. Usually one is advised to run *away* from attackers, but in this case ..."

She trailed off. I gazed mutely at them. My blood was thundering in my ears.

Mr. Dart shook his head. "Mrs. Etaris had just opened the door when you cried out and the dog started to bark."

I didn't recall crying out.

Hal lowered the pot to rest against his thigh. "Dominus Lukel would be very proud."

Dominus Lukel was the fighting master at Morrowlea. We'd had compulsory self-defence three times a week. It was my favourite class.

Mrs. Etaris smiled. "Perhaps Mr. Greenwing would like a cup of tea," she suggested. She crossed the space between us and touched my arm. "Come, Mr. Greenwing."

The world snapped back into its normal muddled confusion. I stared wildly from one to the other and then frantically for the poor dog. She wagged her tail and whined when I looked at her. "Good girl," I said, going to pet her and then stopping when I realized I was still gripping the arrow and a sword in a fighting stance.

"Where did these come from?" I said a touch hysterically.

Mrs. Etaris glanced sympathetically at me, then returned to kneeling over the body of my attacker. I stared at first the weapons and then the man in horror. "Did I *kill* him?"

"Not for want of skill," Mrs. Etaris said. "You obviously know exactly where to hit someone's temple to knock them unconscious."

"I don't think I do!"

Mr. Dart was shaking his head. "Jemis, you jumped up—that's when we saw you. You grabbed the arrow and sprinted up here after the dog, then, uh ..."

"Then took out two ruffians with considerable poise," Hal

supplied.

The events of the past five minutes seemed as if they belonged in a book I had read years ago. But I was holding the arrow and the sword and however oddly I could feel every motion in my body, and my heart surely would not have been thundering this loudly if that hadn't happened. If I hadn't done that. This. This.

I took several deep breaths.

Hal took a step forward. "How were you not on the fencing team at Morrowlea?"

I forced my gaze away from the highwayman. "Same practice time as cross-country."

"Their loss."

Mrs. Etaris was examining the dog, her hands competent and gentle. She said, "You were on the cross-country team?"

"Long-distance running," Hal supplied again.

My voice came out in the same strangely distant tone. "This was so different. Everything was so perfectly clear and simple. I didn't have any doubts about what to do at all."

Mrs. Etaris stood up. "I had a friend once who experienced a similar sort of battle madness. He'd start singing and you knew things were about to become … interesting."

"*You* did?" Mr. Dart said in amazement.

Mrs. Etaris sighed and smiled and patted her hair into place. She was wearing a sensible light grey apron over a blue dress and did not look as if she had ever done anything more untoward than—

—Than show a remarkable flair for espionage when sneaking around the Talgarths' manor house last week.

"I had a somewhat *wild* youth," she said mildly. "Mr. Dart, you're still holding that line? Excellent. Let us truss Mr. Greenwing's captive until we decide what to do with him. Mr. Lingham, you look to be a stout sort of gentleman—could you bring Poppy with you? That is to say, Magistra Bellamy's dog."

Hal nodded and crouched next to the dog, then looked a bit uncertain as to what to do with the pot. I fumbled sword and arrow into one hand so I could take the pot. I couldn't seem to let go of the arrow.

"Thank you," Hal said, grunting as he took the dog in his arms and stood up. We turned to see that Mr. Dart and Mrs. Etaris had tugged the unconscious man to a seated position slumping against the trunk of a willow. I frowned at him more carefully.

The man was dressed in rough clothes of neither fashion nor fit. He was scruffy, dark hair tangled and straggling past his shoulders, face mid-brown from dirt more than ethnicity, facial hair beyond stubble but not quite thick enough to be a beard. He smelled rather sour.

"Ruffian," Mr. Dart suggested, wrinkling his nose.

"Perhaps," said Mrs. Etaris, and efficiently bound his wrists behind the tree. We all stared some more.

"It must have been a *very* wild youth," I ventured.

"You would be amazed at what goes on at a finishing school for young ladies, Mr. Greenwing."

Hal laughed abruptly, and the dog (evidently taking this to be directed at her), licked his face. "My sister said the same thing. She went to Dame Elwen's Academy in Kingsbury."

"And you?" I asked as we started to walk back to the cottage. It seemed an absurdly long distance to have crossed: *why* had that been my first reaction? It was so *obvious* that I ought to have run to the cottage. Or around the shrubbery. Or anywhere but straight *at* two attackers.

Hal raised his eyebrows. "Odlington, of course. Elianne and I may be twins but I'd be hard pressed to pass for a girl."

***

I managed to pry my fingers off the arrow long enough to take the ring Mr. Dart handed me, and we went inside the cottage for the next round of conversation. Mrs. Etaris led us into the kitchen, where the cupboard under the sink had its hinges off and a large amount of the plumbing removed.

"I would suggest that you take off your ring *before* you start doing the dishes next time," Mr. Dart said.

"Or just don't do them in a witch's cottage," Hal added.

"Where did you come from, Mrs. Etaris?" I asked, trying not to shiver too obviously.

She gestured us to seats at the table. Mr. Dart and I sat down, but Hal moved to help her mend the fire. "The Magistra decided it would be prudent to visit her aunt in north Fiellan while things calm down here. She asked me to look in on her cottage, as she left quite hastily after last week's events.—She's our only open local witch," she added to Hal, "and although she had very little to do with it, there was a fair amount of magic flying about last week."

Mr. Dart and I both looked at his stone arm. I twisted the ring, the little garnets sparkling in a stray shaft of light coming in the window. I felt trembly and strange after the fight.

"Too bad there's no training salle in Ragnor Bella," Mr. Dart murmured. "It seems a waste of talent. Perhaps you'll be able to take lessons at Inveragory. There's a naval academy in Isternes, isn't there?"

Hal looked up sharply from the arrow, which I'd set on the table once I was able to pry my fingers open. "Are you planning another degree, Jemis? I hadn't thought you wanted—not to mention the end of things at Morrowlea—that is—"

That is, failing out of Morrowlea would require more than a small fortune to make Inveragory accept me for a second degree.

Mr. Dart raised his eyebrows. "I'll tell him, shall I? Since you had yet to write with your news. Mr. Greenwing has received a letter from Morrowlea informing him that as a result of his courageous defence of the truth and other scholarly virtues, he was awarded first place."

"Oh, well done! The least they could do after letting Lark work everyone into such a froth. Inveragory for Law, is it?"

"Seems the thing to do," I agreed unenthusiastically, then turned abruptly to Mrs. Etaris. "I'm sorry, Mrs. Etaris, but I simply cannot believe you had a *male* friend who sang songs into battle at Madame Clancette's Finishing School for Girls in Fiella-by-the-Sea. Even before the Fall. Tying people up—perhaps. Creeping around houses—all right—espionage—quite likely—even tossing daggers—but *battle*?"

Mrs. Etaris smiled serenely as she set a large pot of peppermint tea on the table. "No, I suppose that was during my university years."

"Where did you go?" asked Hal curiously.

"Galderon over in East Oriole."

"Of course," he said, eyes glinting.

"Ragnor Bella must seem very quiet," Mr. Dart said. "Well, apart from the various affairs of the Greenwings. And the cult."

Hal chuckled. "Not to mention this harvest fair. I am eager to participate in such a notable event."

Mrs. Etaris poured the tea, expression quietly amused. "Oh, there is always much more going on under the surface of a quiet country village than the uninitiated anticipate. Which is why I'm glad you're here, gentlemen. The Embroidery Circle needs your assistance."

"Oh?" said Mr. Dart, eyebrows rising again.

"Yes: we need you to spike a gambling ring."

Chapter Seven
The Dragon has an Idea

"I CAN JUST see your Mrs. Etaris manning the barricades of Galderon," Hal said once we were on our way at last to the Old Arrow. "You must be enjoying working for her."

"I am, as it—wait, barricades?"

"The barricades of Galderon! Surely you know about the Scholars' Revolt?"

I poked at some herbage with the ruffian's arrow, which I found even more puzzling than the fact that when we'd gone back to check on our captive, he'd disappeared. Mrs. Etaris had merely said, "Of course, he did have a collaborator," and suggested we go on with our day. She said she'd make what representations were necessary to the authorities. Since I was not in any good odour with said authorities, I'd agreed with alacrity. But the fact that the highwayman had been using a longbow puzzled me.

Mr. Dart frowned. "That was back in Eritanyr's day, wasn't it? Decades before the Fall, even."

"Mrs. Etaris is the right age to have been at university then. And if she had a *wild* youth that involved friends who sang going into battle ..."

"What on earth happened in Galderon?" I asked. "What Schol-ars' Revolt?"

"The university tried to secede from the province," Mr. Dart said, taking the arrow from me so he could swipe dramatically at innocuous seed heads of wild carrot and cow parsley.

"Not tried to; did," said Hal. "It went all the way up to the Emperor eventually—the Last Emperor, that was, after more than a decade of riots and revolutions and counter-revolutions and all sorts of excitement. The university made the argument that the provincial governor of East Oriole was abusing her position, un-fairly taxing the town—it had a press so she was triple-dipping, I think was the complaint—and was also interfering with academic standards and the governance of the university."

"Still, to turn to violence?" I said skeptically.

"The governor forced them to make her nephew their chan-cellor, I believe. He promptly threw out one of their most import-ant Scholars in a show of blatant bigotry. The faculty and students revolted, overthrew the Chancellor and upper senate, and persuad-ed the townspeople to form the Free and Independent Republic of Galderon with them."

"I can't imagine the governor was very happy about that."

"No, the more she wasn't. She sent in the Army against them, but the university held out against a multi-year siege before they finally got an embassy to Astandalas. The Last Emperor instigated an independent investigation, which revealed gross negligence and misconduct on the part of the governor. He awarded Galderon the status of a client state."

"Huh," I said, wondering at what point in my studies I ought to have learned this.

"I'd feel your education was lacking in local history, except that East Oriole is about a thousand miles away from here. I only know so much about it because my housemaster at Odlington was a student at Galderon during the revolution. I believe he ended up as a general of some fashion before the siege ended."

"Mrs. Etaris was probably the spymaster," I said, and made them all laugh.

"She's certainly got us hopping on behalf of this Embroidery Circle. Do you reckon they secretly run the town?" Hal asked.

"You've read too many of Jemis' romances," Mr. Dart said severely. "The Embroidery Circle consists primarily of the wives of the most thoroughly respectable middle-class men of the town."

Hal whooped. "In short, the answer is yes. Come now, Mr. Dart, I am an imperial duke, I know very well who really runs things. Gossip and business are the two real engines of society."

"That perhaps explains Mr. Greenwing's activities—is revolution coming, Jemis? Shall we enter *that* in the betting-books for the fair?"

I decided to ignore the worrisome fixation everyone was displaying on my role in the upcoming fair events. I'd fallen into the pond on a dare to swing across on the rope of bunting once, and—

And that wasn't at all the reason why people were so intrigued at what might happen this autumn.

"People have such stories," I said after a few moments of ignoring their banter but appreciating the fact that my two closest friends were enjoying each other's acquaintance.

"What do you mean?" Mr. Dart asked.

I took the arrow back from him so I could trail its tip in the running water of the ditch beside the road. Hal would know all the roadside weeds' names, I thought. I tried to recapture my initial idea. "I mean ... you look at Mrs. Etaris and think how ordinary and quiet a life she must have had. Wife of a tiny market town's chief constable, owner of the only bookstore, she embroiders and cooks and rescues the odd lost soul out of pity and compassion. Then you find out she had a *wild* youth and that doesn't just mean she went and gambled away a fortune in Orio City, but was probably a major actor in a successful revolution."

Hal was looking at me. "Do you consider yourself a lost soul, Jemis?"

"More of an errant one," I replied lightly as we climbed over another stile and onto the back lane leading to the Old Arrow.

Hal suddenly stopped so he could examine some pincushion-effect flowers in a soft lavender. "Hold up, Mr. Dart," I said, "Hal's found something."

"Lesser devil's-bit scabious," he said, then turned his head to smile up at Mr. Dart. "Why are you the only one we're still calling *Mister*? Am I scandalizing you with my informality?"

"Oh, no," said Mr. Dart, going rather pink. "If you must know, I don't like my given name! And Perry's almost as bad."

"What, you have a name other than Perry?" I asked, surprised at this confession. "I don't think I knew that. Your brother's never called you anything but Perry."

"No one ever has, and no one ever will. Hamish and Tor know better. And I like how Mr. Dart sounds."

"Well, if that's the case ..." Hal got up, with a specimen carefully uprooted to be put, even more carefully, between the pages of the notebook he always carried in his waistcoat pocket. "Why don't you go by a nickname, Jemis?"

"I don't *always* mind my name," I said, and they laughed, so I didn't go on to say that my father had called me Jimmy, though I was about to when we came to the back side of the pub, and with one accord stopped.

"Any inexplicable tendency towards heroics?" Mr. Dart said, lightly.

The dragon was coiled into the space between malthouse and garden hedge. An incongruous line of washing flapped above it, adding a festive air. The air was warm down here, though above us the wind was rushing white clouds against blue skies.

The dragon was the colour of the green jade crock my mother used to keep honey in. For a moment the memory of the jar was so strong that I thought I could smell that honey, the honey of the wild woods, thick, heavy, perfumed with flowers perhaps even Hal could not name.

The dragon was scratching the edge of its head against the wall of the step, but its brilliant blue eyes were focused on me. Tiny flakes of scale and stone were rising up like dust, glinting brilliantly in the sunlight.

I walked unhurriedly up to it. I felt as I had when facing the ruffians: as if the world had ceased suddenly to be confusing. It was no longer confusing. It was—it was *opened up* to me—

I had a sudden thought of dancing lessons with Violet, that first autumn at Morrowlea, before the Winterturn Ball when Lark had caught me neatly as a tame pigeon.

And then back another handful of years, or longer—for no one knew how long, exactly, the Interim had occupied—to my mother and me in the dower cottage on the Arguty estate, on one splendid spring morning when the world felt alive with the promise of life and coming sanity, and my mother had said it was time to dance the Green Lady in.

Danced we had, in the garden when the flowers of the ancient hawthorn tree fell down on us white as the White Lady's snow, when the sky was opalescent as the Kingdom Between Worlds, when the bees rose around us like in the stories of Paradise, and my mother took my hands and we sang the hymns of coming summer.

In some way the world was holding its hand out to me to partner in the dance, and I—how I wanted to take it—

The dragon finished scratching and rattled its wings to resettle them, like Mr. Dart with his sling. In the sunlight its eyes were blue diamonds.

I bowed formally, hat in hand.

The dragon had a crown of golden horns, each a foot long, pointed sharp as a hawthorn spur. Its tongue was gold. It uncoiled what seemed an endless length towards me before stopping at just the point where I could have reached my hand out to touch the tiny beaded scales of its nose. Its breath was warm and heady, even more honeyed than the air, with the faintest and strangely pleasant bitter undertone to it.

I felt perfectly aware of everything around me, the glittering raindrops on holly and hawthorn hedges, the wind rushing importantly through the canopy of the woods behind the pub, the faint scrape of scales against stone, the yet fainter calls of distant birds, the buzz of late insects, the still astonishment of my friends.

The dragon appeared to be able to regard me face-on, both eyes boring into mine.

Some part of me said:

There is a stone by my right foot.

Another part answered:

Drop right knee, weight balanced. Left hand to hat: right hand to stone. As its head follows movement, raise left hand—hat over its eye—explode upward. Left hand carry past hat to left-central horn, right hand bring up stone to right-central. All weight forward following stone: somersault over horns, full weight on right-central, cracking it at weak joint. As dragon lifts its head to throw you off, land on pub steps. Spin, right hand stone to box ear-hole, left hand carry broken horn around into soft skin at base of jaw.

We had had four weeks on dragons in Self-Defense. But the dragon made no move to attack, and my father had taught me not to pick fights without good purpose.

It said: "Your ring. It is of interest to me."

I closed my right hand so that I could feel the smooth cold metal with my thumb. "It is not mine to give away."

The dragon withdrew its head a fraction so that it could look more intently at me. I saw a better rock a foot over and shifted position.

"Then," said the dragon, "it appears I must ask you for something that *is* yours."

Its voice was clear and ironic and tremendously intimidating.

I drew a deep breath. "What do I have that you could possibly want?"

The dragon drew back its thin reptile lips into what was almost certainly a smile. "Between the green and the white is the door. Between the race and the runner is the lock. Between the sun and the shadow is the key. In the bright heart of the dark house is the dark heart of the bright house. And therewithin, if the sap of the tree runs true, is the golden treasure of the dark woods. Bring that to me ere the Sun and the Moon are at their furthest remove."

"And if I do not?"

The dragon snorted a pouffe of white smoke that filled the air between us. "Then, sir, you will have only the dark treasure of the golden woods to comfort you."

Chapter Eight
Hal has an Idea

"BUT YOU LIKE riddles, Jemis. You wrote your final paper on how all the most obscure parts of that unbelievably long poem were a riddle about the size of rooms in some prison."

"It was a puzzle poem giving the solution to the architecture—" I stopped as Hal and Mr. Dart both laughed at me. "Can we have a drink now, please?"

"You were the one provoking dragons into giving you riddles," Mr. Dart said.

"It was only *one* dragon."

"And only *one* riddle?"

He laughed. as he led the way past a deeply affronted cat, which had appeared, hissing, when the dragon flung itself up into the sky in a kite-tail of laundry and whirling dust. We entered the pub to find a tall saturnine man lounging before the fire with a tankard of beer in his hand.

"What ho," he said amiably to Mr. Dart, before faltering on seeing me coming along behind. After a moment he nodded. "Mr. Greenwing."

I bowed silently.

Sir Hamish Lorkin was my father's cousin, given a knighthood by the King of Rondé in honour of his splendid portraits. He was in his forties now, a thin muscular man, balding a bit and unfashionably dressed in country clothes.

Abruptly he smiled. "What a pleasure to see you!" He gestured to a table towards the back of the room, away from the only other patrons, who were huddled near the fire. As we moved towards it he added to Mr. Dart, "Your brother will be along, he was talking to Linkett about the lower fields. Mr. Greenwing, you are a stranger."

"Mm," I replied, not at all sure how I was supposed to take that.

"You've learned to guard your tongue. A good habit, if not one I ever bothered to learn. Fortunately I don't have half the barony baying for my blood. Whatever did you do to Sir Vorel to excite him so? He was swearing about you over his port yester-eve. It can't all be on account of everyone betting on whether you'll fall into the pond again this year."

I flushed. "That was only once."

"And only *one* dragon," Mr. Dart murmured. "Oh, hullo, Tor."

"Perry, Hamish—Mr. Greenwing."

I rose again to bow to Master Torquin Dart. Shorter than Mr. Dart and stockier, as well as twenty-odd years older, he had the same auburn hair (made somewhat roan by age) and freckled pale skin. He was dressed as practically as Hamish in high-quality Rondelan tweed. Indeed its cut suggested decades of use lay behind the single leather patch on each elbow.

"Master Dart."

He gave a thoughtful grunt. "Perry's been glad to see you."

I was suddenly deeply curious what Mr. Dart's given name was, if not Perry. He gave me a look I interpreted as *don't you dare ask*, so (although tempted) I didn't. Sir Hamish said, "Hear any new gossip, Tor?"

"Don't be absurd," Master Dart replied, which I interpreted as *plenty*, especially as he then added, "What's this I hear about you wanting to run in the three-mile race, Mr. Greenwing?"

"No!" cried Sir Hamish, loudly enough that several of the farmers looked over from where they were solemnly discussing scrapie and hardware disease and other improbable-sounding ailments. "What, you think you can take Tad Finknottle?"

I was fairly certain I could handily beat the barony champion, but a snippet of conversation about poachers emerged out of the background noise in the pub, and I remembered that the game was not just the race. I grinned sheepishly and shrugged. "Better than falling into the pond."

"Roald was baiting him," Mr. Dart said, which was obviously an understandable motivation, for Sir Hamish hastily swallowed a laugh and Master Dart snorted with magnificent unconcern. I was grateful for the interruption offered by the belated arrival of Hal, his hands full of plants.

He was accompanied by the plump inn-wife, who was explaining something. He bid her a pleasant farewell and came over to our group. "Look, Jemis, the innkeeper gave me some of her speedwell! This is an extremely rare variety—oh, my apologies!" He grinned at Master Dart and Sir Hamish, who were both looking at him in astonishment. "I do get carried away at times when I see new plants."

"This is Hal Leaveringham, my good friend from Morrowlea,"

I said, remembering as I began speaking that the proper etiquette would have introductions going the other way. I grimaced apologetically, but Hal didn't seem to notice. "Hal, Master Torquin Dart, the Squire, and Sir Hamish Lorkin."

Both men bowed. Sir Hamish said, "I hadn't heard much news of you at court these past three years, but if you were at Morrowlea that explains it, your grace."

Hal made a face. "I'm not very good at this travelling incognito, am I?"

Sir Hamish chuckled. "I'm a portraitist, your grace. I'd hardly forget someone I've painted, even with the difference between sixteen and twenty-one."

"Please, less of the gracing—I've abandoned my poor valet and most of my clothes, and I can hardly dress the part. I'm the Duke of Fillering Pool, Squire Dart. I don't believe we've met before. Here, Jemis, take these, will you?"

He thrust the plants into my hands. They seemed entirely unprepossessing. I raised my eyebrows at him. "What do you want done with them?"

"Don't lose all the soil! The inn-wife is bringing a container. I'll wrap them up and take them back to Fillering Pool, obviously. What else would I do with them?"

I obediently closed my hands so that the earth didn't fall between my fingers. "Consign them to the compost-heap?"

"Bah. You have no sense of the important things in life."

"What, weeds?"

"It's a *very rare* type of speedwell," he said earnestly, then laughed with the resonant whoop that always surprised. "Oh, before I forget, Jemis, my mama sends her regards. She did like you this summer, even without knowing that you were Mad Jack Greenwing's son. I can't *wait* to tell them. It's such a pity my sister's affections are already engaged."

I choked.

"Anyhow," he went on before anyone else could respond to his stunning blitheness, turning with a brilliant smile to the inn-wife as she arrived with the promised tin. "Thank you, ma'am. What did you say this was called here?"

"'Tis bred from hoary eyebright, my lord, though some as will call it creeping speedwell, and my ma, who gave me that piece when I wed, called it Blue-eyed Veronica. She's from the Woods, my lord."

I reflected that Hal really wasn't very good at travelling incognito. He ignored the *my lords* and set the plant into the tin, pressing soil gently around the roots and even over some of the branches. He looked as if only strict training was keeping him from cooing as the inebriated and half-enchanted Mr. Dart had cooed over the geese in the Talgarths' pond last week.

"Hoary because of the ciliate leaves, creeping because of its prostrate habit, and blue-eyed must be its flowers—though Veronica I am unclear of. Do you know its history, ma'am?"

"My ma always said that Veronica was a name for the Lady down in the Woods."

"Indeed?" Hal smiled down at his treasure. "There must be many wonderful variant names down here."

"In the Woods, to be sure," said the innkeeper, who had arrived with tankards of ale for Master Dart and me. He laughed. "Different words for all sorts of things. Make the runner turn the race, eh, Bella?"

His wife laughed good-naturedly. "It's a more colourful way of saying 'turn the handle on the pump', now, isn't it?"

"Aye, put a story into every sentence."

There were far worse ways to behave, I thought, turning the phrase over in my mind and enjoying it.

"There's a story in every plant-name," Hal said happily. "Pity it's autumn and I'll have to wait till the spring for the flowers. I'm sure it will be well worth the wait."

We all looked at the plant in its tin. The inn-wife said doubtfully, "'Tis a very humble plant, my lord. "

"But of course it is! Nevertheless, it is superb in its own way, and of course it has many interesting properties ... the clarification of the sight being only the beginning of its magical virtues. Oh, yes, ale, sir, unless you have perry?" He winked at Mr. Dart. "I understand that to be a specialty of the region. I have been hearing about the pear orchards of Ragnor barony. And some water, ma'am, for my eyebright."

"We have Arguty pear cider, my lord," the innkeeper said, and bustled his wife off.

Hal set his tin down on the table quite carefully and turned with a disarming smile to Master Dart and Sir Hamish, who were still staring at him. "I don't think I had ever truly realized that the Woods Noirell were so close to Ragnor Bella. Geography was never my best subject, eh, Jemis?"

"You're the one sponsoring expeditions across the Western Sea," I replied, taking the tray of drinks from the innkeeper. He'd added some of the little sweet cornmeal cakes the Old Arrow was noted for. At the sight of them I realized I was famished.

"*Plant hunting* expeditions," Hal replied as earnestly as before, then laughed again. "Not that I don't expect them to come back with maps, mind. Who knows what they'll find out there over the old border?" He dribbled a little water from a small ewer on the tray into his container. "There. Now, Jemis, leaving aside questions of plants and plant-hunting—"

"For the nonce."

He grinned at me. "I'm sure I'll find some more to tell you about later. Anyhow, perhaps one of you gentlemen will be able to tell me—how do I get to the Woods from here?"

We all looked at him. Finally I said, "Er, why?"

"I want some honey," he said, taking one of the cakes, then took in our expressions. "Why, is that so strange? At least three of the other people on the mail coach were coming to the Fair hoping to acquire some. That Madam Lezré seemed certain she had a source—but then it occurred to me, when the inn-wife was speaking just now, that of course I have every right to go call on the Marchioness and ... and it seems as if there are reasons no one else suggested that?"

I swallowed a long draught of my ale and started to cough when some went down the wrong way. Mr. Dart rolled his eyes, but his mouth was full with cake, and Sir Hamish was snickering softly, so it was left to Master Dart to say: "The Marchioness is, ah, somewhat eccentric."

"Hasn't left the Woods in *years*," Sir Hamish put in. "Actually, come to think of it I haven't seen anyone from the Woods in years—the Hornes used to come to the Fair with a wagonload of honey."

Master Dart nodded. "Sometimes the Whites—they're the inn-keepers there—would come with their mead, too."

"Mr. White's mead was *superb*," Sir Hamish said, closing his eyes reminiscently. "It made you think of Paradise like the song. Alas, they haven't been by, oh, since Perry and the others went off to university."

"They're not on the list of vendors this year," Mr. Dart agreed, then cocked his head at me. "Have *you* heard anything from the Marchioness, Jemis? We were interrupted earlier when we were talking about that article in the *New Salon* about the dearth of honey."

I swallowed another mouthful of ale. "No. Not since my mother died. Why do you want Noirell honey, Hal?"

He was looking back and forth, brow furrowed slightly. His expression didn't clear as he answered. "It's my mother's favourite, and I wanted to give her a crock for Winterturn. We need to turn her up sweet—my sister wants to marry an unsuitable party, you see." He grinned; his frowns never lasted long. "Not that I care, and I am technically the head of the family, but Mama ... it is a pity, Jemis, that ... well, never mind. Is there a particular reason you'd hear from the eccentric Marchioness? Family connection?"

"She's my grandmother," I said, rolling a stray leaf of his hoary eyebright between my fingers. "She didn't get on well with my mother."

"She was a right old witch," Sir Hamish said, snickering again. "Do you remember, Tor, when we went in for Jack and Olive's wedding? She made them have it at that absurd ruined temple right in the middle of the Woods, and half the wedding party couldn't find it. It ended up just being you and me, Jack and Olive, the Marchioness and her March—"

"Her *Marquis*," said Master Dart. "Oh, what was his name?

Looked like a jockey."

"He looked like Jemis—or rather, Jemis looks like him. Udo, that was his name."

I took another drink. "I'm so glad to know that not only am I named for a horse, but that I look as if I ought to be riding one professionally."

"Could be worse," Mr. Dart said. "You could look like one, too."

"Thank you, Mr. Dart."

"Mind, she was *literally* a witch," Sir Hamish went on, gesturing at Mr. Long the innkeeper for some more ale. I decided I was better off resisting the temptation to keep drinking, and drew my tankard away. "Always used to think that was the only way she managed to find a husband."

"Hamish!"

"An imperial title is quite attractive, even these days," Hal murmured.

"Point," said Sir Hamish, grinning. "Now, this is all to say that you may wish to rethink your plan of calling on the Marchioness to ask her for honey. It's quite possible she'd turn you into something, fashion or no fashion, and then where would your sister be?"

"Duchess of Fillering Pool," Hal said, smiling imperturbably. "As it happens, I have a small talent in that direction myself, but never mind that. Imperial titles get passed down by primogeniture, not by gender. Which means—"

But Sir Hamish had choked on his ale and we had to wait while he spluttered himself into good order again. Several of the farmers looked over curiously. "Well now!" he said, focusing in on me. "I had *entirely* forgotten that."

"What?" I retorted cleverly, and then my mind started to work through what Hal had just said. "Hal—what—what do you mean?"

"Unless you have any aunts or uncles?" Sir Hamish said.

"No, my mother was an only child ..."

"And you're *her* only child."

"Hal—don't—"

"Which makes you, if I am not much mistaken, the Viscount St-Noire."

Chapter Nine
I have No Idea

SUPPER AT DART Hall was excellent and washed down with co-pious—one might even say extravagant—quantities of even more excellent Arcadian red. I kept trying to explain how I couldn't possibly be a viscount (a *viscount!*), but everyone else seemed to feel the matter was settled. Eventually I gave up on trying to change the subject, and listened to Hal's account of his journey.

"I was in Isternes to see off my ship on her expedition," he explained as the second remove was removed and the Darts' butler, Mr. Brock, came in with port and cheese and then over to the side-board for cigars. "That's when I heard that my great-uncle, whom I was planning on visiting, had gone walkabout."

"He doesn't live in Fillering Pool?" Mr. Dart asked.

"No, he's an advisor to the Lady on Nên Corovel. So there I was, with everything arranged—at home, I mean, my sister's look-ing after my duties for the autumn—for me to be away another month or more, and nowhere to go. I was buying presents when I discovered that no one had any Noirell honey for love or money."

"The *New Salon* reported that the last barrel in Kingsford went for three gold emperors," Mr. Dart said, accepting his pipe from Mr. Brock. He was already remarkably proficient using his left hand for all the tasks he'd formerly done with his right; it wouldn't be much longer before no one, watching him, would realize he wasn't naturally left-handed.

"Distracted, Mr. Greenwing?" Master Dart said, and I started, realizing that the port had come to a stop before me. I put a small amount of port in my glass for appearances' sake and slid the decanter along to Hal.

"Lord St-Noire," murmured Sir Hamish.

"*Mr. Greenwing*," I said, in what nearly amounted to a growl. Mr. Dart, his pipe successfully lit, raised his eyebrows at me. I glowered at him and poked at a cracker with my knife until it crumbled into pieces.

Hal slid the decanter along to Sir Hamish. "Anyhow, I couldn't find any honey in Isternes or Orio City, and when I got to the turn to Fillering Pool I decided I'd keep on to Fiellan and see whether I could find any here. I was a bit worried about Jemis, who hadn't written me in a while, and it occurred to me that my uncle might have come to Ragnor Bella, so I set off hither."

Mr. Dart blew a smoke ring. "You said earlier you went into the river at Otterburn?"

Hal cut himself a piece of Blue Yrchester and examined it carefully before spreading the cheese on his biscuit. "My coachman can get quite puffed with the consequence of driving the Duke—he hasn't had the, er, privilege very often since I've been at Morrowlea—and he was too busy preening for a passing landau full of ladies to watch where we were going, and off the road we went and into the river. It's not as if it was a high-perch phaeton or anything."

"Did you lose the horses?" I asked, knowing that Hal would not be telling the story so lightly if he had lost any of the people.

"No, fortunately the Otterburn isn't a very dramatic river—it was only about three feet deep, and basically all that happened was that the coach tipped over and one of the horses sprained a tendon, and Filbert—that's my valet—and I got a ducking. As did all my belongings. Which is why I ended up on the mail coach—I decided I was still in the mood for adventures, and after walking this summer, Jemis, travelling in the crested carriage, et cetera, was rather boring. So I told Criotte, the coachman, to see to the horses and fix the axle of the carriage or whatever it was that was wrenched out of alignment, and sent Filbert back to Fillering Pool with the damaged luggage and a letter to my sister. Then the mail coach came by, and I got on it, and … came here."

He grinned at me. "There were some minor adventures on the coach, but I can see that Jemis is still hoping to persuade us there is no way whatsoever he, his grandmother's sole living relative, is not also her heir."

"I have two half-sisters," I said.

"Younger, I presume?"

"Yes," said Sir Hamish, "and not from a legitimate marriage."

"My mother entered into her second marriage in good faith," I said hotly. "It's not her fault that my father turned out to be alive and she was a bigamist—"

Sir Hamish said levelly, "I meant, not from a marriage contracted within the Woods. I seem to remember there was something about inheritance conditions involved in why the ceremony was at that temple."

"Oh, yes," said Master Dart, puffing thoughtfully at his cigar.

"Yes, that's true. I do recall Jack saying something about that … Some of the Imperial titles get passed down through strange conditions."

"So it's possible I'm not eligible?"

Hal started to laugh. "You sound so hopeful! Why don't you want to be a viscount, Jemis? I know you're a much keener radical than I am, but I have to say that money and a title can be very helpful."

"How am I more of a radical than you?" I replied, gesturing at him, neatly but not exactly well-dressed from his cravat to his water-damaged boots. "You're an imperial duke who went to Morrowlea."

"And you're a viscount who went there, too, and was one of the most impressively high-minded idealists. The fact that you didn't know notwithstanding—although I'm not quite clear *how* you didn't. Didn't your mother tell you?"

Hal had known all through university that my parents were dead, though I hadn't given him any specifics as to how. I'd known his father was dead, that he loved his mother dearly, that he had a twin sister whom he missed fiercely and wrote every week, that he had a number of aunts and uncles and cousins.

"No," I said slowly, trying to get past the lump of pain that thinking of my mother always brought close to the surface. "I … when my mother died, I wrote to tell my grandmother, and she wrote back, *My daughter has been dead these five years since*, and—and that was that. I haven't had any communication with her since then."

"No letters? Nothing from her lawyers or agents or men of business?"

I felt a sudden hollow sensation. I had no idea—*none*—what was involved in an imperial title, any title. Agents for what? Mr. Dart was his brother's land agent ... I pushed around the crumbs on my plate. "Nothing. I didn't—I didn't pursue, and I'm sure Mr. Buchance didn't."

"He's your stepfather?"

"Was. He died this past summer."

"While we—?"

"While I was wandering around Ghilousette not writing to anyone," I said glumly. "People think I missed his funeral on purpose."

"How absurd." Hal cut himself some more cheese. "Does that mean you missed the reading of the will at the Midsomer Assizes?"

"There was that, too. And now my uncle is the sitting magistrate for the autumn session—"

"And he thinks you're all set to set off a revolution," said Sir Hamish, snickering again.

Master Dart made a noise suggestive of warning and reached forward to take another cigar. Mr. Dart said sharply, "Not that one!"

There was a pause. Master Dart moved his hand to the cigar one over. "This one all right, Perry?"

Mr. Dart was flushing pink behind his beard. "Er, yes, that one's fine."

"You haven't done that in ages," Master Dart observed, carefully examining the acceptable cigar. "When you were a little boy you were forever telling us not to touch this or that thing, that this one wanted us to use it and that one didn't."

"Oh, that's right," Sir Hamish cried, pouring himself more port and topping up Mr. Dart's while he was about it. "I'd forgotten—

you must have been, what, four or five? And your papa would come up and say in a deep, deep voice, '*Now then, Peregrine*'—"

He stopped, but not soon enough. Mr. Dart gave him a fulminating glare, and spoke with haughty precision. "Do tell us the gossip, Hamish, I was in the fields all morning."

Sir Hamish was rather red, his bearing apologetic. He coughed. "Most of it is about Mr. Greenwing, naturally."

"Naturally," I said, but they ignored me.

"Baron Ragnor is convinced he's here to bring magic back into prominence and destroy both his careful equilibrium of power and the calm prosperity of the fiefdom, though as he thinks everyone he dislikes is doing that I shouldn't worry."

"Oh, good," I muttered.

"Justice Talgarth is certain that you have something do with the incident at his house last week, though he is amusingly inconsistent as to which part, and he's too canny a lawyer to try a suit against you, even with Sir Vorel in the magistrate's chair this session."

"He did nothing wrong," Mr. Dart said stoutly, thus neatly glossing over the numerous crimes we'd committed last weekend, which ranged from gambling to impersonation to assault to entry under false pretences—I had to suppress a smile when he winked at me.

"Lady Flora—"

"My sainted aunt," I put in for Hal's benefit.

"—is utterly sure you returned for no purpose other than to murder her husband, and probably herself as well, in their bed so that you can claim his property, which may or may not legally be yours, anyhow—"

"Depending on his acknowledgment by the Marchioness?"

asked Hal.

"No, this is the Greenwing side," I replied, deciding I would have some port after all. "The situation with my father's inheritance is complicated."

"And Sir Vorel himself," Sir Hamish went on, slightly triumphantly in the face of Hal's visibly growing confusion, "is trying to pass off your return to Ragnor Bella as nothing less than the first sortie of the coming revolution."

"Does he say I am against any particular system? Or am I simply revolting?"

"You went to Morrowlea, I think that's quite enough for him," said Mr. Dart, chuckling. "I don't think he can get over the fact that you made it on merits. It throws off all his direst mutterings. Did you tell him about Mrs. Figheldean's theory, Hamish? That's the one where you're responsible for the summer's flooding."

I gritted my teeth, though that just added the increasing likelihood of a bad headache to my day. "And just how does she think I accomplished that, since apart from anything else I wasn't in south Fiellan this summer?"

"Oh, Mrs. Figheldean doesn't *think*," Sir Hamish said comfortably. "No more than any of that lot, outside their pet hobbies. Sir Vorel is very sound on ornamental carp, you know."

"As it happens, I wasn't aware of that."

"How little interest you take in your neighbours and near relations," Mr. Dart said, choosing two cakes. "Yet everyone's in agonies over how to bet on you—for the Fair, of course."

"You're not much like your father," Hamish observed, when I took a deep gulp of my port and regretted treating the fine old liquor that way. "He would have hit someone by now."

I swallowed tautly. "I'm told I don't favour either of my parents except in my general intransigency and propensity to cause chaos."

"I hear also in your skills at table." He chuckled. "Shall I tell you why *I* think you're back here?"

"To dethrone the King of Rondé, no doubt."

"Or recreate the Red Company," Mr. Dart suggested, having finally managed to swallow.

Hamish smiled. "Ah, you see, I'm not one of the fashionable *ton*, Mr. Greenwing. I'm a simple artist and farmer. I don't come up with elaborate theories to feed my folly if I can help it, and I'm not one of Sir Vorel's cronies to be beholden to him for my opinions. I reckon you came here because this is your home and your stepfather's died."

"And you need to be here for the will to be read at the Winterturn Assizes," Mr. Dart said, bracing his pipe against his plate so he could tamp the tobacco down properly.

"Assuming Sir Vorel doesn't find a way to prevent it," I said glumly. "I can't believe they all spend that much time thinking about me."

"Well, you did come back and try to be polite to everyone," Mr. Dart said, striking a sulphur match and lighting his pipe. I sneezed mildly at the initial burst of smoke, and sighed. He waved the pipe vaguely in the direction of the door. "Is that Brock answering the front door?"

"Sounds like it," agreed Master Dart, turning in his chair as the door to the dining room opened and the butler came in to ask in sonorous tones whether the Darts were at home to Sir Vorel Greenwing, magistrate.

Chapter Ten
Sir Vorel has No Idea

MY UNCLE GAVE them no time to decide, as he stomped through the door in Mr. Brock's wake. A footman bobbed behind him, trying to take cape and hat, both of which were dripping wet.

"Ah, good evening, Sir Vorel," Sir Hamish said urbanely, nodding at Mr. Brock. "Pour the good magistrate some port, will you? We have already dined, but do you need any sustenance? I believe there's some Blue Yrchester left."

Sir Vorel fought his arms free of his many-shouldered cape and glared indiscriminately around the room until his gaze found me. "Not at the same table as that—that—" He shuddered all over, as if words could not come anywhere close to expressing the revulsion he felt looking at me. "How can you be so lacking in all finer sentiment? I thought you men of *sense*."

Master Dart rose from his chair, walked unhurriedly around the table, and placed his hands firmly on my shoulders. "Are you suggesting we should be anything but glad to offer hospitality to my brother's best friend and the son of one of *our* closest friends?"

"You should know better than to harbour the degenerate offspring of a traitor!"

Master Dart pushed me back down into my seat as I tried to rise. He frowned severely as I protested incoherently. "No, Mr. Greenwing, this is not the time."

"A coward and a fool, like his father," my uncle spat.

I wrestled with Master Dart's grip, but he was immovable.

Sir Hamish spoke with a kind of cool amusement. "And does that come down your father's side, or your mother's, Sir Vorel?"

Sir Vorel swung, eyes bulging, face reddening furiously. "How *dare* you, sir! If I were not the magistrate, it would be pistols at dawn, sir!"

"For pointing out that Jack Greenwing was your brother as well as Jemis' father? You cannot rewrite all the barony records to suit your fancy."

Sir Vorel's jaw worked, his chins wobbling over his too-narrow cravat. His face was no longer so red that I feared (oh, all right, hoped) for an apoplexy, but his eyes were terrifying. His voice hissed with rage. "So you show your colours at last! You would have harboured the traitor, too, would you not? You will let him have the freedom of the barony, will let him besmirch his name and his family, will let him pretend to a rank he does not have and make us all a laughing-stock and an object of scorn and mockery!"

"Are you talking about Jemis or his father?" Mr. Dart asked after a moment, his tone one of polite enquiry.

"You watch yourself, young man! You will regret—"

"Here now," Master Dart said. I squirmed under his iron grip. Pain was radiating out from his fingers. "Watch your tongue, Sir Vorel—you have no call to be threatening either my brother or Mr. Greenwing."

"Is he not pretending in public houses to be a Viscount?" Sir Vorel cried. "Is he not threatening to race with all the commoners? Is he not claiming his father was no traitor, though all the letters of proof were come? Is he not—"

"Excuse me," said Hal, in a quiet tone that nonetheless cut easily through my uncle's bluster.

"Who the hell are you?" Sir Vorel cried. "Some rapscallion crony of my degenerate nephew's?"

I stopped struggling against Master Dart so I could twist to look at Hal. He had not stood, was leaning back in his chair, but every line of his body, from the angle of his chin to the way he'd crossed his legs at the ankle, said—

"I am Halioren Lord Leaveringham, the Duke of Fillering Pool," he said, in a tone I had never heard from him before. I'd never heard *anyone* speak like that, though I'd certainly heard people try.

Sir Vorel gaped and spluttered and looked as if apoplexy was still a viable possibility. Hal slowly uncrossed his legs and stood. He held himself without any pretence or affectation, but if he had been dressed in cloth-of-gold and ermine he could not have looked any more impressive. I gaped almost as badly as my uncle. I had shared a room with Hal for three years, and never seen even a hint of this.

"Sir Vorel," he said, his voice soft, so that we all instinctively leaned to hear better. "You may perhaps have noted that my given name is Halioren; I am named for General Prince Benneret Halioren, commander of the Fourth Division of the Seventh Army of Astandalas. He is my great-uncle; my father's mother was the younger sister of King Roald of Rondé, and the General is his youngest brother."

Sir Vorel opened his mouth, then closed it again when Hal took one not-particularly-aggressive step forward. I had never noticed how short my uncle was before.

Hal smiled slightly. "I am sure you recognize his name. The General was, of course, Jack Greenwing's commander at both Orkaty and Loe. In my family, Sir Vorel, we have been regaled with stories about Mad Jack Greenwing—how he took a border at Orkaty and won thereby the Heart of Glory from the Hand of the Emperor—and how he rescued my great-uncle from death by torture by the Stone Speakers at Loe."

"He was the traitor of Loe," Sir Vorel whispered, face very white.

Hal actually chuckled, not his usual whoop but a civilized kind of noise that managed to convey a deeply sophisticated knowledge of the world, a sadness with its follies, an aloofness to its rough tumult.

"Sir Vorel, I assure you I will be doing everything in my power to find out how this tragic misunderstanding was able to occur and to persist. Major Jack Greenwing was not the traitor who opened the castle of Loe—he was not even *in* the castle when the betrayal happened."

Master Dart's hands clenched on my shoulders, sending darts of agony through my neck.

I cast my thoughts back to those crazy three weeks when my father came back to find everyone confused, suspicious, unrelentingly doubtful. What had my father said? He'd been over the border on a scouting mission, that was it—but I couldn't remember details, I had been so angry with everything—and all my memories were washed over with the fury that my father had been so hounded—that he, who had made it all the way home, after the Fall, from across the other side of the Border—three years it had taken him—and he came home to find everyone thinking him a traitor—

"Do you not know the true story?" Hal said, still in the light, thoughtful, disinterested tone. "My great-uncle tells it, oh, almost every time he comes for a visit."

"Please enlighten us, your grace," Sir Hamish said, his voice nowhere near as sardonic as usual.

Hal smiled again. "With pleasure. The fortress of Loe was in the sixth valley of the Seven Valleys over in far eastern Alinor. The Seventh Army was pushing the Border eastward. The Fourth Division was always the vanguard—at Orkaty they earned the motto of 'We hold the Sun', when my great-uncle commanded Jack Greenwing to take the next ridge, and when he planted the Sun Banner at the top discovered an ambush."

My father had held the banner firm. General Halioren had come up second behind him, and the rest of their patrol after, and they had held the ridge until the rest of the division came to relieve them.

"In the Seven Valleys campaign they were again first, and ended up pushing farther than anticipated, all the way to the capture of the fortress of Loe. The Valleyites then collapsed the mountains behind them and cut them off from the rest of the army. They were sitting out the siege on the other side of the Border—until at least the fortress was betrayed and most of the officers and men slaughtered immediately. My great-uncle and those of the command staff who survived the initial assault were captured and led in chains up into the uncharted mountains and eventually into a secret fastness hidden by magic inside a mountain."

We had not heard this story.

We had received the letter stating that Jakory Greenwing had been shot in the back running away from court martial for the betrayal of Loe.

And two months later—after my mother lost the baby she had been carrying, after my elder uncle Sir Rinald had broken his neck out hunting, after the inheritance had been decided in favour of Sir Vorel, for a traitor forfeits his patrimony—we had received the letter stating that Jakory Greenwing was reported dead on a scouting mission.

And three years later—after the Fall of Astandalas, after my mother had married again, after I had started slowly to let myself love my new stepfather, after Lauren had been born—I had opened the door to a knock and discovered there on the step my father.

And three weeks after that had come the visit from the constables to tell us that his body had been found hanging in the forest.

Hal said, voice clear and unemotional, "The magic-users of the Valleyites were adherents of the Dark Kings, and they hated the soldiers of Astandalas. They used three of the commanders in their evil rituals. My great-uncle, as the ranking officer, was forced to watch, and then while they worked on the other two, they broke his hands and put him naked in a hole on the side of a cliff and left him there to die of starvation and cold."

I firmed my lips against disgust and fury that anyone could do that to anyone else.

"My great-uncle said he decided he would die defiantly, and all through the night, as long as he could, he sang the anthem of Astandalas. Some time before dawn he heard something scrabbling on the outside of the cliff, and he did his best to lift his head and prepare himself to die—but it was not death, it was Jack Greenwing come to rescue him."

"Yes!" whispered Mr. Dart; when I looked over at him I saw his cheeks were silvery with tears.

"No," said Sir Vorel, but it was a protest against the world, not against Hal.

"Yes," said Hal even so. "Jack had been sent on a scouting mission before the siege closed in. Only he and two others of his patrol had made it, but they saw the fall of Loe, they saw the command staff marched out, they followed them all the way up. No one knows exactly what happened to Mad Jack between leaving his two soldiers to wait for his return and when he reached my great-uncle, because there wasn't enough time afterwards for him to give a full report. He had been caught, been imprisoned with the corpses of the other officers, had fought a giant ice serpent with the hairpins that one of the officers had in her hair. He gave the mercy cut to the other officer. He made his way through the walls of a fortress made of stone and ice and magic.

"He used his belt to lift my great-uncle out of his hole. My great-uncle's hands were broken, and they were halfway up a thousand-foot cliff. He says he fainted from the pain and exhaustion as Jack carried him down, didn't see much more than that Jack had nothing but his hands and his feet and a short rod of metal to use as an anchor."

"They got down?" Mr. Dart said.

"All the way down. Jack's men were waiting, and led them to a safe spot to rest, then to the only pass they could hope to make before the Valleyites found them—Jack had heard that they planned a new sortie. They came to the Gate of Morning—"

"Dear Lady," Mr. Dart breathed, leaning forward in his chair, intent on every word. "The pass into Bloodwater. They said the river ran red for weeks after the battle there ..."

Hal looked at me. "They could see the Valleyites coming up the valley when they reached the pass. They knew they had to leave someone to hold them back as long as possible—and the General had knowledge he needed to pass on, one of the soldiers was a wizard and they needed him to perform the spells to open the Border, and the other one was badly affected by the altitude. So ..." He looked solemnly at me. "So they left Jack to hold the pass as long as he could, knowing that—"

"That no one would be coming to relieve him," Mr. Dart said quietly. Hal nodded.

"Until this spring, when I heard the story of the so-called 'Traitor of Loe', my family had never heard anything of Major Jack Greenwing than his superb heroism and self-sacrifice." He glanced at me. "That is why I thought my great-uncle might be coming here, to find out the story of Mad Jack's return home and ... and subsequent fortune."

He looked back at my uncle, whose face was blank with some negative emotion I couldn't otherwise decipher. "Sir Vorel, I will assure you once more that I will be doing *everything* in my power to redress this unspeakable travesty. My great-uncle will certainly vouch for him, and if I must go to Zunidh to seek a benediction from the Last Emperor, I shall do so."

"Thank you," I said quietly, when my uncle still said nothing.

Hal smiled very faintly, still every inch an imperial duke, radiating the assurance that if he did have to cross the borders between worlds to seek an audience with the Last Emperor, there would be no problem whatsoever in being granted one.

"As to the other matter, Sir Vorel, it is my understanding that Jemis is the grandson of the Marchioness of the Woods Noirell, eldest son of her only child. As imperial titles are passed through primogeniture, and it appears from what Sir Hamish and Master Dart were telling us earlier that any peculiar requirements arising from the customs of the Woods themselves were met, then yes, it is my belief that Jemis' proper title is the Viscount St-Noire. There will no doubt be some legal matters to clear up, and of course he shall have to confirm the inheritance requirements of the marquisate, but I very much doubt those will prove a problem."

The dragon might, I thought. Master Dart's hands were still heavy on my shoulders.

My uncle stared silently at Hal for an uncomfortably long time, then essayed a sketchy bow, turned on his heel, and stomped out of the room.

"I wonder," said Hal, once again in his normal tone and posture, "whether he is aware that he is already a character in a melodrama?"

Chapter Eleven
Night Ideas

"WE THOUGHT YOU might want company."

I looked up from where I'd been sitting by the fire in my bedroom, trying to read a favourite book I'd left there, but not heeding the lines. It was late, but I'd kept the fire blazing.

I blinked at Hal, who'd opened the door without ceremony and was smiling down at me. "I beg your pardon?"

He edged in, followed by Mr. Dart, who let the door swing shut behind him. "'No knocking, halloos, crying that there were elephants, nothing.'"

I smiled at the quotation from *Aurora*. "'And not even a pot of wine for the visitor.'"

"Whatever *would* we do without Fitzroy Angursell? That's all right. We brought our own."

It was the old bedroom I'd had whenever I'd stayed over at the Hall, with wallpaper in green and gold stripes and furniture in comfortable brown leather and dull gold velvet. It had always made me think of being underwater. After my excursion the week before, which had involved a period of time submerged in the Talgarths' moat, I revised my thought to 'being underwater on a sunny after-noon'. Midnight in the Talgarths' moat had been like being in an inkwell.

Mr. Dart gave Hal the choice of seats; he chose the other up-holstered chair before the fire. Mr. Dart tugged over the footstool for himself. Neither of them said anything. I thought of all the times they had stood up for me, stood beside me, stood behind or before me. I swallowed and drew the cloth of the old dressing gown Mr. Dart had lent me tighter around myself.

"He was still a suicide. Nothing changes that."

They exchanged glances. Then Hal said, "Forgive the imperti-nence, but are you sure?"

I stared at him, unable to collect his meaning. "There was a note."

"There was also a brother who inherited due to his disgrace."

I stared at him some more. Hal looked very serious. I made an involuntary noise somewhere between a cough and a cackle. "Are you implying—do you mean—how can you *suggest* such a thing?"

"Your uncle would not be the first person in history to take steps to … ensure … a succession he was not, properly speaking, otherwise entitled to."

"He would not be the first *uncle* to do so," said Mr. Dart.

"Has this honestly never occurred to you?" Hal said, giving me a hard look. "The moment you said that your older uncle was kind to you and your younger uncle was glad to inherit on your father's death I wondered."

"I suppose you'll suggest Sir Rinald's death by hunting was Sir Vorel's doing, too."

Hal shrugged. "Most people take advantage of situations, rather than create them. All he needed to do was promise your mother he would write to the command staff at Eil and be as mystified as anyone when they never replied. He might even have intended to have gone farther, but then there was the Fall. He wouldn't have needed to do anything else after that."

"But ..." But I stopped there, for I could see Sir Vorel smiling down at me as he explained to my mother that *of course* we would keep staying at the old dower cottage, that he would see his brother's widow not be left destitute and alone now that the sordid truth was out. She need not return to her own family: *he* was the head of her family now, and he would protect her.

And my mother, trying not to cry.

And then the Fall, and when we made it to Arguty House, him saying that now more than ever we should stay at the dower cottage, for the Woods were right on the Border and had assuredly become dangerous as well as strange with all the magic rearranged by the Fall. But still making us beg for every scrap of food or assistance he gave us.

And my mother, telling me over and over again that she loved me, that it didn't matter what anyone said, that my father had been a good man, that Sir Vorel was doing his best with a bad situation.

I realized I was saying this out loud. "He was always so *jolly* about it," I said. "I hated him."

I had never said the words aloud. I flushed, but refused to put my hand over my mouth in childish reaction. I glared defiantly at them.

Mr. Dart pulled out a bottle of wine from the pocket of his dressing gown and filled the glasses that Hal produced from somewhere. He passed me one, then said quietly, "And when your father returned?"

I frowned. "He was even jollier then. He acted as if nothing had ever given him greater pleasure. He was full of enthusiasm and plans for helping—*how* had I forgotten? He kept coming by, he insisted my father stay at Arguty House, he was all full of plans."

"He always was a hypocrite," Mr. Dart said, then looked as if *he* wanted to cover his mouth with embarrassment.

When had we gotten so mealy-mouthed? You read old novels from Astandalan days and it was as if no one had any manners at all, just elaborate ritual ceremonies and ribald wit.

Mr. Dart coughed. "He always acts as if it was his doing that the Arguty estates are so profitable now, that he was so clever in building it up again after Jemis' grandfather nearly broke it, when it was all Sir Rinald's doing. Sir Rinald did all the work, and then he broke his neck hunting and Sir Vorel reaped all the benefits."

"Hmm," said Hal. "He wasn't so jolly to you in town, Jemis."

"He's not happy I returned to Ragnor Bella. It upsets his wife to see me, apparently. I'm a reminder of our family's most terrible scandal, you know, and certain to come to a worse end than my father."

"Is he actively trying to drive you away?"

"He did tell me outright I should leave town."

"The devil he did!"

I smiled crookedly. "He's not the only one."

"It will be interesting," Mr. Dart said thoughtfully into his wine glass, "to find out his reaction to the story you told tonight, Hal. Confirmation from an Imperial duke that Major Greenwing was *not* the traitor of Loe cannot be something he will welcome, if we are correct in our suspicions."

"But what about my father's note?" I asked, trying not to sound pathetic.

It was all too easy to imagine my uncle—but that was a dreadful thing to think about anybody, and I disliked him far too much to be able to think about it clearly.

"I thought *your* last letter to me in the spring had an elegiac quality," Mr. Dart said. "If something had happened to you I would have thought it was that sort of good-bye. I wouldn't have thought *murder*."

"Oh," I said numbly.

There was a pause, then Hal said, "Well, this has been a most diverting day. What did you have planned for tomorrow? Now that I know that Ragnor Bella's reputation is entirely undeserved, I am eager to help uncover its secrets."

"Well," said Mr. Dart, "since there doesn't seem to be anything to do but wait and see Sir Vorel's reaction to your story, and you can't sign up for the Fair competitions till Sunday, perhaps we might work on the dragon's riddle. I reckon we should try the Woods Noirell."

"Oh!" said Hal, enthusiastically. "Then we can find out why there's such a dearth of honey."

I rolled my eyes, sipped the wine. Found my eyebrows raising. "This is excellent wine. We never used to get given the good stuff."

"Your friend the imperial duke helps. Also I think Brock's very impressed that you went to Morrowlea on merits."

Hal looked at me. "You were the Rondelan Scholar at Morrowlea?"

"The Fiellanese one," I muttered, though I was pleased, for that triumph had come before Lark and the wireweed and the bright and brilliant Jemis Greenwing that had not been the real one, after all.

"Morrowlea's the smallest of the Circle Schools. They only take one scholar from each country in Northwest Oriole." Hal shook his head in admiration. "I always knew you were smart, Jemis, but that is an extraordinary achievement."

"We're making him blush," said Mr. Dart.

"Oh, that's no feat, Mr. Dart," said Hal, and they both laughed heartily.

"Oh, go away," I said, and threw them out so I could go to bed and pretend to sleep.

Chapter Twelve
Sir Vorel has an Idea

INTENDING AS WE were to go chasing dragons, of course Saturday dawned as sodden and wet an autumnal day as anyone could imagine.

We sat in the breakfast room staring out at the grey rain sheeting down. There was no chance of seeing the dragon; there was barely any chance of seeing the other side of the front lawn.

"Well," said Hal philosophically, "we are men of Alinor. Perhaps you have some books on magical fauna, Master Dart? We might as well do some research."

But Mr. Dart had not entirely been joking, on another occasion, when he told me that his brother's library was arranged by colour. It was not quite as bad as that—it was not that all the red books were together, and all the blue ones elsewhere—but it had been organized with a strong eye to aesthetics and much less to any desire to actually find anything.

"I'm afraid it's my fault," Sir Hamish said, as we stood in the middle of the room admiring its appearance and trying not to be dismayed at the utter incoherence of its contents. "It's such a beautiful room … and we're not a very bookish family."

"History is over here," Mr. Dart said, striding over to the brass-chased mahogany shelves between two gorgeous Collian scrolls depicting the famous islets crowned with contorted trees of the Sea of Ten Thousand Pinnacles. He ran his good hand lightly across the spines. "General Astandalan, Alinorel, Collian, Voonran, Ystharian, Zuni … even some outworld tomes …"

I walked over to stand beside him. The history books were completely clean and well-used, unlike most of the other bays of the library. But then Mr. Dart had always been keen on the subject. He used to ask my father for stories even more than I had.

Still, as Hal had said, there wasn't much else to be done—and I did like little better than delving into a good library. Hunting for dragons could take many forms, after all.

***

"My dear nephew," said a familiar voice.

I looked up unthinkingly, mind still bemused by the intricate rhymes and glorious thundering momentum of Fitzroy Angursell's *Kissing the Moon* (a work only slightly less well regarded than *Aurora*, and considerably more far-fetched, even though the latter was a comic satire and the former purported to be a true account of the Red Company's visit to the Moon's country).

"My *dear* nephew," repeated the voice.

I blinked. My uncle stood there, damp hair curling becomingly, several chins tucked unbecomingly into the thin neckerchief, starched shirt-collar points wilting from the wet. A maid was just closing the door to the library behind him.

"Sir Vorel," I said blankly.

He was holding his hands outstretched towards me. While I watched in total disbelief, he crossed the room, ignoring the arrested figures of Sir Hamish, Mr. Dart, Master Dart, and Hal, and took my hands in his own. *Kissing the Moon* slid down my arm and fluttered to the floor.

He was smiling back tears. "My dear *nephew*, words cannot express my feelings at this juncture."

"Oh?" I said weakly.

Words, he declared, failed him: but yet they came pouring forth. How astonished he had been last evening by the young Duke of Fillering Pool (with a bow to Hal, whose face was back to its hauteur). When his dear lady wife had come home from a dining engagement with the Terrilees (who were the Terrilees?), she told him how she had been stopped and regaled by not fewer than *seven* different parties along the way with the story of how the young Duke of Fillering Pool knew me from Morrowlea and had come to visit, —and when he had shared the Duke's story of how my father was the *hero*, not the *traitor*, of Loe—how he had tossed and turned all night, thinking what he could *possibly* do—how Lady Flora had insisted he wait until the rain relented before he made even the two-mile ride to Dart Hall—

"But how could I wait, my dear boy," he said, "how could I wait? When I think of how *wrong* I was—when I think that if only I had *listened* to my brother, he might still be with us—with *you*—when I think of how I have *treated* you—"

At this point words did fail him, and he choked up, finally let go of my hands, and plunged to stand with his elbow on the mantelpiece and hand over his brows in a gesture as affected as it was fine, breast heaving with emotion and oratory.

I looked at Hal and Mr. Dart, who had identical expressions of incredulity on their faces. Master Dart and Sir Hamish were in the middle of exchanging a look I could not read, but which caused Sir Hamish to nod sharply and Master Dart to go to the door to murmur something to a servant on its other side.

I massaged life back into my hands, and picked up *Kissing the Moon* from the floor, then stood there, smoothing out the bent corners, and had no idea at all of what to say.

Presently Sir Vorel suppressed his heaving bosom (the words came unbidden to mind; for some reason they were in Violet's voice), wiped his eyes with a handkerchief, and came back over to me. This time he took my right hand in both of his.

"My dear nephew," he said again—making me wonder irresistibly whether he had forgotten my name—"*let* me make things right for you. I have done what little I could under the circumstances for the love I once bore my brother, but with such unimpeachable support for his character—my dear boy, you must be angry with me. No, do not speak! Not yet. Not until I have said my piece. You have every right to be angry with me. I have not treated you well, my boy, I am ashamed to admit. You have always been a memory to me of—I should not say such a thing, to *you* least of all—but perhaps you *most* of all have the right to know—"

He sighed heavily, and squeezed my hand. "My dear boy, your mother was like the Green Lady in springtime. It will not astonish you that Lady Olive of the Woods had many suitors ... but perhaps you did not know, could not know, that I was one of them. She chose my brother ... then she chose that *merchant* ... and I confess I was angry—for I had offered her everything I had, everything I *was*, but I could see that although it was not love such as she had known with my brother—she did love the man, merchant though he was—and I resigned my heart to another wife, and was glad only to see *her* happy. ... My dear boy, when your father returned and caused such distress to your mother by his reappearance, and his story was so incredible and he was so—well, *changed*—from the brother I had known—I was angry, and did not listen to his protestations that the story of his treason was false, that there had been a mistake."

He sighed even more heavily. "You can think how that has haunted me, how that has *tortured* me. When I think that if I had merely listened to him—if I had merely *believed* him, as was my duty as his brother—oh, my dear nephew, if I could only go back to that time and recant all the dreadful things I said to him—perhaps he might not have been driven to take his own life. And perhaps I might have been able to forgive him for having a son by *her*, when I never—"

He smiled tremulously up at me. "My boy, I could not forgive him for the shame he brought to *her*. And I cannot forgive myself for not listening, for playing a role—however small, however large, only the Lady knows—in his last act. I have taken out my anger and my sorrow on you, who were innocent of all but loving your father, as a son ought. As any son ought," he repeated, shaking my hand with both of his for emphasis, his eyes welling once more with tears. "Oh, if only I had—it is too late for that. But it is not too late—I pray it is not too late—to make amends to *you*."

"Sir Vorel," I began, trying to tug my hand free.

"Too long," he said thickly, "too long have I insisted on this formality, as if I could thereby keep distant from the strength of my feelings. Too long have I hidden my—dare I say it? I must, I must, for if I do not *now*, my courage may fail, and I retreat once more behind the mask of courtesy and duty—too long have I hidden my *love* for you, my thoughts that you are my brother's son and the son of the woman we both—loved—"

"Sir Vorel," I began again, as he began once more to sob, and this time when he raised his hands picturesquely to his face he took mine with them. I jerked my hand free. "I am astonished," I said finally. "I do not know what to say."

"Words fail," he said meaningfully.

I rather thought they did.

"My dear nephew," he said yet again, "give me no answer now. We must—oh, there are so many things we must discuss. Where you are to live, for one. It is not suitable for you to stay with Mrs. Buchance."

Indignation managed to break through the mass of emotions threatening to suffocate me. "Mrs. Buchance has been the soul of courtesy and kindness."

I did manage to shut my teeth on, *Unlike you*, but the effort left my tone and sentence very abrupt.

Sir Vorel gave me a smile that was indulgent to the point of condescension. "My dear boy, you are still very young, and un-versed in the ways of the world. Your—stepmother—well—*quite* apart from the fact that her social class is not quite the thing—she is *very* young, and a young and very wealthy widow—well—people talk, you know."

Icy rage swamped every other sentiment. I was so angry I couldn't breathe, and groped automatically for a handkerchief that was not in its right place, for I was wearing an outfit of Mr. Dart's and not my own—

"Your sentiments are very proper," he said, smiling even more indulgently. "You can, however, and *will*, I am sure, look much higher. And you are very young to be settling down so ... domestically. Dear boy, you have barely seen the world! We must discuss many things—your allowance, for one—and of course, Lady Flora was saying only yesterday that perhaps it would be for the best if you were to come live with us, for you *are*, you know, my nearest living relative."

He daubed at his eyes with his handkerchief again. "I am too overcome with emotion to speak of practical details." He reached out and took my hand again—I seemed incapable of keeping it from his grasp—and pressed it to his heart. I permitted him with a sort of horrified fascination to see what he would do next.

"I am sorry I cannot stay for luncheon," he said, looking at Master Dart. "But I have said my piece, and words fail me. Words fail me." He sighed hugely. "How *happy* I am to know my brother's name can be cleared of the ignominy that has attached to it. My dear nephew—we will speak again soon. Very soon."

And he plunged out of the room, through the door the footman was holding open, and left us all staring at one another.

I wiped my hands thoroughly with the handkerchief I had finally extracted from Mr. Dart's waistcoat pocket.

Chapter Thirteen
The Dragon has Another Idea

WE WERE NOT able to discuss the matter, because even as we trailed out after Master Dart to ensure that Sir Vorel had indeed left the premises, the footman on duty turned back to the front doors and opened them on the resplendent figure of the Honourable Roald Ragnor.

"Hullo the Darts!" he said, taking off his hat politely and shaking out his golden curls in a spray of water drops like diamonds. I tried to suppress the wave envy that always arose at the sight of the baron's son (for I was never going to be so handsome, so broadly muscular, or so tall, whatever else I might manage to make of myself), but I was feeling unsettled after the strange interview with my uncle, and woefully inclined to rejoice in the sight of the Honourable Rag's sodden appearance.

"Come for lunch, have you?" Sir Hamish said genially. "Your grace, may I present to you the Honourable Roald Ragnor, Baron Ragnor's son and heir? Master Roald, this is Mr. Greenwing's friend from Morrowlea, the Duke of Fillering Pool."

"How d'ye do, your grace," the Honourable Rag said, sweeping a bow.

Hal nodded with a suspicious access of ducal hauteur. "Master Roald."

"Did I see Sir Vorel cantering off down the drive?" the Honourable Rag said, following us to the dining room. "It's a wet day for calling."

"And yet you're here," Sir Hamish said.

The Honourable Rag laughed robustly. "So I am."

But he declined to explain.

Over lunch the conversation turned largely on the likely after-effects of wireweed seedlings in the Dart bottomlands, the autumn flooding having washed down seeds from the Talgarths' into their fields. I didn't have much to contribute to this topic, since Hal knew far more than I did about the botany. Once I'd said my piece about reading that wireweed was a perennial legume from Kilromby, and that the Rag flooded in early autumn after the snow melted from the mountains, he launched into a thorough lecture on the varying properties of legumes vis-à-vis removing the seedlings, and only the protestations that the bottomlands would be ankle-deep in mud from the morning rain prevented him from leaving the table to go investigate the matter.

It felt decidedly strange to be back in the role of a proper young gentleman, familiar as the comfortably elegant dining room at the Dart manse was. The week at Mrs. Buchance's, working at Mrs. Etaris', doing my best to be bourgeois, all that fell away. Even the Honourable Rag spoke to me on equal terms with the others, calling me Greenwing and guarding nothing of his speech.

My thoughts fell away to wondering about my uncle and his effusions. It was far easier to believe he had somehow arranged for my father—

But I couldn't condemn the man on no proof simply because I disliked him and because he used to make my mother cry.

"You're woolgathering, Greenwing."

I looked up from the pile of walnut shells next to my plate. The Honourable Rag was smiling genially at me. "Penn'orth o' herring for your thoughts?"

There was something so *odd* about the Honourable Rag now, I thought.

I didn't think I wanted to say 'Why *are* you behaving so much as if you haven't a thought in your brain?' to him, and was not much more inclined towards further public discussion of my uncle, so instead I smiled with an effort of lightness. "Oh, just woolgathering, indeed."

"Thinking about the Fair competitions?" the Honourable Rag asked, smirking.

Life is a game of Poacher, I reminded myself. And Mrs. Etaris had asked me to string him along. "Yes, Hal and I are thinking of putting our names in for the cake competition. I was contemplating which recipe we should try."

"Your mother used to make that honey cake," Mr. Dart said, giving me an appreciative grin. "What was it called again? Beehive Cake?"

"Bee Sting Cake," said Sir Hamish, his eyes quizzical, smile sardonic. "Always something special, with honey from the Woods. I don't think she ever made it for the Fair, did she, Tor? Even though the best were always with the autumn honey."

Master Dart was also looking from the Honourable Rag to me, as if he were reading lines from a book I couldn't see. He snorted softly. "Not the Lady Olive, no. And there won't be much honey from the autumn blooms if the weather doesn't clear soon."

"Oh, it'll clear," Mr. Dart said confidently. "It's clearing already, actually. It'll be dry enough for the oats in the early part of the week."

Hal looked at him. "Weather-working in your family?"

The Honourable Rag laughed with more exuberance than the question, or the answer, permitted. "Don't ask him that, your Grace. M'father's not keen on magic, not keen at all."

I raised my eyebrows at him. Mr. Dart and I had seen him wandering the woods by the Talgarths' house last week with a wer-elight—which if he'd bought it was one thing (though still problematic), but if he'd made it himself was quite another.

He kept smirking, dropping his eyes meaningfully to my right hand, which was resting around the stem of my goblet, and to the ring I wore there.

To my annoyance, I was fairly certain he'd won that round.

Master Dart, apparently oblivious to this interchange, smiled at Hal. "The winter rains will be settling in soon. We tend to have rain in September, then the Emperor's Summer for about three weeks starting a fortnight or so after the autumn equinox. Dartington's held the Harvest Fair the second week in October since, oh, time immemorial."

"Since the accession of the Empress Zangora the XIII," Mr. Dart said, "who declared a jubilee year throughout all the empire as a thanksgiving for her coming to the throne safely after the successive deaths of her four elder siblings. Northwest Oriole used to run to Midsomer fairs and Winterturn markets in honour of the Lady of the Green and White, but the harvest fair caught on in many principalities. The Empress' Accession Day was the tenth of October, and Dartington still keeps its fair on the week-end closest to that date."

"I didn't know that," I said. It was perfectly obvious no one else had, either.

"It's in the *History of Northwest Oriole*. Diggory Ezalinel of Avalen."

We all nodded appreciatively. After a moment, Hal said, "Is your weather really that regular? You *always* have the Emperor's Summer? Even since the Fall?"

"Since the Interim finished, yes," Master Dart said. "The rains come after, then snow the week of Winterturn."

"How extraordinary."

"Accidents of geography, no doubt," said the Honourable Rag, pushing himself back from the table. "And I have some geography to cover this afternoon, so I'll bid you g'day." He made a careless bow to Hal, nodded at the rest of us, and loped off, tall, handsome, muscular, and confident as always.

I sighed.

Hal said, thoughtfully, "He should have bowed to you, Jemis. If the weather's clearing, we should definitely go call on your grandmother this afternoon."

***

"Where did you learn that?" I asked abruptly as we rode down the long carriageway from Dart Hall to the road. "To be all—ducal—like that? Were you *taught* that?"

Hal gave me a strange look. "Was I being very ducal just then? I'm sorry if I was."

"I think he probably means last night," Mr. Dart said, nudging his horse up along my other side. "When you told off Sir Vorel so thoroughly he came crawling back this morning."

"And wasn't *that* interesting. We shall have to talk about what it means further. No—well, I suppose the answer is 'yes', because I was taught how to comport myself, how to behave. But not that, specifically. My grandfather—my mother's father—was an extraordinary man. A gentle soul, generally very kind, very interested in everyone, always listening regardless of rank. Except sometimes he forgot ..."

"To be gentle?"

Hal chuckled, looking out at the meadows sloping down towards the hidden course of the East Rag on our right. "If you startled him when he wasn't expecting anyone to be there—he loved insects, was a great entomologist, loved to spend the day by himself in the meadows looking for butterflies or beetles—*how* he reacted. Those first moments before he caught himself—it's hard to explain. He would just *look* at you, with this expression of ... outrage? Outrage isn't quite right. He would look at you as if the idea of someone daring to interrupt him was inconceivable. As if every time he was startled he was shocked to the core of all his philosophies."

"That sounds a bit strange," I said.

Hal grinned. "We must all have these eccentric relatives, eh? My grandfather was something of an enigma. He'd repudiated his family, his rank, his name, everything."

"To be an entomologist?" This was Alinor; such things happened.

"To be ... something. He never told us the whole story. We

never learned who he was—who he had been, anyway. He'd had some sort of argument with his brother, and he used to say, sometimes, that court was his brother's domain. But he never told us who his brother was, why court came into it, except for how obvious it was he was from a very important clan. I remember there were a lot of discussions about it, just before the Fall. We were supposed to go to Astandalas so Elly and I could be presented to the Emperor when we were sixteen, but we wanted to go earlier—so we could learn some 'polish', I think was our argument." He chuckled. "We so wanted to see the capital."

And that, right there, was why my uncle had come back grovelling this morning. He must have gone and looked up the Duke of Fillering Pool in the *Peerage of Northwest Oriole*. Hell, an Imperial Duke would be in the *Book of the First Thousand Families of Astandalas*.

"And when you want to channel the most intense aristocratic behaviour possible?" Mr. Dart said, grinning.

Hal whooped. "Yes, exactly. He didn't get angry very often, but when he did … Oh, look!"

Mr. Dart and both jumped at the sudden change of tone, looking wildly around for dragons, ruffians, wicked priests, the Lady knew what else.

But Hal was swinging off his horse, landing ankle deep in mud. He ignored the damage to his boots and plunged forward to examine a dozen or so light purple crocuses blooming in the dry lee of the hedge.

"I thought crocuses bloomed in the spring," I said finally, knowing we weren't going to get back on any other topic until Hal had taken his fill.

"Most do, but there are several autumn-blooming species, of which this is by far the most famous—the saffron crocus. Do you see the stigmas? They must be an inch long."

I grinned at Mr. Dart, who was shaking his head in amusement, and obligingly said: "They are a splendid orange."

"They're not native here," Hal said, pulling out a pen-knife from his waistcoat pocket. He cut one perfect blossom from the small patch and folded into his little notebook, a page or two on from the lesser scabious. "Do people grow them commercially anywhere roundabout?"

Mr. Dart shrugged. "Not that I've ever heard."

"Most curious, since the saffron crocus is almost entirely vegetatively propagated—that is, it doesn't set seed," he clarified at our blank looks.

I filed this piece of information away (for you never knew when I might need to know that fact about the saffron crocus). "So someone planted a few bulbs here?"

"Corms. Yes … though conceivably a bird could have—some jays are known to plant acorns and such—or a squirrel—but even so—where did they *come* from? I haven't heard of saffron being grown this side of East Oriole."

"Indeed, it's almost as strange as Jemis moving from 'under no circumstances whatsoever' to 'hmm, well, perhaps I shall insinuate myself into the Honourable Rag's gambling ring'."

"That wasn't what I was doing!"

"Wasn't it?"

My horse blew out its breath in a great whuffle. I felt this thoroughly expressed my sentiments.

"Look," I said, as Hal stowed away pen-knife and notebook

and remounted his horse. "When the other topics of conversation were my father, my uncle, my grandmother, or myself, I felt that the Harvest Fair was preferable."

"You didn't think we should go back to the dragon or the ruffians or—"

"—Or the peculiar behaviour of your local witch?" asked Hal, grinning.

"Not with Roald Ragnor. He'd've wanted to go dragon-hunting."

"Or witch-hunting?"

Mr. Dart made a face. "The Honourable Roald Ragnor wouldn't be caught dead fraternizing with witches. It'd be against his father's express wishes."

"Tight leash."

"Not tight enough, apparently," I said, "not if Mrs. Etaris is concerned. Mr. Dart, what are we going to do about this gambling ring?"

"Do? Why, you seem to have done most of what's needed already, and I believe—along with Mrs. Etaris—that the rest will follow naturally."

I tried not to grind my teeth. "Why does everyone *care* so much about me?"

"Well, you *are* from nearly the only interesting family in South Fiellan, Jemis. No one else has plays written about them."

I muttered a curse. "And what about Magistra Bellamy?"

"Not much we can do if she's gone away up North."

Hal shook out his reins. "Why does it matter so much about this Magistra Bellamy? Her housekeeping is atrocious."

"Hush," I said, as we came abreast of the Old Arrow—this time *sans* dragon, though the cat was lying curled in a patch of sunlight on the short wall along its garden side.

"You've grown very circumspect," Hal said, casting me a teasing glance. "No talking about magic at all?"

"It's not the witch so much as why she's gone," I replied awkwardly, just as Mr. Dart exchanged greetings with a farmer heading home with a jug of ale from the public house. Two women in middle-class garments turned, saw us, bobbed curtsies to Mr. Dart and Hal, and openly gawked at me. I sighed, and nudged my horse to go a little faster.

We came to the crossroads, and turned to the bridge, leaving behind the small flow of traffic leading to the village. Hal twisted in his saddle to look back at the village. "Why isn't the village built closer to the river? Does it have a tendency to flood?"

Mr. Dart clopped up between us. "Not along here—our bottomlands do, upriver where the meanders are. This is the East Rag—the South runs past Ragnor Bella. No, it's the old tradition in south Fiellan that nothing's built at crossroads. Even hostelries are always at least a furlong away."

"Whyever not?"

We clattered over the hump of the cobbled bridge. Mr. Dart looked at me. I said briefly, "Crossroads are sacred to the Dark Kings. It's where you bury criminals and suicides. What do you reckon, Mr. Dart? Teller Road?"

Teller Road led to the White Cross, where the Imperial Highway was crossed by three other roads, where the Arguty and Dart estates met the Commons and the baron's home farm, and where my father was buried. Mr. Dart made a face. "Let's try the Greenway. It shouldn't be too wet for the horses under the trees."

I turned my horse accordingly onto the lane running behind a cluster of dovecotes. The doves—white and cinnamon and grey—were sitting on their doorsteps like so many neighbours taking in the air, but our passage disturbed them and sent a flock wheeling up in a clatter of wings.

"The problem with Magistra Bellamy," said Mr. Dart, ostensibly to Hal beside him but loudly enough that I could hear him clearly, too, "is that Jemis needs a magic teacher."

"Is she the only practitioner in the barony?"

"She and Dominus Gleason are the only acknowledged ones, and Jemis has taken an unaccountable dislike to Dominus Gleason."

"It's not unaccountable," I said, but didn't clarify.

We passed the last farm on that lane. The muddy ruts turned into the farmyard, leaving us with a greensward as firm and fair as any ride I'd ever been on, sprinkled liberally with pink and white daisies.

"How lovely," said Hal, as we came to the pair of standing stones that marked the place where the lane entered the Hildon Wood and the Greenway proper began.

The Hildon Wood was not as large or as venerable as either the Arguty Forest or the Woods Noirell, nor nearly so mysterious nor dangerous, but it was beautiful in its autumn finery. The Greenway was bordered on either side with hawthorns and hollies, both bright-berried and even the hawthorn still green.

"Let's gallop," I suggested, feeling a sudden urge for speed. Without waiting for their responses I gave my restive horse her head.

The Greenway was as straight and level as an Astandalan road, though far older. It ran a good three miles through the Hildon

Wood from Henring Farm at its northeastern gate to the Green Dragon at its southwestern. There were no houses, no crossroads, not even any branching paths; the only human work you could see was the roofline of the Woodhills' manse through the trees about halfway along, though there was no connecting path to Holtwood.

The only break in the long straight ride, in fact, was the place where the path forked to curve around a standing stone set into a perfectly circular pool just before you reached the Green Dragon.

I pulled up my horse about fifty yards from the pool, for the dragon was there.

After the morning's rain the wind had freshened considerably, but the trees on either side of the hedges were absorbing the brunt of it. Although I could hear the wind, down in the green channel between hawthorn and holly the air was still and close and unexpectedly hot.

It didn't occur to me to look behind to see where Hal and Mr. Dart were. I dismounted and tethered my horse to a convenient branch, straightened my coat and neckcloth and hat, and walked slowly and deliberately along the remaining thirty or so yards before the pool.

The Lady's stones, as a rule, consist of a flat offering stone, placed usually just above the water's surface, to the eastern side of the man-size or taller upright stone anchored in the centre of the pool. The hawthorn and holly hedges continued around the circular glade, leaving perhaps five feet between the shrubs and the stone coping of the pool.

If the Ellery Stone, up in the Coombe by the Lady's Pools, was where the children of Ragnor barony went to scare themselves silly with ghost and monster tales, the Dragon Stone along the

Greenway was where youths went to pray for assistance in matters of the heart—and the loins. Heart, loins, and feet are sacred to the Green Lady of Summer; head, lungs, and hands to the White Lady of Winter.

I had always vaguely assumed that the Dragon Stone took its name from the nearby tavern, but from the way the living dragon was perched, I was no longer so sure. It fit neatly into the space: haunches on the offering stone, tail coiled around the lip of the basin, neck curved into the surfaced of the upright, wings arcing perfectly to fit the space, casting green shadows on the grass, underlit by wavering ripples of light.

Perhaps tavern and stone were named for real dragons, not the other way around.

I looked at the dragon. It looked at me. I bowed, politely, slightly extravagantly, slightly ironically.

The dragon inclined its head. Paused a moment. Spoke.

"Between the green and the white is the door. Between the race and the runner is the lock. Between the sun and the shadow is the key. In the bright heart of the dark house is the dark heart of the bright house. And therewithin, if the sap of the tree runs true, is the golden treasure of the dark woods."

It paused there, the riddle like the first lines of a haiku, awaiting the turn, the twist, the closure.

The demand, the reward, the cost.

And then it said, its voice soft, incongruously reasonable, "The way of the woods has many turns and few branches. The branch of the woods has many turns and few ways. The turn of the woods is the way of the branch, for good, young sir, or for ill."

"Whose good?" I said. "Whose ill?"

The dragon unfurled itself from around the stones in a single sinuous movement, head motionless, eyes on mine, horns gleaming polished gold. It smiled, even more disquietingly, its eyes too aware, too cold, too ironic, even as its wings lifted green and gold in the sunlight, against the rushing clouds, white and blue.

"That is, of course, up to you."

Chapter Fourteen
Mr. Dart has Another Idea

"WELL, OBVIOUSLY THE first thing to do is go to the Woods Noirell," said Mr. Dart.

"I don't know my grandmother," I replied, trying not to take my aggravation out on them.

"What has that got to do with it? If anything, that increases the adventure."

I glared up at Hal, who had said this last—not that Mr. Dart was not evidently also thinking it—knowing he was right, and not finding the knowledge appealing. "I don't want an adventure. I don't want to be embroiled in the Honourable Rag's folly, I don't want my uncle making trouble with Mrs. Buchance for my own good, I don't want everyone to bet on me for the Fair, I don't want to knock on my grandmother's door, and I sure as hell don't want to be playing games with a dragon!"

I laughed harshly, then regretted it when I started to cough. I sat down on the edge of the pool coping, trying to govern my emotions, or at least my face.

Why did the world have to be so bloody confusing?

Hal and Mr. Dart were arguing above me. I propped my chin on my hand and looked into the water of the pool. It was still moving wildly in reaction from the dragon taking flight.

"But how," I said presently, after both pool and inner self had calmed down, "does it know this about me?"

They looked down at me in equally arrested surprise. It was quite a long way down, as they were still both mounted, Hal leading my horse by her reins behind him. Mr. Dart, of course, had only the one good arm, and couldn't manage two horses. I felt deeply shamed by his courage—but—

But perhaps I was a coward, I thought glumly. I was grasping at reasons not to go to the Woods.

"How does it know I am connected to both the Woods Noirell and Arguty?" I clarified.

"Everyone knows that about you," said Mr. Dart.

"Even dragons?"

"Especially dragons," he replied with unperturbed good humour. "Come, come, Mr. Greenwing—a name never so apposite— you can't want Roald to hog all the glory. Where is your sense of adventure?"

"I seem to have lost it somewhere between Morrowlea and Lind," I said wearily, wishing for the coherent clear world of mortal danger back again. That mood or mode or what-have-you had broken with their arrival, when the dragon winked at me, uncoiled itself the rest of the way from the standing stone, and launched itself aloft.

"Jemis." Hal sounded distressed.

"I need to keep my head down until the Winterturn Assizes. I can't—if anything else happens—I already missed my stepfather's funeral and the Midsomer Assizes. I can't do anything to jeopardize the reading of the will this time."

"Are you in such high expectations?" Hal asked, a question so far removed from proper discretion I nearly laughed at his following embarrassment.

"No, not more than a small competence, but the law in Fiellan is that the will can only be read in the presence of all named parties at one of the Assizes. No one else—my stepfather's wife, his business partner—everyone else has to wait until—"

"I see."

I swallowed down a lump of regret and cowardice.

(Was I not my father's son?—He had come home to ignominy and disgrace, and he—No. No. He was the hero of Orkaty, the *hero* of Loe, the man who had come home against all the odds.)

I touched my hand into the water and silently asked the Lady's blessing. She did not reply, but after a moment I felt better, and was able to look up and smile. "But no. I don't want to let the Honourable Rag win."

"Good man," said Mr. Dart, grinning.

***

We went back to Ragnor Bella first, Hal having agreed with me that we could not in good conscience pay a call on my eccentric grandmother in yesterday's battered clothing, however well the Darts' housekeeper had brushed and mended it. Mrs. Buchance and all the children were out, meaning the house felt eerily quiet after the previous day's chaos.

We left the horses tethered in the back garden, where they could lip at the grass and contemplate whatever horses contemplate when left alone by their riders. "My room's upstairs," I said, leading the way to the chamber Mrs. Buchance had allotted me the fortnight before. It still didn't feel like home, but then nothing did, really.

Hal and Mr. Dart looked around curiously as we went through the upper hall. I realized that Hal, at least, had probably spent very little time in a bourgeois gentleman's residence.

"They bought the house while I was at Morrowlea," I said, opening my bedroom door. Mrs. Buchance had given me the best guest chamber. Hal and Mr. Dart looked around the sparely furnished room; I had about as many belongings at Dart Hall as I did there.

"There wasn't much to acquire at Morrowlea," I said into their silence. "The university supplied all the books and materials and even the robes, and the village hadn't much in the way of stores. Then this summer I was walking, and didn't get more than a handful of books for disinclination to carrying them home with me."

Hal made a snort of laughter, walking over to my desk to look at the portraits there. "Did Sir Hamish paint these? They must be your parents."

"Yes," I said.

"They look very happy."

"Yes."

Mr. Dart wandered over to sit on my bed, while I looked around the room and tried to think. "I suppose I should take a gift to the Marchioness."

"Nothing very grand," Hal said.

"I don't have anything grand to offer," I replied, hoping that didn't come out as bitter. I had a dozen books added to the few left from my childhood that had not yet migrated to the girls' nursery, an embroidered hanging that had been a gift from Mrs. Kulfield after my mother's death. "Roald still has my pen," I said, frowning at the blank notebooks awaiting some inspiration that had never yet been forthcoming.

"What are in those chests?" asked Hal.

"My inheritance," I replied, kneeling before the three small wooden chests set under the window.

The first and smallest held a book of haikus. I took it out and placed it carefully on the desk beside Hal. "This was my mother's wedding-present to my father," I said, turning over the pages.

The shadow-cut illustrations were as sharp and clear as they had ever been, the Old Shaian ideographs in calligraphy both superbly beautiful and superbly legible. There were items pressed between the pages: a curling red feather, a fern frond, a spray of cherry blossoms, a handful of tawny petals still sumptuously and hauntingly scented of the yellow rose of Ysthar.

"My father took it with him through all his campaigns," I said, moving the wafer-thin cross-section of a lotus seed-pod to find the grebe half-hidden in the waterlilies. "He was so pleased to go to West Voonra and walk where Lo en Tai had walked, see the poems inscribed on the waystones of the narrow roads. When he came home he used to tell me the stories behind the poems, show me the feather he had won from a red-tailed hawk, the rose from when he went to Astandalas to be presented to the Emperor ..."

I swallowed hard. "He brought it home with him when he came back, but he left it when ... it was where I found the note."

The note was still there, the last insertion into the book. I had not been able to throw it away, that last communication from my father. I passed it to Hal, my eyes feeling full, my head light. "Read it aloud. I can't."

Hal looked doubtfully at me, but he unfolded the thin paper, cleared his throat, and spoke:

"*Jimmy–I'm sorry. Take care of your mother. She needs you to be strong. Your papa Jack.*"

"I would have gone with him anywhere," I said. "My mother had Mr. Buchance, and Lauren and Sela. I had ..." I stopped hard there, my voice breaking. I fished out one of my handkerchiefs from their basket, and did not even try to pretend I was sneezing.

"I'm sorry, Jemis," Hal said quietly, when I had control of myself.

"It was a long time ago," I said. "Almost seven years." I closed the lid of the first chest and set it on the floor next to the second, which was rather larger. I hadn't opened these since I went away to Morrowlea, did not remember well what had been put in them in the days following my mother's passing.

The second chest held three items wrapped in heavy felt. I set them on the bed next to Mr. Dart, and unwrapped them one by one. The first was a pair of silver combs set with tiny blue stones, the geometrical pattern looking deeply foreign. Some gift to my mother from somewhere far away, I thought, wrapping them away again. There were so many things I did not know of my father's life, who he had been, why he had done what he had done, good and bad.

The second item was the Heart of Glory, the great golden pectoral my father had received from the hand of the Emperor. It looked like a theatrical prop sitting there on the plain grey coverlet, a fortune of gold and black diamonds and yellow topazes. The sun-in-glory etched into the central plaque was the size of a dinner plate, and inset with tiny yellow stones. It spattered the whole room with sunlight.

"By the Emperor," breathed Mr. Dart.

"And they dare suggest your father was a coward and a traitor," Hal said, spreading out the links in the chain so we could admire the workmanship of every detail. "Emperor Artorin presented *five* of these in his whole reign."

"I thought that had been sold," I said, staring at it, and feeling better to know it was still there.

Hal clasped me on the shoulder. Mr. Dart braced the third object, a squat cylinder, against his stone arm, and used his good hand to unwrap its felt covering. "What is *this*?" he asked, in almost equal surprise.

"It's my mother's honey crock," I said, as the green and white jade was revealed. "It *is* the same colour as the dragon. That was what the dragon reminded me of, this jar. I wondered what had happened to it. Mr. Buchance made containers, you see, Hal, that was where his money came from."

"And he didn't like this? This is almost as superb as the pectoral."

"It's true," said Mr. Dart, running his fingers along the pattern etched into a band near the top and bottom of the crock.

"I'd forgotten about the white portion. There were stories she'd tell about the pattern." I reached out to the crock. the smooth striations where green jade became white, feeling the carvings that were nearly invisible to the eye unless you held it to a candle.

When my hand touched the jade, the red stones on my ring flared, and the ring itself felt suddenly warm. I sneezed.

"Magic?" said Mr. Dart, eyes lighting.

"Or dust."

The third chest held bundles of letters tied up with green ribbons. Each bundle had a tag in my mother's hand, saying things like *From West Voonra, 11-12 A.Ar.* or *From Orkaty, 14-15 A.Ar.*

A.Ar: *Aitune Artorin*, the years of the reign of the Last Emperor.

I closed my eyes against the press of tears, and for good measure added my fingertips.

"You don't have to read them," Hal said gently, taking the bundle I was holding and placing it back in the chest. I could hear the rustle of the papers, the slight thunk as he closed the lid. "They'll be there when you're ready."

Chapter Fifteen
The Way of the Woods

"DEAR EMPEROR," SAID Hal, reining in abruptly.

We had crested the last rise of what were somewhat euphemistically known as the Foothills and there before us were the Woods.

The *real* foothills to the Crosslain Mountains began somewhere deep in the Woods, out of sight until they suddenly reared into the upper slopes of the mountains. We crested that last rise and everything between the edge of the Woods and the glaciers was green.

"Dear Emperor," Hal said again.

This was not the Hildon Woods we had traversed earlier that afternoon, friendly with holly and hawthorn and the sounds of birds. It was not even like the Arguty Forest, whose trees were ancient and huge and mysterious but whose thickets were crisscrossed with paths made by animals and people, where you might turn a corner to run into bears or boars or highwaymen.

These were the Woods Noirell, where if you took a wrong turn you might end up in another world.

On the northern slope of that last rise, and all the way back north to Ragnor Bella, the landscape was the familiar patchwork of pasture and arable field, interspersed with small woodlots and clustered farmsteads. As we had ridden south from town the land had grown emptier and wilder, until the last half-mile or so had seen primarily abandoned and semi-ruined buildings, overgrown pastures, fields overrun with weeds. No one really wanted to get close to the Woods any more, Mr. Dart had said into my silence. I was still fighting to keep my emotions in check, and ascribed the uneasiness I felt to half-a-dozen causes, of which magical malaise was low down in priority.

On the southern face of the last foothill, the land was a smooth green lawn as perfectly manicured as if it lay before a gentleman's manse. Close-cropped and daisy-free, it ran up to the deep swift stream that formed the boundary of the Woods. On one side, lawn: on the other, trees. There was little undergrowth, but even so we could see only a few yards in.

The Imperial Highway ran due south from its northern terminus at the old military city of Yrchester in Middle Fiellan. Made of huge blocks of pale stone, it was as smooth and level and straight now as it was when it was first built three centuries before the Fall. Ahead of us it ran dead straight to the stream, as it did at any river or stream or lake to our north, and the bridge looked much the same as any of those built by the Astandalan road-makers, the same great square blocks with the graceful balustrades carved with the runes and ideographs of all the spells attendant on such strategic elements of infrastructure.

This bridge had one element I had never seen otherwise, though my father had said it was what marked the Border crossings throughout the Empire: the Sun Gate on the other side of the stream. This was a perfectly round archway, twenty feet in diame-

ter, made of something—what exactly depended on many conditions—covered entirely in gold leaf laid on in layers (so I had read
in one of my History of Magic texts, before Lark turned me away
from them to Architectural Poetry), each of which was accompanied by chains of spells.

The Empire of Astandalas had covered five worlds, bound together by the great highways, and this was the beginning of a Border crossing.

"Well," I said," here are the Woods."

"Dear Emperor," said Hal for the third time, but he was no
longer looking at the gate: he was looking at the trees, and his expression was thunderstruck. "Those are Tillarny limes."

***

"There will be five gates between here and the Border," I said,
a bit nervously. We had stopped with one accord on the bridge to
look at the great round archway looming over us. The gold leaf was
bright and untarnished, though the runes were blurred and scored
with decades of disrepair. "One for each of the elements. This is the
water gate."

"There are four elements," Mr. Dart objected.

"Not in Astandalan magic," Hal answered absently, his eyes riv-
eted on the trees before us. "Water, metal, earth, air, fire. How far in
is your grandmother's place, Jemis?"

"I have no idea," I replied, trying to remember my father's
stories, the accounts in those History of Magic classes. Surely there
wasn't anything to worry about this far from the old Border—people had crossed *easily* between the worlds in Astandalan days—or
people who had guides had. That was one thing the people of St-

Noire had been, back in the old days. They used to say the bees were so special because bees were sacred to the Emperor, symbols of the Sun-on-Earth himself, and there, in the Woods on the Border between worlds, with the Kingdom potentially just around any corner, behind any tree—

"What do you mean, you have no idea where your grandmother's house is?"

"It's the Castle Noirell," Mr. Dart supplied.

I sighed. "I've only been there once, when I was nine. My mother presented me to my grandparents—my grandfather was still alive then—and, well, that was that."

"Your grandmother must be seriously aristocratic," Hal said. "Even my mother's family didn't keep *that* custom. My father's, on the other hand … But you don't look at all Shaian—which side carried the Noirell line? Grandmother or father?"

I frowned. "I don't know, actually. My mother never talked much about her family, and I never asked her. I always assumed it was my grandmother, because she's still the Marchioness, but I don't actually know."

Mr. Dart looked at me, then thought better of it and asked Hal instead. "What custom are you talking about?"

"The upper aristocracy of Astandalas maintained that it was bad luck for children to be out in public, so the tradition was for them to be raised very quietly at home until the age of nine, when they could be presented to society. It wasn't the same as coming out—that was at sixteen, same as it is now—but before then people didn't talk about children in any specific way. It was considered very bad form even to hint you knew someone had children, and obviously women were very discreet about whether they were increasing."

"So if Lady Olive took Jemis to meet his grandmother at the age of nine …"

"The Marchioness must be *exceedingly* starchy."

"Oh, joy," I said. "Hopefully having an Imperial Duke with me will help with my reception somewhat."

***

Nothing happened when we passed through the Sun Gate.

Nothing happened when we rode into the shadows under the trees.

Nothing happened at all, in fact.

I was obscurely disappointed.

***

We rode for perhaps half an hour in silence, three abreast with me in the middle. Hal was looking earnestly at the trees; Mr. Dart was gazing dreamily at the farther distances of the Woods; and I was looking between my horse's ears at the smooth surface of the highway unspooling before us. After about ten minutes I realized what we were doing, and was faintly amused.

Unlike its arrow-flight straightness outside the Woods, the highway on its approach to the Border was designed to curve and twist and nearly double back upon itself. We had spent perhaps a full week on the Imperial highways in my History of Magic class, for they were the bridges between the worlds of the Empire. It was quite extraordinary to ride along and have all the features and details Domina Issoury had described come flooding back to me.

Each block of limestone was three cubits square and half a cubit deep, set into a roadbed whose layers of gravel and stone were interlaid with bespelled chains to carry the magic unbroken. The wizard-engineers had followed the armies as they conquered new lands and new worlds for Astandalas.

Once a highway was laid, resistance crumpled. Part of that was to do with all the things that came down the highways, the trade goods and money, the people and ideas and arts, the soldiers and clerks and wizards and governors—and part of it was to do with the roads themselves. They were a major component of the binding of wild magic into the Schooled magic that made the Empire the height of civilization.

We rode through a golden afternoon. The Tillarny lime trees had started to turn, though they were blossoming, their leaves green and imperial gold, and the sunlight slanted through to glitter on the limestone and the motes of dust dancing before and behind us. It was a very quiet wood, carpeted in brilliant green moss and fallen leaves, and few and unfamiliar were the birds that sang.

We coiled our way through the Woods, the white road ahead and behind us, no sign of any passage on the highway, no sound but the soughing of the wind in the canopy above us and the chiming clatter of our horses' hooves on the stone. The limes were blooming, the scent of their blossom reminding me irresistibly of my mother, of the honey that had been sovereign remedy for every minor ailment of my childhood. After a while I started to feel less tense, and said so.

Hal looked at me for a long moment. "Do you really?"

I felt immediately as if I should be defensive, but the wind was warm in my face and the air smelled of good things, and I said, "It seems wonderfully calm."

"Indeed," said Hal.

I shrugged—and then, off to the right, I saw the flicker of white movement, and even as I reined in Mr. Dart said: "It's a deer—"

The deer bounded silently between grey trunks and green moss, white as a handkerchief, somehow finer-boned and longer-limbed than ordinary deer. She was pursued by a rider in full armour.

His horse was enormous, hands larger than our riding hacks, and his armour was antiquated, dull, even rusty in places. The visor on his helmet was worked into the shape of a snarling wolf, and both his tattered surcoat and his dented shield bore a wolf's head on white as his device. The white deer canted sideways suddenly, towards the road. The knight thundered in pursuit, lowering his lance even as he came out of the trees and onto the narrow band of moss that bordered the highway.

The deer gathered speed and with a superb thrust leaped the highway, and three things happened:

Even as her front hooves touched the ground on the left-hand side of the road, she disappeared.

The rider hauled back his horse to a halt so fiercely that the great animal reared, neighing loudly, before it quite touched the road.

And my ring flared hot on my finger.

"The Emperor!" said Hal.

The rider—the *knight*, if not exactly in shining armour—stared balefully at us through the visor of his helmet. At least, it felt a baleful stare; and I assumed it was a man; but both could well have been the effect of the snarling wolf.

Because I had been well-raised on a diet of adventure stories, I doffed my hat politely. "Well met, sir knight."

I felt, rather than saw, my friends' surprise. The knight continued to stare. His horse shook its head so bits of slobber flew off.
The bits that landed on the road made a strange hissing noise.

"We are seeking the Castle Noirell," I went on, gesturing
vaguely at the basket tied to my saddle. It contained the wine and
cakes we'd bought from Mr. Inglesides' bakery on our way out of
town for want of any better gift-offering. "I have something for the
Marchioness."

"You'd do better to stay clear of that accursèd house," the
knight replied, in a gravelly voice matching his appearance.

"The Marchioness is my grandmother," I replied with an attempt at insouciance.

"Then twice cursed are you," he declared, "once in the blood
and once in the land that once was host to the golden bees of fair
Melmúsion."

I could think of nothing else, so I said, "I beg your pardon?"

But with a sharp cry he yanked his horse up rearing and then
set it snorting and plunging back off into the woods in the direction from which he'd come.

I realized my jaw was agape, and closed it.

"I feel quite disappointed that my family has no intriguing
mystery about it whatsoever," said Mr. Dart.

"It's not *mysteries* that are the problem," I protested.

"No? An accursed castle!—pray excuse me: *accursèd*. A knight
out of an old ballad. A disappearing hind—and not just any hind,
mind you, but a *white* one—I am full of astonishment and delight.
How could you have even jested that you were uninterested, Jemis,
I cannot imagine."

"Can't you?"

Hal looked sharply at me, brows drawn together. "What's the matter with you, Jemis? You seem positively plunged into gloom and cynicism."

Mrs. Etaris had also called me a cynic. It was not a school of philosophy I had hitherto admired.

"And what of it?" I replied lightly, looking ahead to see if I could see anything besides the trees. I couldn't, which felt as if it should be of some symbolic assistance, but it wasn't.

"What of it?" Hal repeated, scowling even more ferociously. Mr. Dart, riding on my other side, gave him a meaningful shrug out of the corner of my eye. Hal ignored it. "Should I not be concerned that you have changed?—that you are more courteous in mortal danger than you are to your friends—that you are cynical and sarcastic and grim—when you used to be full of laughter and energy and delight and—"

"The Jemis you knew was a delusion composed of lies, stolen magic, and drugs," I said, and nudged my horse into a trot.

It was bone-jarring: of course.

Chapter Sixteen
The Doorkeeper has an Idea

ANOTHER TWENTY OR so minutes after the encounter with the knight, the road performed a complicated sequence of curves around a series of man-made embankments and knolls before taking us through a cleft between two high banks, in the middle of which was the second sun gate.

"The gate of earth," I said, gesturing at it.

"Ah," said Hal, without elaboration.

"Do you have *any* idea how far it is to St-Noire?" Mr. Dart asked. "We may be caught here by nightfall if we don't find the castle soon."

Hal said, "There's someone gathering wood over there we can ask. Hola, good sir," he added more loudly, angling his horse over.

"Nay, halt!" cried the man. "Do not leave the road!"

Hal reined in obediently, but I could tell his curiosity was raised. Well, so was mine. "Why not?"

"By the road you came, by the road you must continue," the man intoned.

We looked at him. He was middle-aged, with dark curly hair

and mid-brown skin and a countenance that seemed more frank and concerned than anything malicious or even mischievous.

"What happens if we don't?" Mr. Dart asked.

The man shook his head.

I rode up to the edge of the road, careful to stay within the bounds of the stone. "We are going to the Castle, sir. Can you tell us the way?"

"Why would you go to the accursèd castle?"

I sighed. Explaining about the dragon seemed ridiculous. All of this seemed ridiculous. "We are going to call on the Marchioness."

"You'd do better to leave the Woods before nightfall."

"What if we want to break this curse?" asked Mr. Dart, with a look at me I interpreted as *you should have thought of that first.* I shrugged.

The man spat on the ground. "There are those who have tried." He picked up his bundle of faggots and turned to go.

"Wait," I said.

He turned his head, expression skeptical.

"Do they still keep bees in the village?"

Without any hesitation at all the man turned away and hurried off into the woods, where he was quickly invisible.

"Curiouser yet," said Mr. Dart. "Why the bees, Jemis?"

I was not at all sure why the question had passed my lips. "The lack of honey ..." I looked down at my hands resting on my thigh, reins held loosely. The golden ring felt warm. But then I had always had warm hands.

"It must be four years since my mother started complaining how expensive the honey was getting," Hal said. "So whatever it is started a while ago. Yes, I remember now, the cook always makes this honey syllabub at Winterturn, and when I went back from Morrowlea in first year she mentioned how hard it had been to get the Noirell honey my mother wanted."

"You had enough of a holiday to get to Fillering Pool?" Mr. Dart asked, glancing at me. "I thought it was short, since Jemis never came home."

Hal winced, offered apologetically: "Ragnor Bella is a long way from South Erlingale."

"I went to Stoneybridge," Mr. Dart said, frowning. "That's at least as far."

I pursed my lips, then when that didn't work, said, shortly, "I didn't want to come back."

"Lark?" asked Mr. Dart in a slightly gentler voice.

"What did I have to come back for?" I asked, voice sharper than I intended. I gestured around at the woods, the heady air billowing around me, motes of pollen gleaming, the silence glaring. "My uncle's hatred? My grandmother's neglect?"

"Your stepfather—"

"My stepfather had a new family. A—an *uncomplicated* new family. What was I, to him? A constant reminder that he had connected his life to a traitor, that his first marriage was unlawful, his first wife dead, his daughters illegitimate, that I was not *his* son."

There was a pause. Mr. Dart said cautiously, "I always thought you liked him."

I scrunched up my face, tried to make my voice calm. "He wanted a son to carry on his name and his business. He wanted to adopt me. He wanted ... He wanted everything I was doing, everything I *was*, for my father. Why do you think I'm not inheriting anything? I made it very clear to him I was always going to keep my father's name—and so I keep my father's inheritance. For good and for ill."

I stopped, the dragon's second riddle echoing in my mind. Looked around at the Woods, ignoring the alarmed faces of my friends.

"What the dragon said …" I said, turning my horse around in a circle. "*The way of the woods has many turns and few branches. The branch of the woods has many turns and few ways. The turn of the branch is the way of the woods, for good, young sir, or for ill.*"

"What are you thinking?" Hal asked intently. "Tell us your thoughts., Jemis."

"The way of the Woods—look at the road. *Many turns and few branches*. But think of the words, this is like literary criticism of the Calligraphic School—"

"We'll take your word for it," said Mr. Dart, the historian.

"Every word is significant, means something, means more than one thing. *The way of the woods*—all right, the highway through the Woods. But what else could that mean? The tradition of the Woods? The customs?"

"The line of inheritance," said Hal, the Duke.

"*Many turns and few branches*. It's line of primogeniture, shifts male to female, Marchioness to Viscount, Viscountess to Marquis. But few branches—my mother an only child, *her* mother an only child—there were no aunts, no uncles, no cousins on that side."

I felt dizzy, realized I was still turning the horse. I relaxed the pressure of thigh, heel, hands. The horse snorted. "*The branch of the woods* … I don't know the literal meaning, though Hal—"

"The famous trees of the Woods Noirell are the Tillarny limes," Hal said, looking up at the green-and-gold trees all around us, the golden bracts around the creamy pollen-rich puffs of blossom. "Look at them: many turns and few ways. The silhouette is unmistakable, that upright trunk, the way the branches arch up and then down and then curve up again at the tip. Each ramification the same."

"Unlike in most of life," Mr. Dart muttered.

"But what else does *branch* mean? *Scion*, right?"

"Back to the question of inheritance. And your life is one of many turns?" Mr. Dart paused to consider, nodded his head judiciously. "I can grant that. You've had more turns of fate's wheel before one-and-twenty than most people have in a lifetime."

"*Many turns, but few ways.*"

Hal was still looking at the shape of the trees all around us, the heart-shaped leaves in green and gold, the flowers with their heavy, heady scent, unworked by the bees that should have been filling them.

I swallowed. "What do you think that means?"

"A life of many turns, but few options? Few paths ahead of you?"

Mr. Dart took a deep breath. "Or the ways you choose are significant, that you have a few moments at which your choice will change things."

"What things?" I asked intently. "I am no one important."

Hal looked down at me, his face somewhat sympathetic. "Jemis, everyone from Yrchester south was talking about Mad Jack Greenwing's son."

"*The turn of the branch is the way of the woods, for good or for ill,*" quoted Mr. Dart. "Like it or not, Jemis, this is your inheritance: the Greenwing name and the Woods Noirell."

***

"I don't quite understand how I've never heard anything much of the Woods," Hal was saying when I once again started attending to the conversation. "You'd think that they'd be much more famous quite apart from the honey."

"Infamous," I muttered.

"They don't usually get named," Mr. Dart replied. "Most of the time they are just—the Woods." He grinned at Hal. "You have heard *one* story about the Woods Noirell, I trust—and about the Castle at its heart: 'Where stood at the window, white stone and ivy, / The silent watcher'—"

"'In her high tower, / When we rode the high way / To the golden city / The city of roses'. *That* was the Castle Noirell?"

"That was Jemis' mother!"

"I had no idea that was a real place. I always thought it was somewhere far away and long ago."

"Long enough ago that Jemis wasn't even a twinkle in his father's eye."

"But your mother is in one of Fitzroy Angursell's songs! Wait--how do you know she's the subject?"

"She saw the Red Company go by," Mr. Dart said. "Jemis used to make her describe them over and over again."

"Do you mind?" I began, half-laughing, but we had turned another corner and there before us was the village. And the villagers.

They stood poised as if to begin a celebration—or, I realized, as we sat our horses and watched expectantly, they stood *posed*.

St-Noire was the village of the Castle Noirell: so much I knew. It was the only village within the bounds of the Woods, so far as I knew. It had once been considered a very picturesque and beautiful place, its architecture running to two-storied timber and white plaster buildings in comfortable, gracious proportions, the roofs covered not with the thatch commoner out in the barony but with wood shingles weathered to a pleasant silvery-brown. The windows were diamond-paned, the coloured glass here and there evidence of the wealth flowing into the village from the travellers passing by on their way to Astandalas the Golden.

I just remembered, from that one visit to my grandmother, that the village had been warm and welcoming and full of flowers even though we had come the week of my birthday. My birthday was in the spur weeks between winter and spring, on the come-and-go day meant to stop the seasons from precessing too much. Even so, St-Noire had been full of sunlight and honey and the singing of the bees working all those tiny jewel-bright flowers of the earliest spring.

Today it was full of sunlight and flowers, but the air was heavy and still and silent and smelled of nothing other than some faintly pleasant bitterness.

"More saffron," Hal murmured.

"Are they ... asleep?" said Mr. Dart.

I blinked again at the scene before us, my mind switching as if from the mode of mortal danger to the mode of ordinary confusion (though neither seemed quite appropriate in this case), and I saw that the village was ... still.

"Are they ... stone?" said Hal.

The houses were in good repair, the plaster glowing gold in the slanting light, the timbers pleasingly dark in contrast, the windows gleaming without hint of dust or cobwebs. Each window had an overflowing window box of flowers, each doorway a half-barrel full of blooms, each yard blazed with colour. And yet there was no breeze: no bees: and then there were the people.

I dismounted and led my horse slowly down the highway. On each side of us were the houses, windows gleaming, doors open to the lambent air, people posed as if caught in a moment of time.

A woman leaned over her fence as if to speak to us: but her smile was for some distant vision.

A boy sat on the step of a house with a great bowl of peas he was shelling, but though his hand was reaching into the bowl, his fingers never closed on the pods.

"It isn't pea season," said Hal.

Three little girls, about the age of my sisters, in the middle of a game of marbles, the player with her finger curled back to flick the white tolley, one of her admirers with her hands clasped anxiously.

"There aren't any bees," I said.

"I don't think that's the only problem here," Mr. Dart said.

"Actually, a lack of pollinators would lead to—" Hal stopped when Mr. Dart and I looked at him. "Probably not this."

They followed me up the road, not leaving the Imperial Highway, our shadows shifting before us as we came in and out of the houses, across the green. There were gnats and flies; but there were no bees.

St-Noire had been known for its honey. But the highway no longer led to Astandalas, and the Gentry had always coveted the Woods.

At the other end of the silent village we curled around another artificial knoll, this one with a tiny chapel to the Emperor as Sun-on-Earth on its crest, and on the far side we saw suddenly looming above us the Castle.

"Are you still feeling this is a welcoming place?" Hal asked.

I rubbed the ring with my thumb and stared up at the Castle. It was made of the same white stone as the highway, but where the road gleamed, the Castle looked scabrous and diseased. Its pennons were flying in the wind, but they were tattered and faded, no longer the brave white bees on the green field. Only the upper windows of the highest tower caught the reddening light, like the echo of that famous song.

"Do you think anyone is there?" Hal asked. "There's no smoke or anything."

Mr. Dart touched his stone arm with his good hand, but stopped as soon as he saw me looking. "Perhaps they're also, uh, cursed."

I might not have been the bright and brilliant Jemis of Hal's fond memories. Nevertheless, I found that even if I could not precisely call myself *eager*, I did have the niggling sensation that—quite apart from anything so inconvenient as family sentiment—I was the grandson of the Marchioness of the Woods. If she was no longer capable of doing her duty (whether through disinclination, illness, enchantment, or death), then as her eldest living descendant it was my responsibility to do so. No matter how erratic my education as a gentleman might have been, the villagers of St-Noire were clearly under the Marchioness' care.

"I am going up to see," I said. "Will you come with me?"

They exchanged a look, and then Hal smiled and Mr. Dart quoted Fitzroy Angursell: "'We may be children of a lesser age, but we should not let that inconvenience us altogether.'"

"In our search for adventure?" I said dryly, remounting my

horse and setting her down the road to where the Castle approach met it.

"In our search for greatness," said Mr. Dart, following me.

I was about to retort that greatness was not really my ambition, but just then I turned my horse onto the Castle lane, and the sunlight winked out in an immediate and quite thoroughly impressive thunderstorm.

A stuttering flash of lightning revealed clouds boiling out of nowhere into blackness. The thunder cracked like a whip. Our horses bolted straight up the hill towards the Castle. We reached the postern gate in what must have been record time. The thunder must have made it impossible for our knocking to be heard clearly, but I had not thumped the knocker more than three times when the door opened.

We tumbled inside to find ourselves in a rain-blasted courtyard of near-night gloom. A figure in a strange green hooded robe stood there, face hidden in shadows. He or she held a flaring torch that hissed in the rain like the wolf-knight's horse's slobber. Thunder cracked in crazy echoes around the stone court, making our horses restive.

I dismounted so I could take mine by a firm grip on her bridle. "We have come to see the Marchioness," I said after I'd caught my breath. "Where can we stable our horses?"

The green-robed figure stared at us in what seemed total shock.

"I am Jemis Greenwing," I added.

At this the figure gave me a long and dismissive once-over—it was amazing how expressive the shadowed hood was—and said, in a voice as gravelly and rusty as the wolf-knight's: "Another one."

Chapter Seventeen
The Marchioness has an Idea

"IT SEEMS," I said a little later, "that not only is my family life literally the stuff of melodrama, it is in fact the stuff of high gothic melodrama."

Mr. Dart turned from his intent perusal of the dusty and shrouded furnishings so he could grin at me. "You sound so surprised, Mr. Greenwing. For a day that has included a dragon's challenge, a knight, a cursed village, and mysterious warnings from a strange peasant, it would be decidedly disappointing if it did not take an even stranger turn when it came to the accommodations. You can't have been expecting things to be *normal.*"

"I was not expecting this."

"Nobody was expecting this," murmured Hal, who was standing with his back to the sputtering and smoking fire. This left me to stand awkwardly in the centre of the room, directly beneath a discoloured and mildewy plasterwork medallion surrounding a tarnished and unlit chandelier hanging somewhat askew. On that thought I took a step away. My boots seemed to be sticking to the carpet. I clutched at my basket of comestibles for fear they would be immediately contaminated if I set them down on anything, then for good measure covered them with my hat.

Hal went on, sounding as if he were discussing the merits of a dubious wine. "It *is* the most revoltingly filthy place I have ever seen. Worse than the witch's cottage."

"Too bad it's Jemis' grandmother's," Mr. Dart said, chuckling. "Come now, Mr. Greenwing, don't be sour."

"Sour? *Sour?*"

"Or have an apoplexy. You were the one who wanted an adventure."

"I don't think I was."

"No, that's true," he said imperturbably; "I suppose that was me and Mrs. Etaris. Do you think the gatekeeper is ever coming back?"

"What do you think she meant by saying 'another one' like that?"

"Do you think that was a woman?" Mr. Dart asked doubtfully.

"Yes," Hal said immediately and somewhat surprisingly. "It sounded as if there were more than one person claiming to be Jemis Greenwing."

"I can't imagine why."

Mr. Dart uttered a short cackle and came over to join Hal by the fire. "Your life isn't that awful, my boy. It's tremendously interesting. And you *are*, as Hal reminded us, the Viscount St-Noire."

I uttered a few choice words, and then said: "Do you find your stone arm tremendously interesting?"

"It's somewhat inconvenient," he allowed.

"And I have to say, while my life may *seem* tremendously interesting, all those interesting affairs can be more than somewhat inconvenient at times. One might go so far as to say they become tedious."

"Might one?—Hold up, there's someone coming."

We turned as one to consider the door by which the green-robed person had led us into the room. It had presumably once been some sort of waiting room, furnished as it was with worm-eaten chairs and mouldy cushions of Second Imperial Syncretic Style; the typical bargello needlework and hook-and-eye woodwork showed even through the decay and dust and gloom and dirt and cobwebs.

The door swung open to reveal a woman wearing a strange wraparound dress in what had probably once been a very startling orange but had mostly faded to a dull rusty tan. She had salt-and-pepper hair in wild corkscrew curls, her skin tone somewhere between the tan of her garment and Hal's near-ebony. She was perhaps in her late sixties, and though her features were thin her eyes were large, luminous, and quite startlingly lovely.

She did not at first accord me more than a passing and dismissive glance: she focused on Hal and Mr. Dart by the fire, both of them looking like two models of a modern gentleman, Mr. Dart with his auburn beard and freckled pale skin and burgundy-and-silver skirted coat and dark breeches, the short-haired dark-skinned Hal in dull gold and ivory knee breeches and velvet coat. My red-ribboned hat was by far the best; but, alas, we were indoors where that didn't matter, and my bottle-green coat seemed to disappear into the shadows even to myself.

She said, "You will find the Castle does not host guests as often as in the days of yore. The staff will do what we can, of course, but our hospitality is sadly diminished."

"I am sure we will be well looked after," Mr. Dart said gallantly, with a bow.

"Do not be too sure," she said. "The very stones of this house are steeped in grief and guilt."

I found that I was beginning to get irritated with the turn towards the gothic. "Why?"

She swung around to gaze at me with those luminous eyes, her face very stern. It did not seem a face made for sternness. I thought, *She should be dancing*—and a memory flashed into brilliant life around me.

"You're Savela Uvara," I cried triumphantly. "The Beekeeper. I remember, you took me into the garden to look at the bee-house—"

For a moment there was a sharp, arrested sensation in the air, as if I had said something half-magical. The ring on my hand flared, and I sneezed once, sharply. Savela Uvara's glance dropped to the ring, then back up to my face, and she said, very slowly, "But the boy died. They both died."

I spoke with a strong effort to be firm and clear. "My mother was Lady Olive Noirell of this house, my father Jakory Greenwing of the Arguty Greenwings. I am their son Jemis Greenwing. I have recently returned from university and I thought I should pay a call on my grandmother. These are my friends, the Duke of Fillering Pool and Mr. Dart of Dartington."

"You *died* in the Pestilence."

"I am no ghost, ma'am."

My words hung in the air strangely, as if I had said something magical, though the ring felt no different than it had since we entered. Savela Uvara walked over to me, her beautiful eyes wide with conflicting emotions. She peered closely at my face, as if she were searching there for the nine-year-old boy she had met once.

As I looked at her, my memories stirred, woken by her face, by the place, by the electric currents of storm and magic and chaotic emotion. I swallowed.

"My mother brought me here to be presented to my grandparents on my ninth birthday. My grandfather took me for a long walk through the Woods, all the way to the Lady's Heart. My grandmother was arguing with my mother. But we had honey and walnut pastries and you took me into the gardens to see the bees."

"That was a dozen years ago."

"Four years ago I wrote to my grandmother that my mother had died from the influenza," I said, "and received in response only a note saying *My daughter has been dead these five years since.* Since my father's disgrace, it seemed."

Mr. Dart turned his head suddenly to look at a footstool beside him. I blinked, distracted; he flushed and then frowned. A mouse, I assumed, and was about to continue speaking when a voice came from the doorway.

"Nine years ago the Pestilence came, followed by the letter that my daughter and grandson were dead. Shortly after that came the first of the impostors."

It was a thin, elderly, aristocratic voice whose thinness held an undercurrent of pure steel.

I looked past Savela Uvara to the woman who had just entered. She was about as far from a cozy grandmother as you could get: she reminded me in a sudden leap of fear and wonder of what Lark could end up like in fifty years. She was tall and lean and pale, her eyes a glittering sharp brown, her elaborately curled hair streaked icy white and black and pinned up into a high mound anchored with glittering jewels and tarnished silver.

When she was satisfied she had our attention, she stumped in. Her cane was ebony and silver, matching her hair and her dress, which looked as if it had been in the first stare of court fashion a decade before the Fall, and as if she hadn't taken it off since. It was made of dozens of layers of silk and lace, white and black and silver, embroidered with blackened silver and beaded with jet, corseted, tattered, and with six inches of grime at its hem. She wore finger-less gloves of black lace up to her elbows. Her face was painted in fashion of the Last Emperor's later court, familiar from the illustrat-ed plates in a few of the books and old periodicals in Mrs. Etaris' bookshop. Her eyes were heavily outlined in kohl, eyelids and lips both painted a brilliant if now-cracked crimson, skin white with rice powder or arsenic.

I produced an elaborate bow, with heel-click and curlicues slightly hampered by the basket I was still holding. "Lady Noirell."

She ignored my greeting and thumped her way up to me. At closer quarters she smelled overpoweringly of rotting flowers and the heavy bitter-honey odour of the dragon. The hand that was not holding the stick curled like a claw. Arthritis, I told myself firmly; and it had once been the fashion for the upper aristocracy to grow out their fingernails, to show they need do no manual labour. My grandmother's red-lacquered nails were over an inch long.

She lifted her hand to my chin. I didn't resist as she lifted my face, none too gently, so she could examine me even more closely than had Savela Uvara. It was almost impossible to believe I was related to her, except that I had seen those sharp brown eyes a time or two in my own mirror.

She said nothing and did not remove her hand. I gazed steadily back into her eyes, seeing the cracks in the make-up, the way that the lipstick had seeped into the fine lines around her mouth, the great lines of experience and bitterness carved into her face.

There was no warmth and no hope in her eyes that I might truly be her grandson, and even though I had not expected a warm welcome I found that I was nonetheless furiously, bitterly disappointed.

I said, "I presume impostors come for what remains of the wealth of Noirell. Do they leave when they see the enchanted village or the decrepitude of this castle? Do they flee when the man collecting firewood warns them off, or the wolf-knight says they are accursed, or a dragon gives them a riddle? Do they come here and presume upon your grief? Madam, you treated my mother evilly and have ignored me my whole life. I have no interest in toadying up to you or pretending to a respect you have in no way earned. I might ignore your treatment of me, of my half-sisters your granddaughters, of my mother—but I cannot ignore the fact that you are the Marchioness of these woods and you have failed in your duty to your people."

She dropped her hand abruptly. "How dare you speak so to me, whelp?"

"How dare you fail your people so utterly , madam? They stand cursed in the village below. It is your duty to redeem them."

There was a short, sharp, ringing silence, and then the Marchioness began to cackle with laughter. "Fool," she said. "You might be fool enough to be my daughter's son. You want to know what the curse is? How to break it? How to win your inheritance?"

"I care nothing for any inheritance from you."

"The more fool you! Uvara, throw the boy and his friends in the cellars, and let them puzzle out what curse lies on this house of mine. If you succeed, boy, then perhaps we will speak again."

"Perhaps," I said noncommittally, but it was drowned out by another cackle and crack of thunder.

Chapter Eighteen
In the Cellars

I SAT IN the cellar sulkily for a while before I realized that was what I was doing, whereupon I decided that I was not, in fact, fifteen, and decided to stop. At first this was not very effective, as Hal and Mr. Dart were deeply engrossed in their conversation—and the basket of pastries—although for that I couldn't blame them. After a bit I caught the line of what they were saying.

"There can't be all that many Imperial titles still vacant, surely?" Mr. Dart was asking. "Not on Alinor, anyway."

"A surprising number. There were over two score titles in Northwest Oriole alone, and at least a dozen were lost in the Fall. Some because everyone was at court in Astandalas, others during the Interim."

"We were reading in last week's *New Salon* that the Ironwood heir has been found."

"Yes. I expect I'll be meeting her this Winterturn—my aunt was called to Chare to assist in the identification, and tells me she's a 'charming gel and very striking'. Her name's Verity or Charity or some sort of virtue, which must be tiresome for her, but probably appealed to my aunt."

I thought of the Honourable Rag claiming the Ironwood heir must be ugly if the paper didn't mention her beauty in the same breath as her title and fortune, and once more liked Hal's relations.

"Starting to be time to think about the next duke, eh?" Mr. Dart said with a sympathetic smile.

"So I am informed. I'm surprised you and Jemis aren't up to your ears in matchmaking mamas?"

"My brother's certainly trying, with the willing assistance of my aunt. And once Jemis' family is all sorted out, all the mamas currently shunning him will start flocking around."

"I'm surprised you didn't find someone in Stoneybridge," I said, rocking my barrel closer to where they were sitting.

"Back with us, are you?" Hal said, but his voice was warm.

Mr. Dart's was much sharper. "Well, I didn't—and since your taste in women appears to be for dashing criminals, I don't think you're one to criticize."

"I'm sorry," I said blankly. "I didn't mean to hit a sore spot."

Mr. Dart sighed heavily. "I've been getting that all summer. It gets wearying."

"Perhaps *you* should put an advertisement in the *New Salon*," I tried, but he didn't rise.

Hal said, "Regarding the Ironwood heir, my aunt wrote to tell me that the heir had to prove herself in some sort of traditional magical competition before she was granted it—had to be acknowledged by a magical sword, I think it was."

"That's all that I need," I replied with a not-very-realistic chuckle. "A magic sword."

"I fear the Marquisate of Noirell is superabundantly likely to require some sort of magical competition, Jemis."

Superabundantly had been a joke, all second year, when I thought I was on top of the world but was probably just flying nearly out of sight on wireweed.

"Given the riddling dragon and cursed Woods," interjected Mr. Dart, sounding as if he were trying not to laugh.

"Bah, I tell you. Where's the light coming from, Hal? Did you make a werelight, and if so, can it be a little brighter, please?"

"Can't you make a were light of your own, if you want one?"

"I don't *know* any magic. I only found out I might have a talent for it last week."

"Seriously?" he said. "Oh—right—that was why you're so concerned about the missing witch. Hmm."

"I take it you're not making the glow, then?" I said, ignoring this for the moment.

"Is it the moss?" Mr. Dart asked incredulously. "Now, that *is* something out of a tale."

"Jemis' whole life appears to be something out of a tale, and we are caught up in it, Mr. Dart, as loyal friends—companions—possibly even guides."

"Well, loyal friends, companions, possibly even guides, do you want to sit in this cellar all night, try to escape, or see what the mysterious glow down the even-more-mysterious passage is?"

"The last, obviously, being both the most foolish and the most interesting option," Hal replied, laughing.

"I'm sure you spent just as much of your boyhood as we did preparing for the day when the Red Company would require our assistance," said Mr. Dart. "Shall we?"

***

We were presumably still in the cellars, which were extensive and cavernous. Occasionally we passed miscellaneous items, junk of the sort that gets put into cellars: broken furniture, old barrels and jugs and boxes, empty bottles, dusty sacks I hoped were empty. Most of it was identified with brands or stamps showing the bees and skeps of Noirell. The bee was a device of Damara, one of the Imperial houses, but the Marquisate of Noirell had been granted use of the image—though never in gold or silver—as a result of some ancient service to a Grand Duke of Damara, still (in the person of the Last Emperor) technically High King of Rondé.

All this Hal conveyed to us in a low voice. Mr. Dart nodded or murmured at appropriate moments, seeming genuinely interested. I trailed along, no longer sulking—or at least, trying very hard not to sulk—but feeling a little cheated that Hal knew so much more about my family history than I did. On both sides.

But I had spent three years at Morrowlea drugged, enchanted, besotted, beguiled—and beyond all that, very deliberately distancing myself from Ragnor Bella, from being Jack Greenwing's son, from mourning my mother the Lady Olive, whose title I, like everyone else, never thought of as more than an honorific.

"It is the moss," said Hal, "but it's not only the moss."

"It's coming from through there," Mr. Dart added. "Well, Jemis?"

"Why am I making the decision?"

"Your grandmother, your riddle, your inheritance—"

"Fine." I contemplated the glow emanating from what seemed to be a curved passageway. I felt sneezes tickling the back of my nose, twisted the ring as had so quickly become habit.

"Fine, what?"

"Fine, let's go see what the mysterious glow is."

But I had listened to my father's stories, and had read dozens of romantic adventures besides, and so I picked up the broken stave of a barrel from the corner, a makeshift weapon if ever there was one but better than nothing.

**

We didn't need it.

We advanced down the passageway. My action in arming myself seemed to have infected Hal and Mr. Dart with a belated sense of caution, for they came close behind me, broken barrel staves of their own in hand.

I reviewed their skills in my mind. Mr. Dart was a good fencer, but he was right-handed and could not yet have learned to compensate for the petrified arm. Hal was a wicked polo player and acceptable boxer, but although not a disgrace with a sword—he had certainly had the tutors to ensure he wasn't a dead loss—he was also certainly not much more than average.

I did not feel very heroic, but it was nevertheless something of a disappointment to reach the source of the glow and discover no adversary nor any sign of one.

We did, however, find the bees.

**

We huddled in the middle of a large stone chamber shaped like the interior of a skep. It was round, the sides curving up above us to a vaulted ceiling, in the centre of which was an unglazed opening.

A few spatters of rain came through, even at the distance of a dozen or fifteen feet.

I felt the water absently. My thoughts were on the unpleasant crunch underfoot before we realized what we were stepping on, the golden glow coming from nowhere in particular. The light illuminated the lost bees of the Woods Noirell, descendants (so it was said) of the bees of Melmúsion, whose honey gave the gods their immortal youthfulness.

"Are they ... dead?" said Mr. Dart.

"Asleep?" I murmured. My mouth, my nose, my mind was full of the taste, the scent of honey, sweet, heavy, familiar.

"Enchanted, surely," said Hal.

Every memory of my mother seemed crowded around me, as numerous, as heartbreaking, as the thousands upon thousands of stone-still bees on the floor.

The curving walls were honeycombed.

My mind snagged suddenly on how analogy and reality chimed together, jangled with unexpected aptness.

The walls were honeycombed: analogously by some skilled stone carver, literally by the work of hundreds of thousands of bees. Old comb, dull gold, caramel, some of it nearly black; none of the white of new-drawn comb, none of the pure bright gold of autumn honey.

Memories were coming back to me. Memories of my mother in our garden at the Dower Cottage, showing me how to light the censer, calm the bees with the fragrant smoke. Opening the skep to show me queen and eggs and larvae and workers and drones. Laughing when I asked her about the drones, telling me through gurgles of laughter I didn't then understand that even drones had a role to play in the world, microcosm and macrocosm. Showing me wax and honey and propolis, telling me that this was my heritage: sweetness, light, stings.

The first honey of the season; how she could say from the scent, the tiniest taste, the colour, that this was hawthorn, this clover, this borage, this rosebay willowherb; that none of them were the same as the honey of the Woods, for the bees in the Woods Noirell, descendants in how many generations of the bees of Melmúsion, drew nectar from the trees that grew there alone, the autumn-blooming Tillarny limes whose scent had been in the air as we rode on the looping old highway.

"It's not too late for the autumn honey, if we could waken the bees," I said, opening my eyes to find the dim light glaring. I rubbed my eyes with cold fingertips, the ring strangely—or not so strangely—warm on my skin. "Any ideas?"

Hal shook his head. Mr. Dart had his slightly cocked, as if trying to listen to something on the edge of hearing.

"Do you hear something?" I asked him.

He started, shook his head vigorously. "No. Nothing. Just—just thinking—what Hal said about the Ironwood heir."

"I've never even heard rumours of a magical sword in the Woods."

Hal said, "No, clearly it has something to do with the bees—and the dragon—did your mother never tell you anything about this? Family stories, jokes, songs, *anything?*"

There was a kind of raised plinth in the middle of the chamber, directly under the roof aperture. I scuffed carefully along the floor, sat down on the bee-free edge. Tried not to cry.

"We kept bees," I said, turning my face up to the cool drops of rain sprinkling down. "She showed me how to look after them …"

Hal seated himself beside me, Mr. Dart on my left a moment later. His stone arm made a muffled thud as it touched the plinth. Hal said, "She looked after them herself?"

"She loved gardens, growing things, bees. Sweet peas were her favourite flower. We weren't well-off, you know, Hal. My father had his pay, nothing from his father—my grandfather nearly ruined the Arguty estate gambling. My elder uncle managed to repair the damage, but only after many years. And my mother's people … she had a small independence, nothing else."

"I think we might now have a better understanding of why that might have been a strained situation," Mr. Dart murmured. "Do you think it would hurt them if I smoked?"

I explained about the incense, how smoke rendered bees sleepy, calm.

"Renders me calm as well," said Mr. Dart, and spent a few minutes fussing with pipe and tobacco and lucifer.

"Perhaps it was a special incense that wakes them," Hal suggested.

"No, the incense was to calm them. She did use a special kind, before the Fall. We ran out during the Interim. After that she just used what we could find in the house, the garden. We were caught in the Dower Cottage, she and I. I—I don't know how long it was before we got across the grounds to Arguty House, let alone to Dartington."

"It was hard everywhere," Hal said, fairly matter-of-factly. "We could see Zabour fall into the sea from the upper tower of Leaveringham Castle. It seemed to take forever."

Zabour, once one of the Circle Schools, now, like so much else, lost.

Hurriedly, moving us all on from dark memories, I said, "I remember when things got better, when we felt the world was no longer spinning adrift. My mother told me it was time to dance the Lady in, and we sang in the garden under the hawthorn blossom. It was a song she used to sing often, a lullaby, a bee song, a gardening song. We used to dance to it in the garden sometimes. That time—I remember—I remember thinking it was like the world reached out to dance with us."

It was such a private, intimate, *safe* moment, there in the heart of a stone hive surrounded by hundreds of thousands of sleeping bees, there with my two best friends, there with the scent of my mother all around, that I added: "That was how I felt facing the ruffians, facing the dragon. Like they had set up the music for a waltz and the world just reached out its hand for me to take."

"Will you sing for us? The song your mother sang?" Mr. Dart asked, blowing smoke rings into the strange golden air, where they glowed like clouds at the edge of sunset, dawn.

"That is a very good idea," said Hal, and so—since I was trying not to sulk—I cleared my throat, closed my eyes, and with a few mistakes found rhythm, melody, words.

> *Wood of the golden trees*
> *Home of the golden bees*
> *Where lost Melmúsion*
> *Sings one more song.*
>
> *Gifts of the Lady Green*
> *Sweetness of the seasons*
> *Summer in wintertime*
> *Sings one more song.*

Gifts of the Lady White
Light in any darkness
Winter wisdom in the spring
Sings one more song.

Heart of the golden trees
Wood of the golden bees
Where lost Melmúsion
Sings one more song.

"I think there's another verse," I said, frowning, eyes still closed, hearing my mother's voice in my mind's ear, echoing softly.

"I think they want to dance with you," said Mr. Dart in a strange voice.

I opened my eyes to see that I had woken the bees of the Woods.

Chapter Nineteen
The Bees of Melmúsion

THE CHAMBER WAS no longer silent.

All those hundreds of thousands of bees—no longer stone-still, no longer silent, no longer—safe? It was hard to find words.

The bees were golden, caramel and gold, their wings visible as glints, the mysterious light still not seeming to emanate from anywhere but nevertheless increased in strength, in luminosity, tenfold, a hundredfold, as if every wingbeat of each of those hundreds of thousands of bees made it grow.

The room no longer felt cold, dank, damp. It was warm, glowing, fragrant with the scent of old honey, old pollen, old beeswax.

It came to me that they would want new nectar, new pollen, new honey, new wax, and that the Tillarny limes were blooming.

I pushed myself off the plinth. The bees were no longer motionless on the floor. The flagstones were clad in the glinting carpet of moving bees I remembered from peeking into our skeps when my mother did the ceremonies that had been such an integral part of Astandalan life.

Some of the bees were in the air. They were not flying purposefully, they seemed confused, adrift, perhaps even expectant.

Waiting to dance?

I had not seen the queen, but now that the bees were moving I knew where she must be, in the centre of the thickest swarm, on the wall opposite the entry where the bees moved across the deeply carved shape of a Sun-in-Glory, emblem of Astandalas.

I bowed to the carving, the queen hidden at its centre, heels clicking, extravagant gestures, hat off.

I sang the old song again, eyes open this time. With each verse, each iteration, the light grew stronger, the buzz grew louder, more and more bees rose from the floor, the walls, found their wings, filled the air.

I danced as my mother had taught me, singing the song over and over again, leaping around the room, hands and feet moving into spaces suddenly *there*, opened for me by the bees.

Their movements were so quiet taken one by one. You could hear a single honeybee in a flower, flying by, if you were listening and nothing louder or more attractive caught your attention.

A hundred, a thousand, a hundred thousand bees? On a still day in summer, they said, you could hear the bees of the Woods Noirell clear across the Border.

I wondered what it had sounded like, smelled like, felt like, to ride up the highway from Astandalas to Alinor, to feel the wind blowing magic across worlds to meet you, to hear the great mysterious hum from the other side of the sun.

Inside that secret room, that stone hive, my voice at its loudest was fully absorbed into the sound of the bees, those hundreds of thousands, waking up so we could at last dance the Lady in.

I danced, sweat pouring down my face, sweat sweet like honey, imagining as I moved my hands that there was someone else there in the room with me, someone in the spaces between the bees, someone whose footsteps matched mine, someone whose hand touched mine, someone whose voice sang somewhere in the harmonies between beesong and mine.

I danced until the room was bright as day, until that other voice started the verse I had not remembered.

> *Honey of the golden woods*
> *Sunlight caught in sweetness*
> *Light of lost Melmúsion*
> *Shine another year.*

And with the last word we all stopped: the bees, and the ghost, and I.

I stood in front of the Sun-in-Glory, the same pattern as the Heart of Glory, the pectoral my father had won for his bravery, for holding the Sun banner firm at the edge of another Border. In the centre of the Sun was the queen of the hive and her attendants and those drones that had a role to play that I understood a little better now, microcosm and macrocosm.

I held the last movement, arms out, foot pointed, and then, knowing the dance was over, feeling somewhere deep inside that the curse was broken, I bowed again to the queen, to the Sun, to the memory of my mother.

I felt a soft hand across my forehead, brushing a stray hank of hair back into place, a gesture I knew far better than the song. And then in a brush of air scented of summertime the sense of someone else was gone.

I fell to my knees and put my hands to my face and wept for

my mother, while the bees she had so loved streamed out into the Woods to start that mysterious alchemy by which they distilled the essence of summer sunlight for the long, dark nights of winter.

Chapter Twenty
The Villagers have an Idea

I PRESUMED SAVELA Uvara fulfilled her promise to let us out, but we had already gone.

We did not want to be late for church.

It was a very long tradition that the Dartington Harvest Fair contests were announced, and competitors' names taken, at the White Cross after the Sunday morning service the week before the Fair.

Mr. Dart abruptly remembered this fact—or pretended to—after I had finally composed myself to see that the golden light had faded into the pale grey light of dawn. The bees, he said, had all streamed up out of the ceiling aperture. Their departure revealed a door on the wall halfway between the entrance we'd used and the Sun-in-Glory. We tried the handle and were surprised to find that, although stiff, it wasn't locked.

It led us into the castle courtyard, which looked thoroughly washed-clean. We decided with unspoken accord not to waken the castle and instead sought out the stables.

"I'm glad to see the horses were cared for," Hal said when we found them. They had all been fed and groomed, tack cleaned and neatly laid out on racks near the stalls.

"Better than we were," Mr. Dart agreed.

I felt strangely stung. "I'm sorry."

Hal paused in the midst of lifting down a saddle pad. "Really? Why? It's hardly your fault your estranged grandmother is mad as a Toulornie diver and lives in a cursed castle."

"Besides, whatever she lacked in hospitality you more than made up for in entertainment."

I gave Mr. Dart an ironic bow. "In that case, I am much relieved."

There was no sign of a groom, so we saddled our horses ourselves, opened the gate ("Somehow," said Hal, "I doubt that they are in much danger from anything outside these walls"), and rode down the hill towards the village.

"Hey ho," said Mr. Dart as we reached the road, "I think you've lifted the curse."

***

The villagers were not far removed from their earlier poses, but now they were looking around in befuddlement. We walked the horses down the highway through the centre of the village. I was tired from the sleepless night, my mother's old song lingering in my mind, the bees in the lime blossoms above and around us sounding loud enough indeed to be heard across the Border.

The villagers were talking madly to each other, or at least they were until we started to ride through the centre of the village. Then they stopped and stared and followed us silently to the little open green where the villagers presumably held market-days and meetings. There did not appear to be anything like a town hall; ordinary houses formed three sides of the green, with the fourth largely occupied by a substantial sprawling building whose sign proclaimed it The Bee at the Border, once an inn noted in poems of travellers on their way to Astandalas. It was the last place to stay in Alinor, a week's journey—once upon a time—from Astandalas the Golden.

The inn was not so prosperous as it once had been; several of the wings looked as if they'd been boarded up for a while, though an attempt had been made to disguise that telltale sign by window-boxes and barrels full of flowers, and the plaster was brightly white-washed.

In front of the white inn was a beautiful and intricately carved stone well-head. If you drank from it—so those travellers' poems said—you were destined always to return to the Woods. It was dry now, the water-moved bees stationary, the carved patterns blurred with neglect and dust like the runes on the Sun Gates.

A couple came out of the inn. They were middle-aged and respectable; the wife was the one who looked as if she were from St-Noire, with the curly brown hair and heart-shaped face visible in various iterations throughout the village—along with a wider range of ethnicities than practically anywhere else in south Fiellan. Her husband was ethnically Shaian, brown to Hal's black, his hair silky rather than wiry. A sign, again, that once upon a time most of the travellers from Alinor to Astandalas passed along this highway, called at this inn, were caught, perhaps, by the eye of a local.

I reined up in front of them, curious about their experience with the curse, aware they must have questions for us—for me. "Good morning," I said cheerfully, glancing at them both, liking their faces, wondering if it would be so unseemly if the Viscount became friends with the innkeepers. "Are you the innkeeper?"

"Yes, sir," she said, with a curtsy. "I'm Sara White. My husband, Basil."

Here I am, I thought, evidently the Viscount St-Noire, if dragon and curse-breaking and Savela Uvara and Hal were to be believed. One of a list of claimants, if the Marchioness were. Decidedly uncomfortable, whatever the case. I opened my mouth to introduce myself, but before I could do so an older man stepped forward out of the throng. He glanced at Hal and Mr. Dart, then focused on me.

"Who are you?" he demanded without preamble. "You look like the old March."

I bowed. "Jemis Greenwing, at your service, sir."

"The Viscount St-Noire," put in Hal, not quite in his ducal voice but not far off it, either.

The crowd murmured, nothing quite loud enough for me to decipher. Above and all around us the bees were thrumming loudly. The air was heavy with the Tillarny limes. I felt very sleepy.

The speaker frowned at me. "We heard you were dead."

I bowed again. "There appears to have been some misunderstanding with the Marchioness."

"Wouldn't be the first time," someone muttered.

I cleared my throat. "My father was Jack Greenwing, of the Arguty Greenwings. He died nearly seven years ago now. My mother was Lady Olive Noirell, who died when the influenza hit Ragnor Bella."

"That was when the problems began," a woman said. Others nodded. "All through the autumn the bees were slow and sad and then this spring they didn't come awake at all."

More nodding. I stared at the speaker, wondering if my sudden wild thought was correct. Before I could formulate the question— how *did* you ask whether people knew they'd been enchanted for over three years? It was not a nice surprise, as I could attest—someone else pushed through the crowd.

"I'm Ben Horne," he announced, his hard gaze going from me to Mr. Dart. "I know you—but you look older than you should. And who's this? He looks like that Perry Dart."

Mr. Dart bowed. "I have that honour."

Mr. Horne did not seem appeased. "What is all this? Why are the limes blooming? It ain't their season!"

I opened my mouth, but Hal dismounted before I spoke. "If I may? My friends, you have been under an enchantment or a curse of some form. When we came through the village yesterday on our way to the castle you were still as statues. Last we night, when we found the bees in the stone hive under the castle, they too were still as statues. Jemis, the Viscount, woke the bees and broke the curse— but as you have noticed, it is now autumn. The bees are working the limes, and the Dartington Harvest Fair is a week away."

"It's Sunday," Mr. Dart said, "and I'm afraid we must away if we wish to reach the White Cross in time."

Several people smiled at this, though most were looking confused and perturbed.

"It's been three and a half years," I blurted. "My mother died in the autumn. She always used to sing an old song to dance the Lady in, autumn and spring—the last time was that autumn. And I didn't know—I'm so sorry—I didn't know it was significant—I didn't know. I will do what I can to make up for it, I promise you!"

Everyone looked at me. After a moment Mr. Horne said, "Your grandfather used to follow along behind the Marchioness apologizing for her, too, when it wasn't his fault."

"Come along now," Mr. White added. "You lads had best be off to put your names in for the Fair—and we had all best see to our homes and get ready for the bees when they bring their honey home. Everyone who wants can come to the parlour for a drink this evening—the last batch of mead should be well matured by now, I guess."

He looked at me, as I watched, astonished, while everyone else nodded and started to stream into the inn. Mr. White smiled slowly, a little like Mr. Inglesides, a little like Mr. Dart. "Next time you're by, lad, we'll have a good long talk. You need some of my honey-wine to perk you up afore the winter."

Chapter Twenty-One
Hal has an Idea

"YOU'RE LOOKING PENSIVE again," Hal observed as we rode along the winding curves of the highway. The bees were extraordinarily loud in the trees above us, around us. I couldn't imagine that one ever quite got used to them.

"I was feeling sleepy, truth be told," I replied. "Perhaps a bit melancholy, thinking so much of my mother. Confused."

That slipped out. I bit my tongue, hoping they wouldn't jump on it, which they didn't—or not out loud. Hal looked off, ostensibly at the bee-laden blossom above us, and Mr. Dart shifted his sling slightly so his stone arm sat better across the pommel of his saddle.

"Damn you," I said without heat. "I'm worrying about where to sit at church."

***

There were six houses of worship in Ragnor barony, seven if you count the small chapter-house of the Premonstratensians in Sowter's Circle. As best as anyone could make them out, these were a group of monks from Ysthar who had gotten very lost once and now preached about their god to the shepherds of the Gorbelow Hills and mostly kept to themselves; I had never spoken to any of them, though had once seen the monks marching barefoot along the road chanting in a foreign language.

Leaving the Ystharians aside, there were sundry shrines (such as the one to the Emperor we'd passed on our way to the Castle Noirell), whatever the cult to the Dark Gods got up to when not sacrificing cows at the Ellery Stone, and the six churches of the Lady.

The Little Church at the Lady's Cross had been destroyed in the Fall, and no one but the Woods folk went to the lady-chapel in the Heart of the Woods. As far as I knew no one but highway-men and panicked travellers went to the Wild Saint's chapel near the Wells in Arguty Forest. This left the Big Church, Dartington Church, and the one outside Ragnor Parva in the Coombe.

"So why do you not go to Dartington church?" Hal asked as Mr. Dart recounted this list.

"Ah," said Mr. Dart, looking uncomfortable.

"We used to go there, when we were little—both the Darts and my family, I mean. I always liked the building, and the old priest was lovely."

"But very old, I take it?"

I grimaced. "Yes. Even after my father was reported dead as the traitor of Loe, he welcomed us ... but then he died."

"And the new priest, when he came from Nên Corovel, was—" Mr. Dart scowled. "He's Charese. Violently opposed to anything that is not strictly male-and-female wedded bliss."

"Ah. A fool. Your brother doesn't hold the living?"

"For various convoluted reasons, no. It's held by the Baron of Temby, up past Yellem."

"I like very much how Temby is 'up' from here. So, in retaliation—"

"Everyone goes to the Big Church, and the vicar of Dartington spends all of his time off in Temby toadying to his relations."

It occurred to me, as Hal nodded judiciously at this, that possibly Mr. Dart's lack of a sweetheart—and apparent dearth of close friends—from Stoneybridge had something to do with the Charese prejudice. It made about as much sense to me as the Baron rejecting the Earl of the Farry March as a husband for his daughter because the Earl was a practitioner of magic, but I couldn't deny that that rejection had been made, and upheld. And the Charese prejudice was deep-seated. Mr. Buchance had never quite been able to be comfortable with Ragnor Bella's easy acknowledgement of the Squire and Sir Hamish's relationship, though he had never done more than show a faint discomfort at my friendship with Mr. Dart.

We rode around another curve and were suddenly at the edge of the Woods. The green-and-gold trees framed a brilliant opening, the morning sunlight pouring in long shafts from our right. The bees had reached here: the air hummed with their working. With one accord we paused at the sun gate, but nothing happened: no knight or white deer or gnomic-utterance-uttering peasant. After a moment I nudged my horse into a canter, and we rode silently for a while.

When we slowed back to a walk, on the crest of a rise that permitted us a glimpse of Ragnor Bella's roofs, I could still hear the bees.

"Tell me about this Big Church," Hal said. "Who are its main patrons?"

Mr. Dart and I looked at each other. I shrugged. Mr. Dart said, "The Baron; the Talgarths; the Woodhills; Jemis' uncle Vorel."

"Not your brother?"

"No, the funds had already been raised when the new priest came and proved odious enough to drive us to the Baron's church."

"Hmm," said Hal.

I was half-listening to the bees. I could believe they were audible across worlds … or I wanted to believe they were, had been once. Once upon a time the Red Company rode along this highway one late moonlit night, heading for Astandalas to make one certain party immortal, and Fitzroy Angursell saw my mother at the window of her bedroom in the castle tower, and wrote a song about her.

> *Where stood at the window*
> *White stone and ivy*
> *The silent watcher*
> *In her high tower*
> *As we rode the high way*
> *To the golden city*
> *Down the white way*
> *To the city of roses*

"The easy thing to do," I said, "would be to sit with the Darts."

"Your voice suggests that you don't wish to take the easy route?"

Mr. Dart frowned at me. "You're not worrying about whether you're unwelcome or unworthy again, are you? We've discussed this."

"Your aunt may disagree, viscountcy or no. But more ..." I sighed, shook my horse's reins, realized the ceaseless thrum was fading into something like a low hum at the back of my throat. "I think last night ..." They waited while I tried to formulate inchoate thoughts into words. "Last night, first my grandmother and then the bees ... and my mother ..."

I trailed off again, lifted my face into a breeze that blew from the north, carrying wood-smoke with it. Sneezed half-heartedly, like an ordinary person. Tried to capture my feelings obliquely.

"If I sit with the Darts—if we, you and I, Hal, sit with the Darts—nothing changes."

"It's no declaration," Mr. Dart said quietly, with a strange edge to his voice I didn't understand. I looked quickly at him, but his smile was open and cheerful as usual.

I dismissed its a a trick of my ears, confused with straining after the fading beesong. "Yes. That's it, exactly. If life is a game of Poacher—"

"Is life a game of Poacher?" Hal asked quizzically.

"I suspect it is for Jemis."

"If," I repeated, "life is a game of Poacher, now is the time to lay down the first hand and let the tales start to unravel the way we want them to."

Hal and Mr. Dart exchanged glances, quite as if they had years of friendship behind them, and for a moment my heart rejoiced in the rightness of the moment.

Hal said: "You've already exceeded my knowledge of Poacher."

Then he grinned. "I am, however, very good at the game of social one-upmanship. Tell me some more about our options."

***

We unsaddled our horses and left them to the ministrations of the Baron's groom. Mr. Czizek was a staunch imperialist, a former soldier from somewhere far away in the Empire, and he worshipped his gods alone and at some other time than Sunday morning. We spent a few minutes assuring ourselves that our appearance was respectable—more or less—then entered the church just before the bells finished ringing.

Mr. Dart nodded affably and strode off to the Darts' pew near the front of the church, while Hal and I, accompanied by a noticeable increase in whispers, made our way to the pew on the right hand side and five up from the back, where Mrs. Buchance sat with my sisters.

Mrs. Buchance looked briefly startled to see us join her, but Sela squirmed under a protesting Lauren so she could sit beside me. To halt Lauren's continued complaints I lifted Sela over to sit between Hal and me. She asked him in a loud whisper what the design on his buttons was.

His reply, that it was his ducal crest, fell into the silence between the final toll of the bells and the first notes of the choir's hymn. I was quite sure that Sela was not the only one very impressed by this piece of information.

I was much less sure whether that nonchalant explanation had been so clearly spoken on purpose. I thought I knew Hal very well: but then people were always essentially a mystery, I reflected, as Mrs. Etaris, three pews ahead of me, half-turned in her seat and winked.

Hal was reasonably devout, and Marcan very much so, so we'd

attended services during our travels. Hal liked sitting on the right-hand side so he could see the priest in the pulpit, and towards the back so he was not overwhelmed by incense. My poor abused system was grateful for this preference, though I had been a bit puzzled at his insistence until the discovery that the ducal pew in the church in Fillering Pool was front and centre and got the full brunt of incense and holy water and flower-petals and all the other elements of a Lady-Day service.

Ghilousette's churches had felt deeply wrong to me—or possibly my malaise had made me feel deeply wrong—and after the first Sunday service in the duchy I had not gone again. Then last week, my first back home, well, I had been somewhat overwhelmed by the Fifth Imperial Bastard Decadent dinner party I'd attended under false pretenses the night before, and had not even tried.

It was lovely, all things considered, to be home.

Prayer succeeded hymn, litany and hymn again, the familiar orderly sequence of the seasonal prayers as the Green Lady of Summer began to hand over her duties to the White Lady of Winter. The actual autumn cross-over day was on the night of All Souls; in the spring it was on my birthday, the come-and-go last day of February in the spur weeks between winter and spring.

No wonder I was muddled so often, I thought, standing for a hymn, sitting again for the homily, thoughts drifting as Father Rigby launched into the same sermon he gave every year on the Sunday before the Dartington Harvest Fair. I was child of neither winter nor summer, White Lady nor Green; I was born on a cross-over come-and-go day, the 29th of February, the day of All Fools.

The priest called for the Lady's gift of fair play and a good year for the Fair ahead, the choir sang one last hymn, and we all rose decorously and followed priest and acolytes and choir and Important People out of the church, each of us in our own order from first-ranked to last.

As we waited for our turn to shuffle into the aisle I girded myself for Hauling the Net, the second major stage in the game of Poacher.

Mr. Dart, walking beside Sir Hamish, winked at us as they passed.

Hal leaned over Sela's head to whisper in my ear. "Ready to run the gauntlet?"

Chapter Twenty-Two
Mr. Inglesides has an Idea

THE GAME OF Poacher, as my father taught it to me, has four primary stages: Casting the Lure, Hauling the Net, Laying the Table, and Measuring the Tale.

Early-stage players think the point lies in figuring out what cards to take and which to discard during the first rounds of the game.

Slightly more advanced players try to calculate the effect of the common cards on their opponent and take that into account.

Excellent players are running through the probabilities of which cards are in the discard piles, which are in their opponent's hand, and which is the Emperor Card, the last to be played.

I'm not sure what exactly I'd call myself, except that my father had taught me how to play Poacher as if it were the game of life, and my mother had taught me—well, that there was a game behind the game, and that for the true master of the game, the cards you were dealt didn't actually matter.

The true art of Poacher lies not in how one reacts to what one is given, but in shaping the other player's understanding of what they have in their hand and on the table before them.

I felt as if I had spent my whole summer reacting. Reacting to my stepfather's questions about my future, to Lark's beguilement and betrayal, to Hal's support, to my illness, to *Three Years Gone*, to the weather in North Fiellan and the craziness of Ghilousette. Reacting to Mrs. Buchance's suggestions and my uncle's insinuations, to the town's general opprobrium and the occasional bright spot of friendship. Reacting to finding a fish pie, to being attacked by Violet, to being caught up in cults and magic and organized crime. Reacting to the Honourable Rag's baiting, to my grandmother, to the dragon, to Hal—

Reacting was no way to win at Poacher, nor, as I was beginning to see, at life.

I smiled at Hal, who had agreeably let Sela take his hand, turned to offer Lauren my own, and was surprised by a sudden wondering smile from Mrs. Buchance. "Good morning," I said cheerfully to her, then greeted Mr. and Mrs. Inglesides, who were seated in the row behind us, along with their large progeny and a few strangers.

"Good morning, Mr. Greenwing," said Mr. Inglesides, quiet mischief in his eyes. It occurred to me that I would quite like to play Poacher against him. Last week he had indicated he was of a radical turn of philosophy, but we had not yet had much of a chance to talk. He indicated the woman beside him. "My sister-in-law, Mrs. Eglantine. She's come down for the Fair. Iris, this is Mr. Greenwing, who was Mr. Buchance's stepson. He's just come back from university."

By this time I had made it into the aisle, so I was able to bow to Mrs. Eglantine, who looked astonished. "Greenwing? As in the play?"

I smiled at her, noticing how a few people in the pews behind her, in the aisle around me, were listening. This *was* like Poacher: if you were prepared, you could turn any card to the story you wished to be told. "Yes, although the playwright was unfortunately much misinformed about the true facts of the case."

"Oh?" said Mrs. Eglantine, but her attention was drifting to the conversation going on behind me between Sela and Hal.

"Are *you* a duke?" Sela was asking.

"Yes, I'm the Duke of Fillering Pool," he said easily.

"And you're friends with Jemis?"

"Yes, we met at university."

Sela heaved a great sigh. "I'm not even in *school* yet."

Hal laughed. "Well, I'm sure you can't be all that far off."

I lost track of their conversation as Mrs. Etaris came up to me to be greeted in turn. Her husband, the Chief Constable, had his eyes on Hal as he gave me a short nod before striding off in the direction of my uncle. *Point*, I thought, and bowed extravagantly to my employer. "Good morning, Mrs. Etaris."

"Good morning, Mr. Greenwing," she replied, eyes brimful of humour. "I am somewhat disappointed to see you here; I was eagerly anticipating the wild froth of rumours that would surely be circulating in your continued absence."

I bowed again, less extravagantly this time, and offered her my arm. "May I escort you in the general direction of the White Cross, ma'am? Despite my unanticipated presence, I believe I might be able to supply the barony with a few items of gossip."

Mrs. Etaris laughed and set her hand lightly on my elbow. We ambled forward. I was conscious of the way the rest of the congregation was split between attending to their own concerns (a small minority), casting speculative glances and whispers in our direction, and casting even more speculative glances and whispers on Hal. Hal was still talking enthusiastically with Sela. Beyond him in the churchyard the tableau of all the worthy gentry of Ragnor barony.

"All of them bar one," said Mrs. Etaris as we came to the door to wait our turn to greet Father Rigby.

She was looking out the doorway at that same grouping of gentry. "Oh?" I said, smiling, wondering if she meant my grand-mother—or me.

She grinned at me, well-feathered hat tilting slightly back as she moved her head. "I am glad to see you in such fine fettle, Mr. Greenwing."

We shuffled forward two steps to Father Rigby. The priest was plump, ginger-haired, and full of slightly erratic intensity. He reached out his hands to Mrs. Etaris. "Mrs. Etaris, good morning, good morning. How are you this fine day?"

"Very well, thank you," she murmured politely.

He turned to me and looked remarkably blank for a man who had been my priest for four years. Time to lay the next card on the table, I thought, and on cue Mrs. Etaris smiled.

"Mr. Greenwing, I'm sure you remember Father Rigby. Father, this is Jemis Greenwing; he's recently back from Morrowlea after a walking tour of the four duchies."

"Oh yes," said Father Rigby, his puzzled expression not clear-ing. Perhaps his blankness was for some other reason? I glanced past him, breaking uncomfortable eye contact, and saw that half the congregation was watching this interaction. I smiled brightly at the priest. There were too many reasons for the priest to look puzzled to even begin to count at this moment.

I decided the next move would have to take place outside, so I bowed to the priest. "Good morning, Father. It was so, ah, homely to hear you speak of the Dartington Harvest Fair the way you always have. Now that I'm home in Ragnor Bella I'm sure I will see you more frequently."

The priest frowned briefly. I wondered just what he'd been hearing from his congregation over the last two weeks. "You plan on staying? I mean, since you had not come back from university during the holidays, we—that is, I had heard you would not be returning? Especially after your stepfather's death ..."

That I had missed Mr. Buchance's funeral was a regret I would hold the rest of my life. I bowed again. "I regret very much that I was in Ghilousette and had not given sufficient direction to Mrs. Buchance that she could reach me with the news in time for me to return for the funeral. As for my plans, no doubt they may change somewhat now that I have begun to reconcile with my grandmother, the Marchioness of the Woods Noirell, but as it stands, yes, I intend to stay in Ragnor Bella for the foreseeable future."

Since Father Rigby was one of the great gossips of the barony, anyone who had not heard that directly would certainly hear it very soon. I glanced out into the churchyard, saw Hal and Sela talking to Mr. Dart, and bowed again at the priest. "I must go find my friend, the Duke of Fillering Pool—we want to enter our names in a competition for the Fair. Good morning!"

"Good morning," the priest replied faintly. I offered my arm to Mrs. Etaris again, and we made our way with all decorum across the yard.

In a briefly isolated moment, Mrs. Etaris murmured, "Very fine fettle indeed, Mr. Greenwing. I'm sure the gambling ring has already moved from rigging the choirboys' race to betting on you."

***

"The custom," Mr. Dart said to Hal, "is for everyone to proceed to the White Cross, where the Squire—that's my brother—and the Bailiff of Dartington take entries for the competition."

"I am beginning to comprehend why this Fair is the talk of four baronies. The heart of culture is taking the time to do the unnecessary in the most picturesque manner possible."

"You've been listening to Jemis about his radical philosophers, haven't you?"

Hal laughed. "It was that or participate in the conversations about poetry. I like poetry to read as much as the next man, unless that next man is Jemis in a fit of structural analysis."

"I listened to you explain the history of the development of pollination in plants."

Mr. Dart grinned. "I must admit that sometimes I wish I'd gone to Morrowlea with you, but I wouldn't exchange my tutor for the world."

I wondered, not for the first time, what exactly had made Mr. Dart's tutor that special—and for the first time wondered moreover whether there was a smidgen of more than a student's love for his teacher in the warmth of Mr. Dart's voice. Given his response to my teasing on the subject of matrimonial prospects, I decided to forebear comment. I surveyed the scene around us instead.

The priest was still occupied with greeting his parishioners. Those who were taking part in the next procession were trying to form up, though they were thwarted in this effort by the total disregard of the congregation and the still-conversing priest.

Ahead of us the thurifer decided to begin and strode off down the lane as if using the thurible to whack invisible enemies from his path. He nearly hit the Honourable Rag, who had crossed aimlessly before him to be insistently bonhomous to Dominus Gleason. This pleased me more than it should have.

The thurifer was followed by two acolytes in green cassocks and white surplices. They bore the Lady's banners, Green Lady on the right and White on the left. Behind them came the choir, lustily singing yet another of the harvest hymns, but somewhat ragged in their procession despite Father Rigby's fluttering gestures. I eyed the choirboys' ranks and could see why the gambling ring might be planning on nefarious activity there. There were four rival friends I was glad I didn't have to mind.

Behind the pushing, shoving, and angelically singing choirboys came Mr. Etaris, the Chief Constable, and next to him the Clerk of the Court. They bore respectively the flags of Fiellan and Astandalas—Hal, spying these, asked whether the fact that Fiellan was a part of the Kingdom of Rondé was always so thoroughly ignored.

"Down here it is," Mr. Dart replied cheerfully. "I can't speak for the Middle or the North."

"It never ceases to surprise me how far south we are here. To think that Fiella-by-the-Sea is the far north for you!"

"I saw Rondelan flags in North Fiellan," I said vaguely, watching knots of interested parties clump together, break apart, group elsewhere, all of them talking; all of them, or so it seemed, watching the three of us.

"We don't have much to do with the government," Mr. Dart agreed. "Our problems usually stay here or go all the way to the

Lady on Nên Corovel, like last week with Miss Shipston, the mermaid."

Hal blinked, but before he could respond the priest suddenly recalled that he was next in the procession. The little gossiping knots broke up to follow the priest down the hill, and we were inexorably drawn after them. In the shuffle I found myself next to Mr. Inglesides.

I nodded politely. "Good morning—or rather afternoon. It's a splendid day, isn't it?"

"'Tis." We walked a few yards in silence. It *was* a splendid day, the sky blue with a few puffs of white cloud here and there, the grass bright green, the hedgerows in full fruit—hawthorn, blackberry, spindle, sloe.

For a moment I almost imagined I could smell the heavy-honey scent of the Tillarny limes, but when I turned my head into the wind all I smelled was incense. I sneezed.

Hal, talking again to Mr. Dart, grinned over his shoulder at the noise before angling suddenly across the procession to investigate something in the lee of the hedgerow. Mr. Inglesides watched him squat down, then turned to me. His expression was so difficult to read—was he trying not to laugh?—that I felt my attention sharpen.

Time for the next card drawn from the Happenstance pile—

"Mr. Greenwing, lad, I like you a lot. I think you're turning out a fine man indeed, one to make your folks proud. I'd like to see you settled, at home in yourself. I reckon the barony'd be far the better for you and your ideas."

"Oh," I said, and added, because his tone was almost as ambiguous as his expression, "but?"

He did smile, but it was directed at Mrs. Buchance, who had turned around to corral a straying Sela and waved at us in passing.

"But," he said in a low voice, nodding at his sister, "that is not right for either of you."

Mr. Inglesides was not like my uncle in any particular, but they had both raised the same concern.

It was on my lips to protest that the thought had never crossed my mind except as a result of the warnings against it—for quite apart from my own tendency to fall in love with dashing criminals, it was uncomfortably close to incest; if there wasn't a law against it I rather thought there should be—when it occurred to me that it might not be *my* heart that Mr. Inglesides was concerned with.

So after we'd walked a few yards more, through the lych-gate at the bottom of the hill and onto the Borrowbank Road, I said, "I'm very grateful to Mrs. Buchance for putting me up these last few weeks. Now that the job at the bookstore is going well, I should be in more of a position to find my own lodgings. Have you heard of anywhere?"

We proceeded along the lane, past Hal, who appeared to be taken with some sort of fern, and halted briefly while a tussle between two of the choirboys was resolved by their irate parent.

"You wouldn't think to stay with your uncle, then?"

Ahead of us groups shifted position, revealing all the fine gentry of the barony clustering around Squire and Bailiff at the White Cross—or all of them except one.

Hal joined us, brushing the dirt from his hands and beaming. I smiled at Mr. Inglesides. "Oh, no, I don't think that would suit either of us. Not to mention Arguty Hall is rather far to come into town daily for 9:00, don't you think?"

Mr. Inglesides' eyes twinkled. Hal, tucking his fern away in his notebook, asked, "How far is it?"

"Six and a half miles."

"Well, you run that before breakfast."

Hal was not very good at Poacher.

I shook my head in fond exasperation, contriving—I hoped—to express that Hal was ribbing me.

Fortunately any questions Mr. Inglesides might have been inclined to ask were forestalled by our arrival at the White Cross. In the press forward I held onto Hal's arm and angled us towards Mrs. Etaris, who would surely have an idea for how I might go about looking for lodging.

She was standing a bit apart from everyone else on the south side of the waystone. A few yards closer to us Dominus Gleason stood, similarly alone—except when I looked again at him I realized his manservant stood close behind him. I blinked, wondering how I had missed the looming figure at first.

Dominus Gleason turned his head from the waystone to our approach. A little smirk appeared and did not improve his features. "Mr. Greenwing. Have you had the chance to think about my offer? You are quite enveloped in magic, you know, and must be taught."

"So I have been informed," I replied, with a short, uninflected bow. "Please excuse me—I must ask Mrs. Etaris a question."

The smirk hardened into a sneer; the old magister's nostrils flared; he made his strange hacking laugh. "Mrs. Etaris? A nonentity, a nothing, a woman. Ask her any question and its answer will be domestic; there is no greatness to be found there, no way to learn—" his voice dropped, his eyes almost bulged with intensity—he made what he probably thought was a smile— "No way to learn, Mr. Greenwing, those things worth knowing."

How did the man make me feel so immediately greasy and soiled? I gave him an insincere smile. "As it happens, my question *is* entirely domestic. Good day to you, Domine."

I tugged an unresisting Hal along, feeling as if I were escaping some sort of oozing miasma. The very air seemed clearer and fresher next to Mrs. Etaris. I turned my back on Dominus Gleason and pulled out a handkerchief with which to wipe my hands. I was surprised to feel my muscles trembling, as if I'd just relaxed a great strain.

"That's your potential magic teacher?" Hal asked.

I started. "I'm not—no. No."

"I didn't say you *should*—quite the opposite. Good day to you, Mrs. Etaris."

"Mr. Lingham, Mr. Greenwing." She curtsied slightly, contriving by the movement to shift us all over a few feet farther away from the magister. She went on in a lower voice. "Do you truly have a question for me, Mr. Greenwing, or did you merely wish to escape the magister? His metaphysics is somewhat muddled; nonentities can have their appeal."

Sometimes, in the game of Poacher, one was best served by a straight-forward and frank approach. I nodded. "Do you know where I might find lodging? Until Winterturn, at least."

Mrs. Etaris followed my half-intentional glance to the family grouping on the other side of the waystone: Mrs. Buchance and her daughters, Mr. Inglesides and his wife and children, Mrs. Ingleside's sister and brother-in-law and their children.

One thing I liked very much about Mrs. Etaris was that she

never seemed puzzled by what seemed to me odd and unexpected problems. I wished I felt half so confident or competent as she was.

"Ah, of course," she replied. "It had occurred to me that you might eventually want a place of your own—radical as some will take that idea. If it appeals, there is a flat above the bookstore. I will give you a reduced rent for the first month as you will need to clear it out and clean it up first."

Hal snorted. "I can help. We did enough of that at Morrowlea. Even if Jemis usually managed to get out of lumber-room duty on account of his sneezes."

"The lumber rooms of Morrowlea are much more likely to contain magical items than the flat above my bookstore," Mrs. Etaris said, "though I can't promise for the second room, which was left rather cluttered by the previous owner. I shall get you the keys tomorrow, Mr. Greenwing. I believe the entries are about to be taken."

Hal turned forward again. I tried to focus on the Dartington town crier's announcement of the Fair and the rules for entering the competitions. I had not been to look at the White Cross since I returned to Ragnor Bella. It was not considered seemly to acknowledge the soberer aspects of the waystones.

I forced myself to look at the tall white stone in the centre of the crossroads. The waystone was twelve feet tall and told, to those who could read its symbolism, the history of the barony in stark simplicity.

Pre-Astandalan stonework; Astandalan runes; post-Astandalan cords to bind the broken magic.

I did not know on which side they had buried my father, but I supposed it didn't matter to anyone but me.

There were milestones throughout the Empire—every mile, in fact, along the great highways. They changed material and location by region and sometimes by magical purpose. In Ghilousette they were stone cylinders breast-high on a mounted man; down by Morrowlea they were shaped pyramids not much more than four feet high. Only the numbering system and the glyphs used by the Schooled wizards were the same.

The waystones of South Fiellan were something else. Our milestones were waist-high fluted columns made of the local stones, white limestone in Ragnor, yellow sandstone in Yellem, pink granite in Temby. The waystones were much, much older.

The White Cross was where the Astandalan highway met Teller Road, which followed the South Rag downriver from Ragnor Bella; Dartly Road, which crossed the East Rag on the way to Dartington and Arguty; the Borrowbank Road from the Baron's castle via the Big Church; and Old Spinney lane, which led along the south bank of the East Rag towards the Greenway and, eventually, the Talgarths' house and beyond it the village of Ragnor Parva in the Coombe.

I had learned in History of Magic that most crossroads onto the highway were unremarkable, the Imperial road's magic overwhelming, containing, and subduing any elements brought by a crossing road.

Major crossroads—where two highways met, for instance—were more significant, and like bridges had many extra spells woven into the chains and stones of the road-bed. Those were marked by special cobbles: at the great crossroads in Yrchester the place where the Astandalas Road met the East-West Highway was shown by granite blocks flecked with gold mica.

In South Fiellan the great hundred-weight blocks of stone were not used at crossroads because of the occasional need to dig them up to bury the criminal dead.

The White Cross was built of 6,561 basalt setts arranged inside iron bands to form a sun-in-glory with the waystone at its centre. They were basalt because of how hard it was to enchant basalt (and how hard it was, therefore, to disenchant basalt once the spells were inlaid), set in iron because iron has the curious magical property of binding loose magic into its pattern. That was, so my tutor had said, why the Good Neighbours did not like iron; it interfered with their innate magic.

By use of the basalt and iron bands and spells of staggering complexity, concerned officials of South Fiellan could, when necessary, pry up the cobbles, dig a hole, and without destroying the great chains of spells that had bound the Empire together bury— let us give an example—the body of a traitor and a suicide.

Just then Hal nudged me, and without paying attention to anyone around me I entered my name in the Three-Mile Race and, a little while later, the Cake Competition.

Chapter Twenty-Three
Furnishings

HAL AND I spent the night at Dart Hall, then ambled rather slowly into town along the Greenway (this time *sans* dragon). We had to stop frequently for Hal to look at various plants, as a result of which we did not have enough time to acquire anything from Mr. Inglesides' bakery before I had to go to work. I did learn that the flora of South Fiellan was, due to the isolating effects of the Arguty Forest to the North and the cradle of Crosslain Mountains and Gorbelow Hills to the southeast and -west, quite distinct from other regions in Rondé.

"That explains more than plants," I replied, tickled by the thought.

"You used to be on the highway to Astandalas," Hal observed, tucking whatever-it-was into his notebook. "Surely that brought news and, er, new ideas?"

"You may have noticed that the towns around here are not built *on* the highway ..."

"Because of the customs around crossroads, you said."

"Yes. But it did mean that with the exception of St-Noire in the Woods, travellers had to leave the highway to get anywhere. A few did, of course, but generally speaking Ragnor Bella rejoices in its reputation as the dullest town in Northwest Oriole."

Hal laughed. "Where did travellers stay, in that case?"

I frowned, trying to remember. "The Bee at the Border in St-Noire was a famous inn. The one back up from there … I believe there was a post-stage just on the north side of the Arguty Forest. People on foot usually would stay at the Green Dragon, I think, which is about halfway between."

"Which is where?"

"Ahead of us a few hundred yards—the inn, that is; the creature I am not sure of."

"You shall have to put your mind to its riddle at some point, Jemis, you know."

I frowned at the hawthorn and holly. We had passed the Drag-onstone Pool, and could see ahead of us the gold-inflected end of the ancient road.

"I'm not *ignoring* it," I protested, but the words fell lamely even on my own ears. Hal looked out at the wind-tossed trees around us, oaks and ashes and hornbeam. Some sweet fragrance cut through the air; I sneezed.

"Sweet autumn clematis," Hal murmured. "Jemis—"

But whatever he was going to say went unsaid, for in a great thundering of hooves and kicking-up of clods the Honourable Rag launched his big black stallion into the Greenway at full gal-lop towards us.

We scattered instinctually to the sides. He ignored us with an aristocratic indifference, neither slowing nor changing his direc-tion, and thundered off as heavily and as mysteriously as the grey wolf-knight of the Woods Noirell.

"Nice horse," said Hal.

"He might have paid the tiniest heed to us pedestrians," I grumbled. "He might have hit us."

"He has not given me the impression of someone overly concerned with the common foot," Hal replied, and linked his arm with mine. "Come now, Jemis, cheer up. Why aren't you eagerly attacking this puzzle laid before you? It seems so much exactly what you should enjoy."

This puzzle being the dragon's riddle, naturally, not the riddle of the Honourable Rag's behaviour (which only I seemed at all concerned about, or even interested in). I considered my response. I could not, actually, quite account for my reluctance to put my mind to it.

"Something about having *a destiny* bothers me," I said at last, as we turned away from the Green Dragon onto the main highway. "And a destiny tied in with my mother's people, who are so horrible!"

"Only your grandmother. The other people in the Woods seemed odd, but generally pleasant."

"I'm not related to any of the other people, alas."

"But you are responsible for them."

I considered that indisputable fact. I sighed, trying to counteract the thin frisson of panic that accompanied the thought. "Yes. I shall have to see what books are in the store—on *noblesse oblige*, that is."

"I can help you with that, Jemis."

I smiled at him. "Thanks, Hal. Perhaps you can give me the basics before you return to Fillering Pool. So long as you don't object to sharing my flat with me—though I imagine the Darts would willingly put you up if you'd prefer."

"I shared a room with you for three years, sir! Unless you were fostering a yearning for your own home all that time."

"I was fostering a desire to marry Lark."

We walked on for a while in silence. We took the Town Road (no proper crossroad waystone there; just a milestone with an arrow pointing to *Ragnor Bella, 2*), round a wide bend cloaked in oaks undergirded with ivy, crested a low rise, and saw spilling in the valley below us the silver ribbons of Rag and Raggle, and in the triangle made by their confluence the attractive jumble of buildings that was Ragnor Bella, the dullest town in Northwest Oriole.

"It's such a pretty town," Hal murmured, then added on nearly the same breath: "About you and Lark."

I carefully unclenched my jaw. "Yes?"

The road to Ragnor Bella angled down the face of the hill. Ahead of us two wagons were being driven across the humpbacked bridge over the Rag. Hal said, "I know your betrayal is more than just … the ordinary drama of a relationship."

"She was drugging and ensorcelling me."

"About that." He paused, seemed to be picking his words with unwonted care. "I am, as it happens, a fairly gifted practitioner of magic. Obviously I've not studied it at university, but my mother studied magic at Oakhill when it was more than just fashionable, and she taught me and my sister."

"What are you saying?"

"I'm saying that while—Jemis, Lark was definitely stealing your magic. I didn't sense *anything* from you while we were at Morrowlea, and I should have, from an untaught mage. I haven't made a study of wireweed, but I know that it has concealing effects as well as permitting unscrupulous wizards to steal other people's innate magic. That explains why I didn't see anything more than a certain tendency towards glamour in Lark."

"You didn't say anything about magical glamour."

"When you had fallen that heavily? After so sweetly and tentatively working up the nerve to approach Violet, you plunged headfirst into a torrid love affair with Lark. I presumed at first that it would fade—but it lasted nearly two years, so I presumed there was something deeper than mere glamour."

I digested this. "All right. I grant that I wouldn't have listened to you suggesting Lark was beguiling me."

"I didn't realize she was *beguiling* you. I thought she was just using her magic to exaggerate her charm, which is reprehensible but has never been illegal. And I thought ... Jemis, I'm not expressing myself properly here. I thought that under her influence some of your own tendencies were exaggerated, too."

"Oh, thank you!"

"Please don't snap at me. I mean to say that the wireweed and the magic did not *change* who you are—they, ah, brought out certain aspects more than others. Good humour, cheerfulness, quickness of thought, cleverness—those are part of you! They're not only the effect of the drug."

I bit back a bitter retort, for we had been walking far faster than I'd realized and had come abreast of the carts. I did not wish to discuss my inner life with all the good folk of Ragnor Bella—my outer life was surely sufficient fodder—so I doffed my hat to the farmers and guided Hal to the bookstore. He sighed and let the conversation go, though I was fairly sure he would bring it up again at the first opportunity.

Not that that came for several days, as it happened.

Mrs. Etaris was in the process of mending her fire. She straightened as the bell over the door jangled. "Oh, good morning, Mr. Greenwing, Mr. Lingham. Perfectly on time, as usual."

"Entirely Jemis' doing," Hal said, bowing politely. "I am all-too-easily distracted by intriguing plants."

"Oh, are you a gardener?"

"Studied botany, ma'am."

Mrs. Etaris' face lit up and she launched into a sudden interrogation of Hal's course of study. I left them to it. A half-full box of books sat on the counter. As I moved the box I saw there was an address on the lid: in a beautiful hand was written *Mrs. Jullanar Etaris, Elderflower Books, Ragnor Bella, Fiellan.*

"Jullanar," I said aloud, surprised, then flushed when Mrs. Etaris and Hal both looked at me.

Mrs. Etaris smiled. "My name? Yes; I am of the generation that made it, ah, infamous. You may notice both my husband and my sister avoid calling me by it."

"As if thereby they could escape either the renown, or the notoriety, of the name?"

"There were six girls named Jullanar in my year at Madame Clancette's Finishing School. I doubt you'd find one of them that goes by it nowadays. Now, let me see … we'll put a note on the door and I'll show you the flat."

***

The flat was accessed by a stair winding up past the old shrine (which I had never seen any indication Mrs. Etaris used). It had five rooms: a tiny kitchen, a largish parlour, a water closet, a bedroom, and a large room up another flight of stairs in the attic.

All of them were very well stocked with miscellaneous—

"*Bric-à-brac,*" suggested Hal.

"Junk," Mrs. Etaris replied with cheerful insouciance. "Well, here it is, Mr. Greenwing. Do you think it will suit?"

I had already decided that the flat would suit regardless of its appearance, condition, or character. It was a pleasant surprise that it held none of the air of decrepitude or despair that, I realized unexpectedly, I had unconsciously been expecting. Somehow I had thought it would be like the Castle Noirell, but instead it was very much like Magistra Bellamy's cottage.

"It's lovely," I said belatedly. Flushed at the choice of word, caught Hal's mocking eye, and promptly sneezed. "Ah—what would you like us to do with the, ah, *bric-à-brac?*"

"Anything that seems salvageable you may salvage; let me know if you come across anything of greater interest; true junk you can put in the lane behind the store and I shall hire Messrs. Pinger and Garsom to haul it to the junkyard."

"Splendid," said Hal, and promptly slung down his knapsack into a corner. "Now, Jemis, what time is lunch?"

***

The morning downstairs passed pleasantly. We could hear the odd thump and scrape as Hal moved things around above us, and a snatch of him singing something by Fitzroy Angursell. Mrs. Etaris, unpacking the box of books, listened for a few moments, expression a little wistful, before she asked me to close the door at the bottom of the stairs.

She was, I reflected, the Chief Constable's wife. He probably expected her to preserve the appearances of respectability, even if her own tastes ran to banned poetry and local espionage.

I served customers and shelved books and was occasionally distracted by Gingersnap the cat, a book on gnomic utterances from Northern Voonra that had absolutely nothing to do with dragons, Alinorel or otherwise, and my thoughts.

I was trying to remember what I'd been like, what life had been like, that first term at Morrowlea. Before Lark and her ivory pipe.

Mr. Buchance had insisted that he had business with his partner in Chare and therefore travelled with me and Mr. Dart on our way south. We had taken the rough road running out of the Coombe into the mountains, down the other side into the Farry March, and south on that side of the mountains until Mr. Buchance and Mr. Dart had turned off towards Chare and I had continued south and west towards Morrowlea.

At the time Mr. Dart and I had chafed at this oversight, though I could admit now that we had been grateful to Mr. Buchance for his assistance in terms of doing business with innkeepers and horse-changers and tolls: not so much for the financial help, but for the simple fact that he was experienced in the ways of travel, and we had never been out of south Fiellan. He knew what to ask for, what to expect, what to complain about and what to tip.

I wondered, now that it was by far too late to ask, whether that caution and oversight was some way of my stepfather showing me that his new family did not wholly exclude me. At the time I had felt a little suspicious that he was making certain that I arrived at Morrowlea in order to make sure I was safely gone from Ragnor Bella.

Clutching my precious letter of acceptance I had presented myself at the porter's lodge. I had tried not to stare at the magnificent architecture, at the sophisticated older students in their bottle-green robes trimmed with the colours of their disciplines, the professors in Scholars' black, their hoods the rich green-and-gold stripe of Morrowlea. Marvelled a little at the gardens and workshops filled with students hard at work, for Morrowlea, even more so than most Alinorel universities, was a fiefdom unto itself.

If a fiefdom, then its lord was the Chancellor, Domina Rusticiana, Scholar of Lightning, elegant as a painting of an Astandalan princess.

She had taken my letter and bidden me be seated. I had sat in the chair before her great desk, hat in my lap, looking at the wealth of learning and secular riches in her study—the books, the artifacts, the art. She had looked me over coolly. I braced myself.

"So you are our Fiellanese scholar," she said. She spoke with an accent, which I learned later was that of the Astandalan court. She spoke precisely, softly so that I leaned forward to hear her.

"Yes, ma'am," I replied, trying not to crush my hat, waiting for the questions.

She nodded. "Congratulations. I shall be interested to follow your career here as you come into yourself. You understand that you are not to speak of origins here? Including your status as a scholarship student?"

"Yes, ma'am."

She glanced down at my letter, tapped it with her finger. I was nearly sick with fear.

"You are our only Jemis this year, so we need not fret about distinguishing your name. Welcome to Morrowlea, young man: I hope it is everything you have hoped for and far more."

Thus dismissed, I bumbled my way to the Registrar, who gave me my room key and first month's list of courses—which were taken by all first-year students as a way to ensure they had equal grounding in the fundamentals, to meet each other, and to be introduced to subjects and disciplines perhaps unknown and yet potentially beloved—to the Sartor, who gave me my robes, and finally to my room, where I found Hal.

Hal, dressed already in his robes (grey for first-year students), looked grand, intimidatingly confident. New people never daunted him, nor any social situation, but all the little practical details of common life were strange and occasionally baffling to him. The boots, that first evening; but even before that, when we struck up a tentative alliance in order to find the refectory, he had treated the act of picking up a tray in order to carry his plate to the long tables as the peculiar custom of another culture.

In such little moments was friendship begun and nurtured: in conversations late into the night about the books we read; in early morning chores done so poorly at first; in our mild competition to improve so that Stable-master or Housekeeper or Cook ceased complaining about us useless first-years who didn't know a spoon from a spatula.

I thought about those first months. They seemed duller but yet more concrete than the magic years that followed. Those were dreamlike, or like memories of a book I had read: clear-edged, vivid, brilliant, but with emotions somehow absent, leached-out, gone.

I knew I had felt emotions: remembered how my heart had beaten loudly whenever I saw Lark, how my breath came faster, how my body was flooded by desire and what I had taken for happiness.

But I smiled involuntarily thinking about Marcan and Hal and I getting in trouble for swimming in the fish pond after curfew, and all that remembered froth of excitement left me now cold.

I shied away from Lark; thought instead of later episodes with Hal and Marcan, Isoude and Violet, and all the rest of our friends in the year.

Smiled foolishly at the second-year discovery that the devout and very traditional Marcan—whom I'd pegged as a prosperous yeoman farmer's son until his father's outriders came to collect him—had never read anything by Fitzroy Angursell.

That had been a happy winter and spring, reading the poems, including all the many volumes of *Aurora*.

Perhaps I did not owe the wireweed *all* my happiness.

***

I went to Mr. Inglesides' bakery for luncheon items and to tell him about the flat. Dominus Gleason's man was there when I entered. The cinnamon buns he was purchasing seemed incongruous, but then what did I know of either him—whose name I did not even know—or Dominus Gleason, apart from the latter's propensities to minor crimes?

"Good afternoon," I said neutrally to the manservant.

He turned, expression blankly hostile, eyes flat. Surveyed me from head to toe; visibly dismissed me as a threat; said, in a voice so like a wheel over gravel I had immediately to wonder if he cultivated it on purpose, "Pipsqueak."

I blinked.

He walked out with his cinnamon buns, contriving to loom all the way and still not hit his head on the doorjamb.

Last week I had been given the cut direct by Dame Talgarth in the bakery. That had not ended well for her—though I had not, in point of fact, *intended* to do anything against her. Perhaps there would be some similarly oblique way to return the favour to Dominus Gleason and his man.

It would have to be *very* oblique: the man was not the most dangerous person I had ever encountered (that honour went to the Tarvenol duellist with whom I had played Poacher at the Green Dragon last week, followed in short order first by Violet and then by Lark), but he was certainly in the top echelon. And no one I had heard tell had any idea what Dominus Gleason's skill as a wizard was. He had been a Scholar-wizard at Fiella-by-the-Sea before the Fall, but that said little nowadays.

I paid for Temby pasties, more cinnamon buns, and coffee, and conveyed them all up to the new flat, where Hal had been most busy.

Over lunch he showed me his lists, of things he had found and things we needed.

"Much in the 'salvageable' category?"

"Oh, most of it. Do you know what the previous owner did with the space?"

"No, Mrs. Etaris has had the shop as long as I can remember."

"I'm split—or perhaps they were. I think they might have been either a printer-stationer—"

"Quite reasonable."

"—Or a cheesemonger."

I snorted into my coffee. "I'm sorry?"

"Possibly even a cheese*maker*, except why do that in the middle of town? There are all sorts of pots and things in here."

"They might be the necessities for an illegal still, you know. There are enough of those in the Arguty Forest to float the town down the Rag."

"And yet this is the dullest town in Northwest Oriole. I think there must be a conspiracy of sorts to keep it so."

"Probably. The good gentry seem committed to the reputation."

I winced inwardly at giving Hal this opportunity to return to the conversation about the matters swirling about me, and was glad to hear the town bell ring the hour so I could escape back down the stairs to work.

**

Mr. Dart arrived at closing-time to admire the flat and bear us off to the Ragnor Arms for supper. I had never eaten at the hotel and was unfavourably impressed by the food compared to Mrs. Buchance's cooking or even my own. The wine was adequate and the conversation, since public, general, so I was overall pleased.

We talked about Stoneybridge and Morrowlea's respective attitudes to their neighbours. I was aware, though disbelieving of the fact, that the conversations around us ebbed whenever I spoke. Accordingly I spoke less and less of substance as the meal wore on, until we were on the third remove and the Honourable Rag launched himself from where he had been dining with Mr. Woodhill and flung himself into our company in order, it seemed, to champion Tara on every count.

"It's true we had no city amusements," Hal agreed cheerfully, "but to be frank, Master Roald, what of it? If one goes to a great university, does one not do well to study at least a portion of the time?"

"They are many things to study," replied the Honourable Rag, winking at me. He beckoned the waiter over with a casual snap of his fingers that inspired in me a sudden wash of fury.

"And of what *did* you make a study?" I asked sharply. "Was it only the chase?"

"Merkheld—or is it Merganser?—holds that the chase is the noblest field of study, for by it one learns courage, wisdom, faith, and all virtue—"

"Patience, too? Or no; that's angling."

Mr. Dart snorted and buried himself in his glass. The Honourable Rag took a sip of his wine. "But stay, Mr. Greenwing, surely you learned more at Morrowlea than mere bookishness? You are attracting adventures—"

"And you are attracting trouble, or else I've been sadly misinformed, Master Roald."

"Oh, the art of the chase has taught me when a trail's worth the following, Mr. Greenwing. I have high hopes for the Fair."

"So do I," interjected Hal at this point, while I tried to analyze precisely why I felt so miffed. "I think we can place, at least, with our cake, don't you, Jemis?"

Mr. Dart laughed. "You have great expectations—or perhaps they're low ones for the populace of Ragnor barony."

"Oh, I leave all expectations to Mr. Greenwing, Mr. Dart, along with his patrimony of riddles, relatives, and honey-receptacles."

And something deep in my mind clicked into place; but I did not figure out what it was until several days later.

Chapter Twenty-Four
The First Magic Lesson

"WE'LL START WITH something very basic," Hal said after the three of us had settled into the comfortable old chairs. "Lighting a candle is always a good one. Useful skill, easy to do."

He produced three candles and set them on saucers on the table between us. "Three?" I said.

"I thought Mr. Dart might like to participate."

Mr. Dart made a face. I nodded, not paying much attention to his quibbles, but instead feeling an odd thrill of anticipation and nerves. Magic had been such an ordinary and uncomplicated part of life for so long—until it wasn't. During Imperial days there had been no indication I had any magic in me—I hadn't made lights or made things move or made anything happen at all—and I still couldn't quite believe that Lark had been stealing power from me.

She had stolen my heart, my attention, my self-respect, certainly; but magic?

Hal picked up the candle closest to him. "Note that these are all candles that have already been lit. It's easier to light an old candle—"

"Always is," Mr. Dart said, patting his pocket for his pipe. "The wax is already drawn up into the wick."

"Yes, and the candle *knows* it's supposed to light. All right: Jemis, we'll see how, ah, ready the magic is. You concentrate on light, and say *ivailo ivaro ivo.*"

"'Light, lighten, be lit'," I murmured, picking up the candle to look at it more closely, the Old Shaian words coming clearly to mind. I felt a bit foolish. I had no idea what it was supposed to *feel* like, calling fire. I imagined a point of light gathering around the little bulging edge of the wick, imagined heat gathering, imagined pressure in my mind. Said, "*Ivailo ivaro ivo!*"

To my great surprise the candle lit.

I lowered it hastily. "Well, now, I wasn't expecting that to work."

Hal whooped with laughter. "Really, Jemis! You have magic practically *leaking* out of you."

"I can't tell," I said dourly. "If I blow it out, can I light it again?"

"You can certainly try. Or try *oraino oraro oro*—"

"Is magic seriously just a matter of saying three forms of the imperative in Old Shaian? I'm a little disappointed my tutor never mentioned this."

"Most people don't learn Old Shaian. These are just the fundamentals. It's much more complex once you get past the basics."

I said the words, imagining pinching the candle (despite Hal's words, I couldn't believe that just *stating* the words would work; otherwise why had I not made all sorts of things happen during Old Shaian? I'd started the course before I'd been caught by Lark). The flame obediently went out, then relit itself when I said the other words.

"This is—this is seriously—"

"Magical?" said Mr. Dart, lighting his pipe from my candle.

"Your turn, Mr. Dart," Hal said, smiling encouragingly.

Mr. Dart looked strangely hesitant. "I don't think …"

"Come now, Mr. Dart," I said. "You might learn something. Unless Stoneybridge filled you right up to completion?"

He puffed at his pipe, blew a careful smoke ring up towards the ceiling. Glanced cautiously at his candle, sighed, slowly said, "*Ivailo ivarno*—" He stopped.

"*Ivaro*," Hal repeated, enunciating clearly.

Mr. Dart didn't appear to be listening. He was frowning at the candle in its saucer, attention fixated, the pipe drooping in his hand. Said sharply, "*Tisso!*"

Flame gushed a full three feet upwards.

For a moment I was caught back in the memory of last week's excursion into a burning house, the smell of wood and fire—the heat, the light, the *heat*—

"*Aoro!*"

The flame lowered itself reluctantly, obedient to Hal's command ('now diminish'), dwindled to a torch, to a taper, to a fine point, to an ember glowing in a puddle of wax, to a thin coiling line of smoke.

Mr. Dart's eyes were wild. "What—what happened? Why did that happen?"

Hal unhurriedly moved the two other candles out of the way. "Why did you say that word? It wasn't what I'd told you."

Mr. Dart was still staring fixedly at the remnants of his candle. "I—that was what the candle wanted me to say—"

"Perry," I said, reaching out to grip his shoulder. "What do you mean, it *wanted* you to say that?"

He pushed back against the chair. "I'm—I'm not supposed—I'm not supposed to *listen!*"

"Wild magic," breathed Hal. "It must be. Mr. Dart, when did you first—"

"I'm not supposed to talk about it!" he cried, thrusting back so hard his chair fell over. His stone arm hit the floor with a thud, and he pushed himself into the corner, wrapping his good arm around his knees, hiding his head. His voice came out more softly. "I promised my Papa I'd never talk about it."

"Perry, your papa died when we were six."

"I promised! He made me promise. He told me I must never never tell anyone."

Hal frowned, making a gesture to me that I interpreted as 'keep him talking'. I rose from my seat, lowered myself down next to him. Had a sudden memory of Sir Hamish imitating the late Squire Dart saying *Now then, Peregrine*, when Mr. Dart as a little boy would say something about some inanimate object not 'wanting' something or other.

"Mr. Dart, Perry, you can talk to us … We won't tell anyone else."

He buried his head, voice muffled. "You wouldn't break a promise to your father, would you, Jemis?"

I stopped my initial response, for the answer, of course, was no, I wouldn't.

Hal said, "Mr. Dart, if you have a gift at wild magic, it makes sense your papa would try to prevent you from developing it—in the days of the Empire it was a sentence of exile or death, if it couldn't be controlled. You managed to repress it successfully— that's a wonderful thing. Most people couldn't, you know. But now

... now it's different. The magic is different. You won't be driven mad by Schooled magic—the system is different."

I nodded. "Your papa wouldn't want you to—your papa would be so proud of you!"

"Now that you've called the magic—Mr. Dart—it will come again. You have to learn how to control it. Magic either comes once; or often."

"Even wild magic?" I asked, feeling Mr. Dart shivering against me.

Hal said, "It's wild magic, it doesn't obey rules ... But if Mr. Dart has been suppressing his gift, it will be ... it will be *wanting* to come out. Have you been finding that—things—are speaking to you more?"

"*I don't listen to them!*"

I leaned back from the vehemence, then cautiously put my hand on his shoulder again, glancing beseechingly at Hal.

He made a helpless gesture. "It has to be his decision."

I raised my eyebrows at him. "Would you go against a promise to your father?"

"I promised my father I would take care of my mother and my sister and that I would always strive to be as fair and just a lord as I could," Hal said, scraping at the puddle of wax that remained of Mr. Dart's candle. "I promised him I would always treat people fairly. I promised him I would always try to listen to all sides of the situation. I promised him I would always strive to be a good man."

None of that seemed to be helping. I leaned my head back against the wall. I desperately wanted to try the magic again, but that was selfish. I felt terrible that I had not noticed how much Mr. Dart was hiding behind beard and always-cheerful demeanour.

"My father made me promise things like never to try to cheat Mrs. Henny the Post at Poacher."

"I'm sorry—Mrs. Henny the Post? Why is she called a post?"

"Not *a* post; *the* Post. She's the postmistress. Like Fogerty the Fish is the fishmonger, Mrs. Jarnem the Sweet has the sweetshop, Kulfield the Iron is the blacksmith."

"There's an apprentice blacksmith named Kulfield on my ship. I think he's from Fiellan?"

"Yes, Roddy Kulfield. Mr. Dart and the Honourable Rag were telling me that he'd gone to sea to be draughtsman. You might have heard that the strength contests at the Fair are now wide open; that's why."

"The Honourable Rag?"

"Roald Ragnor, the Baron's son."

"Oh Lady," said Mr. Dart suddenly, still into his knees, "the Baron is going to be so angry that you're studying magic."

I laughed ruefully. "Isn't he just? He's rabidly against magic, Hal."

"So?"

"It's easy enough for you to say that," Mr. Dart said, lifting his head. His eyes were red and he was pale, but he was more composed and his voice was steady enough. "You don't live here and you're an imperial Duke."

"Jemis is an imperial Viscount. He outranks any mere regional baron. As for you, Mr. Dart, Jemis has told me all sorts of wonderful stories about you, and none of them made you sound craven."

"Hal!"

"I'm not learning magic," Mr. Dart said, though his eyes were straying to the candles.

"What do other people do here who have inclinations towards magic?"

"Hide it or leave, I suppose," I said, seeing that Mr. Dart's attention was focused on the candles, though I couldn't tell whether he was listening to us, or just ... listening. "No one talks about it, or at least ... not before. Last week they were not very happy about the magic that came out ... That's why Magistra Bellamy's gone off north for a while, Mrs. Etaris said. The Honourable Miss Jullanar fell in love with an itinerant knife-sharpener who turned out to be the Earl of the Farry March in disguise, but her father refused the match because there's too much magic in the March. Mr. Dart, did you hear what the Honourable Rag's response was? I wasn't here."

Mr. Dart lifted his pipe and puffed on it a few times. "He had an argument with his father, but the Baron holds the purse-strings."

I shook my head, thinking once again what a waste—what a *drone*—the Honourable Rag was turning out to be. "From what Violet said, he was playing far too high in Orio City—he went to Tara, Hal."

"And not on merit," Mr. Dart said, blowing smoke rings. We were still seated on the floor, looking up at where Hal was sitting sideways on his chair, but otherwise Mr. Dart seemed back to his usual self. He smiled crookedly. "All of them play too high—the Baron, Sir Vorel and Lady Flora, the Talgarths, the Woodhills, the Figheldeans—that's what you should do, Jemis, you could play Sir Vorel for the Arguty estate."

"I'd rather get it because I'm legally entitled to it than because I'm better at Poacher than he is."

"You're better at Poacher than practically everyone."

"Yes, that's true," Hal said thoughtfully. "Though I didn't think you liked playing all that much, Jemis. We'd all get out the cards, and you'd just watch ..."

"My father taught me how to play, but he told me to be careful ... I tried to warn Roald before we went to university."

They all looked at me. Mr. Dart said cautiously, "Warn him about what? Playing too high? The Baron's pockets are very deep."

"So, I have been told, were my grandfather's," I replied dryly. He winced. I hesitated a moment longer, then went on: "One of the things my father taught me was what to look for in someone who is ... addicted."

Mr. Dart made a surprised motion. "*That's* what your quarrel was about? He was very angry. So were you," he added conscientiously. "But he's been polite this week."

"You've an interesting notion of polite, Mr. Dart."

"Wait, why did your father decide to tell you all that? *When?* When he came back after—after Loe?"

"No, that summer he pulled me out of the kingschool." I looked up at Hal. "Before my father was called up for the Seven Valleys campaign, he was home for nearly six months, and had me out of school so we could spend the time together."

"We were all so jealous," Mr. Dart said reminiscently. "We used to spend hours wondering what you were up to. And then you'd come by and it was always *better* than we'd imagined. We'd think maybe you'd gone coney-catching, and you'd gone boar hunting up the Rag. Or that you'd gone riding with the Hunt, and instead you'd done the Leap."

I smiled with an unwilling pride, and the memory of sheer astonishment as we'd come up to the famous gap between Fiellan and Ghilousette.

"I don't know if he'd always planned to do it, or if it was just that we were up in the high country, and we came to the old road. There's a very, very old route between south Fiellan and Ghilousette, up in the Gorbelow Hills. It might even be pre-Astandalan, from when people actually wanted to go between south Fiellan and Ghilousette. Anyhow, the road serves a couple of villages on this side, then goes up to the Cleft Pass. They say that the giants broke it in half, but no one knows what really happened. Earthquake, presumably, though now that we've met a dragon I don't know. The mountain is split fully in two and the road goes right up to it—and down the other side."

"I've heard of the Leap," Hal said. "Daredevils die there every couple of years. How old were you?"

"Nine. My father said it would be something to tell my own son one day." I shook my head. "I wasn't afraid—I truly thought my father was invincible—he said that the way to make the jump was to throw my heart over and my horse would follow. It didn't occur to me to doubt him. He went over first and I jumped after, on my old white pony."

"Then what?" Mr. Dart said.

I laughed. "Then we had to jump back, of course, because otherwise you have to go all the way up to the coast. It's weeks around. We stayed the night with some shepherds to rest the horses, jumped back across, and came back home to a great scold from my mother because we'd spent the night away without telling her. I don't know she ever found out we'd done the Leap, actually. My father had been called up, and we never talked about it after we got home."

"You've done the Leap both ways," Hal said flatly. "When you were nine."

"I don't know if I'd have the nerve now to throw my heart over first and presume my horse would follow." I laughed again, more bitterly. "I've learned other lessons from my father since then."

Hal frowned at me. "Didn't you think these were strange things to be taught?"

"Not really. He was very thorough in what he taught me and in explaining the consequences. I didn't understand all of what he *meant* by the consequences, but I memorized them. When he was showing me how to play at cards he took great pains to explain how people cheated, so that I would know. And then we talked about *why* people cheated, how it could be for all sorts of reasons—and he gave me advice for what to do if I were winning too much, or losing too much, or got into games with the wrong sort of people ..."

"Which includes your uncle?" Mr. Dart said, snickering. "And Mrs. Henny the Post?"

"Which probably ought to include dragons, but I don't see how I'm going to get out of that one."

"You're already halfway to answering its riddle," Hal said encouragingly.

This seemed a good change of subject. I stood up so I could fish out the piece of paper where I'd copied out the riddle. Mr. Dart got up a moment after me, righted his chair, sat down again at the table. I spread out the paper, frowned at the dimness, started to reach the unlit candle towards the lit one, then remembered.

"*Ivailo ivaro ivo!*" I smiled foolishly when it lit again. "Oh, goodness, I don't care how unfashionable this is."

Hal chuckled. "We'll just have to bring it back into fashion."

"Only if Mr. Dart will help me."

Mr. Dart muttered something incomprehensible without removing his pipe from his mouth, so I quirked my eyebrows at him and turned to the page. "Here we are. *Between the green and the white is the door. Between the race and the runner is the lock. Between the sun and the shadow is the key. In the bright heart of the dark house is the dark heart of the bright house. And therewithin, if the sap of the tree runs true, is the golden treasure of the dark woods. Bring that to me ere the Sun and the Moon are at their furthest remove.* Standard gibberish, eh?"

"The *golden treasure of the dark wood* must be honey," Hal said.

Mr. Dart puffed for a few moments. "When are the Sun and the Moon at their furthest remove?"

"Full moon," I said automatically; it was a standard element in Second Period Calligraphic riddle-poetry.

"That's Friday, then."

Hal frowned. "What day is it? I've lost track."

"Today's Wednesday," said Mr. Dart. "That's why I'm in town, I had a delivery to meet."

"What I never understand about these sorts of things in the stories," I said, "is how tailored they are. I mean, does the dragon see the future? Make it happen? Does me trying to fulfill the terms make them come to pass?"

"That's the standard rule," Mr. Dart replied, leaning back to stare up at the ceiling, where his smoke was dissolving into a slight haze. I rubbed my thumb on the ring, grateful not to be prostrate with sneezing. "Why do you ask in particular?"

"Well, I'd already decided to run in the three-mile race. So between me and it is the 'lock'—whatever exactly that means. But that presupposes that I am *destined* somehow to be the one to fulfill the terms of this riddle."

"You're making my head hurt," Hal said. "What are dragons, anyway?"

"The physical manifestations of old chaotic magic, according to Domina Issoury."

"And you're the unacknowledged heir of the Woods Noirell, which is a place of serious magic, old and new. Perhaps the dragon comes with a riddle whenever there's a doubtful succession, so the rightful heir can prove himself. Or herself, as the case may be. That might explain the bit about 'if the sap of the tree runs true'—metaphorically speaking, are you of the right bloodline?"

"It seems wrong that we can figure out the second half of the riddle but not the first."

"But you've already solved the third part, haven't you?" said Mr. Dart. "The bit about the branches and ways and turns and so forth."

I'd neglected to write that part down. Added it now. Frowned again. "What does this *mean*? The green and the white—or the Green and the White—does it have something to do with the Lady? What is it the door *of*? Or *to*? Why is it locked? What can the key that falls between the sun and the shadow *be*?"

"And then something about bright hearts and dark hearts …"

"*In the bright heart of the dark house is the dark heart of the bright house.* Is this supposed to refer to bees?"

"There weren't any bees in the Woods until you woke them," Hal pointed out. "They were cursed."

"What is the heart of a house, anyway? In old puzzle-poetry it would be the hearth."

"The one we saw in the castle was hardly *bright*," Hal said, laughing. "I wouldn't stand for it at Leaveringham Castle—nor at Morrowlea, and I had to clean our grates!"

"I helped you," I protested.

"Not after you started sneezing so much, you couldn't get near the ash without coming over all faint."

I laughed. "Oh, Hal, I've missed your company." I looked hastily at Mr. Dart to make sure I hadn't hurt his feelings—he hadn't mentioned any close friends made at Stoneybridge, which now that I thought of it was very strange, he was such a pleasant and good-natured and all round amiable sort of person, he ought to have been swallowed up in gregarious company. Mr. Dart was not, however, paying us much attention. He was still looking at the ceiling and blowing smoke rings.

He seemed to feel our concerned glances, for he dropped his gaze suddenly. "In the castle," he said, "there was something in that first room, the waiting room—every time you came close, Jemis, it wanted you to pick it up. I couldn't help but hear it ... I was trying not to listen, usually I can make myself not hear them, but that one was *shouting*."

"What was it? The thing that was shouting?"

"I don't know," he said, frustration and fear suddenly sharpening his voice. "Jemis, I've spent my entire life *not listening*. I—until today I'd forgotten *why*—my papa never explained that it was wild magic, he just said I'd go crazy if I listened to the voices, that whatever else I did I was never ever supposed to let anyone know I could hear them. Do you have any idea how hard it is—Jemis, you were frightened enough about asking Dominus Gleason for tutoring, and you're already considered a wild eccentric."

"My reputation wasn't why I was concerned—fine, frightened!—of Dominus Gleason. He makes my skin crawl. I fainted going into his house."

"Is there anyone else who can teach you magic?" Hal asked intently.

"Magistra Bellamy, presumably, when she comes back. She's friends with Mrs. Etaris ..."

Mr. Dart sighed. "My brother's not as snobby as some, but he'll not be over-pleased with me taking lessons from her. Dominus Gleason at least was a professor of magic at Fiella-by-the-Sea before the Fall."

"Didn't Sir Hamish say the Marchioness was a witch?" Hal asked. "Perhaps she'll give you lessons—"

"What, if I can persuade her I'm actually her grandson?"

There was a pause. I grimaced. "And so we come back to the dragon's riddle ..."

Chapter Twenty-Five
I have an Idea

FRIDAY NIGHT HAL and I celebrated a more-or-less clean flat and the fact that had been paid for my first fortnight of work. I bought us a bottle of wine from the Ragnor Arms. It wasn't as good as the wine the Darts' butler had served us, but then again, as Hal said, Mr. Brock probably wasn't filling their cellars from the hotel's offering.

"I wasn't sure where to go, actually," I admitted, topping up our mismatched wine glasses. These were courtesy of the young son of some member of the Embroidery Circle, who'd shown up earlier with a box of miscellaneous kitchen supplies and a bashful explanation that his mum, whoever she was, thought we might appreciate them. Which we did. I resolved to ask Mrs. Etaris who it was so I could write to thank her.

Hal ate one of the biscuits he had made that afternoon. "I am still pondering. This week has been one new experience after another for me. Who knew bed linens were so amazingly expensive?"

"I'm afraid my budget is rather tighter than your housekeeper's. Mind you, she'd be buying several dozen more than we needed."

"I don't think she needs to buy them very often. We've all

sorts of antique linens and things. Wool blankets … so many wool blankets. The old duke—my father, that is—was forever sending off for woollens from various places so he could use them in his experiments."

I cut some cheese, ate one of the biscuits. Said tentatively, "Do you remember your father well?"

"Not really. He was … aristocratic, I guess you could say, in the old style. Felt children belonged in the nursery until they reached the age of reason. He was very grand and very proud—and I know my mother cared very deeply for him. He'd take Elly riding sometimes." He smiled ruefully. "Perhaps he was better with women. Or perhaps he felt that as his heir I had to be treated differently, harder, because it would fall on me to make the hard decisions."

I didn't know what to say to this. I was grateful that my mother had not felt the same way.

Hal sighed. "I've always felt guilty that—when he died, I was sad, but also … relieved. He was so hard, the old duke. I don't think I ever called him anything but that. I remember swearing to Elly once that when I had children they would never, ever call me 'your grace'."

There was a note in his voice that suggested he had said enough. I said, lightly enough to move on if he wished, "I think my grandmother also likes the old style."

Hal laughed, poured us more wine. "I think you're entirely correct. But oddly my grandfather, my mother's father, was nothing like that. He delighted in all our pet names for him. He taught me so much."

"You miss him," I ventured.

"Yes. Did you know your other relations?"

"Not my father's parents. They'd died when I was young. I always liked my uncle Sir Rinald. He died in a hunting accident just after—between the letters from Loe."

"The false one first, then the truth, right?"

I swallowed. I could see Hal was done talking about his family. "Yes. I've always—it was so awful that Uncle Rinald died thinking my father was branded a traitor."

"He believed it?"

"Even the accusation was ..."

"Of course. An insupportable disgrace."

I traced a spill of crumbs and wine. "No. No, he didn't think it was true, but all we had was that official letter."

"I have been thinking about that," said Hal. "I hope my great-uncle does show up here soon—he will know the people involved, how such a mistake could have been made. Your father was *famous*, Jemis. He should never have been confused with someone else—unless someone did so deliberately."

"Deliberately? As in, someone deliberately *lied* to us?"

"Perhaps your father had enemies in the army ... people do. And someone *was* the traitor of Loe, after all. It might not have been 'Jakory Greenwing' at all."

I felt very tired. "It's so strange to think of such deliberate wickedness. You don't expect people to be wicked on purpose, somehow. By accident or mischance, yes, but on purpose?" I sighed. "I've spent all summer trying to excuse Violet ..."

"Did she give you any excuses when you saw her?"

"No. She said some things were inexcusable, and she was sorry."

I stopped there, hearing a note of regret, pain, sorrow in my voice. I had spent the summer trying to find a reason to forgive

Violet; not Lark.

Hal said, "Mrs. Buchance sent your things over, by the way, this afternoon. I put them in your room, though I was wondering if you wanted to put the crock out on display? It's so beautiful. The Heart of Glory, too."

I was glad for the change of subject. "I'd be a little worried about thieves."

"Tchah! There's magic for that."

"Really? And you know it?"

"I do have a dukedom to protect, you know."

I smiled, forced myself upright; felt immediately better. Hal came with me to my room, where I found the chests of my inheritance, a box of clothes and small items, and another box of books and paperwork. "Not much of a life," I murmured, pulling out the crock and pectoral.

"The books will come in time, and other things, too. You'll make a good lawyer, I think."

"Prone to arguments as I am?" My eye fell on the topmost letter, the one from Morrowlea awarding me first place. A niggling doubt crystallized. I said, "I am going to write them. Dominus Nidry—the faculty."

"Ask them to sponsor you to Inveragory?"

"That, and to say I'm—I wasn't exactly disinterested, this spring. I wish I were the sort of person who could stand up against—against *that*—for the pure love of truth, but I'm not." I looked at the Heart of Glory peeking out of its flannel wrapping. "I'm not. I thought Violet was, but she ..."

"There will be another time," said Hal, taking the pectoral from me. "And next time, like last time, you will hold the Sun. Do you think your father was unafraid? My great-uncle was. But he still stood there as long as it took."

We went back out to the parlour, where I wrote my letter in many drafts and Hal fussed about with the Heart of Glory, until Mr. Dart arrived—"It being Friday night," he said cheerfully—with a rather better bottle of wine and the news that the Honourable Rag had told everyone it was *my* dragon to deal with.

"Oh, joy," I said, and got up to move the honey crock from the corner table where Hal had set it to the mantelpiece, where my mother had always kept it.

"The wine? You're welcome. Oh, look at the pattern in the candlelight. I hadn't seen it before."

I glanced back at the crock. The candle at the end of the mantle was guttering low, causing the bas-relief to stand out sharply. I smiled.

"My mother used to tell me stories about the pattern ..." I turned the crock so that the curving lines showed themselves a tree, heart-shaped leaves now clearly visible. "There are two bees somewhere, a white one and a green one. We used to have a little game about finding them. My mother used to say that they were racing each other to collect the nectar, like the moon and the sun, like the seasons of the year."

I realized Hal and Mr. Dart were both staring at me: and then the rest of the riddle fell into place.

***

The sun had long since set when I left.

I was not really dressed for running—usually I wore the same clothing as for fencing lessons—but my half-boots were comfortable and snug, my breeches fine wool, my shirt and waistcoat cool cotton. My coat I had wrapped around the jade crock to cushion it inside its sack.

I set out at a brisk walk through the quiet evening streets of Ragnor Bella, passing a few men on their way to various houses, public or private, and two older women I didn't know sitting on a front stoop to catechize the passersby. Arrived (without more than a suggestive few comments about the contents of the sack) at Ragglebridge—bridge, pub, and hamlet in their sequence—where tonight there were no mysterious armed strangers to spark thoughts of revolutions or romance. Once on the other side of the torchlight, I began to lope.

The moon was set to rise at ten-thirty or so, which gave me just about enough time to thoroughly enjoy the run.

Up the long slope out of the valley of the Raggle, the road still damp and a bit churned up from rain and the day's traffic. Around the curve that encompassed the hill on which stood the Little church (walnut tree skeletal against the stars; no sign of Violet, nor anyone else). Past the Lady's Cross, empty this evening of gentry or cultists; turned south onto the fine old imperial highway, and, muscles warm, ran.

Marcan had been keen on meditative practices and had tried on numerous occasions to teach me. Whether it was the fault of wireweed or enchantment or my own personality I didn't now know, but I had never succeeded in calming my mind while sitting still.

Running, though, running I could do.

And running I found myself asking myself the hard questions.

What was I afraid of, Hal had asked me: why could I not rejoice in good news, trust in it?

I ran, the pale limestone road clear before me, smooth, firm, more steadfast than the Empire that had built it.

I was afraid of the good news being withdrawn.

The treed height to my left was the western edge of the Coombe hills, where Mr. Dart and I had discovered cultists and black magic and wireweed and organized crime.

I was afraid I was nothing without the wireweed and the magic.

To my right were the half-abandoned fields and pastures that had once been lovingly tended by farmers who had almost all perished during the Interim, by magic gone awry, by pestilence, by wild animals, by wilder men.

I was afraid of how much I wanted something to fill the void left by the loss of Lark and the wireweed.

I passed one lone farmhouse with a light burning inside, wondered who had braved the loss of all their neighbours, how they kept picking up the pieces of their lives when so few came down the highway now.

I was afraid that I would never again be whole.

Ahead of me the mountains rose against the stars. The peaks of the Crosslains had snow on them, sure sign of the turning season, though frosts had yet to touch us in the wide vale of the Rag.

I was afraid of becoming like the Honourable Rag: addicted to gambling, to drinking too much, to hunting too hard, to trying to drown the inner voices.

Below the white peaks the grey slopes of the Foothills, and below that dark dimness the darker mass of the Woods, silent now in the nighttime.

I was afraid the title—Hal's *good news*—would mean I had to do none of the hard work. That again like the Honourable Rag people would smilingly watch me destroy myself, secure in the eccentricities of the gentry; that I would never live up to my father's legacy; that everything I had learned of myself standing up against Lark would be lost not to my cowardice but to a far-too-easy adjustment to my mother's heritage.

The tall white waystone marking the branch of the road that led off to the west and the Gorbelow Hills and the Leap cast a black shadow across the road, which I felt a superstitious urge to jump.

My father had taught me to play Poacher; to jump the Leap (throw my heart first and be sure my horse would follow); to stand up for what was right, to fight for what I believed in.

My mother had taught me to think through what I believed in; that life was a game of Poacher; that sometimes one had to make compromises to survive, but that one never compromised the heart of oneself, for what survived without the heart was nothing.

I was afraid that the good fortune would turn sour because so often already it had. My father's return leading to suicide and disgrace; my love for Lark imploding into lies and criminal magic; my efforts to do the right thing, say the right thing, be the right thing, for Mr. Buchance ending ... well, ending with him deciding to give me the merest competence and me missing his funeral.

That was a hard thought to address. I gritted my teeth, concentrated on my form, and when I was in the smoothest stride forced my thoughts back to it.

I did truly believe, or I kept trying to convince myself I truly believed—my *mind* believed, though my heart struggled with it— that he owed me nothing more, indeed nothing so much. I was not actually his son; I had made it clear to him that I would not, could not, be his son, not with my father's legacy (the good and the bad) hanging over me. How could I be his son, when I was the son of the man who had been given the Heart of the Glory by the Emperor, and was buried under five roads at the White Cross.

I had not in the least deliberately missed Mr. Buchance's funeral, but missed it I had.

I crested a low rise, started down to the wide plain before the boundary stream, the first Sun Gate a dim circle in the starlight.

So I had: and (I could hear Mrs. Etaris' voice in my ear) what was I going to do as a result?

I would do my best to see that Mrs. Buchance and my sisters had all they needed. They would not need any financial help from me, but there were presumably other things I could do.

It occurred to me for the first time that the heiresses of an upward-climbing Charese merchant would find adult life much easier if the Viscount St-Noire (presumably at some point the Marquis—or possibly March—of the Woods Noirell) acknowledged them as his kin and got his friend the Duke of Fillering Pool to help sponsor them into the world.

Most people, after all, did not go to Morrowlea because they wanted to know who they were without the trappings of name and family and wealth.

Another thing I had learned was people did care for me, even when it felt as though no one in the world did, and it was unkind to them to get out of all communication. How unhappy I would be never to hear from Mr. Dart or Hal again—or Marcan—or indeed Violet.

I mused about potential ways to communicate with Violet for a few hundred yards before I arrived at the Sun Gate and realized what I was doing.

No. I was not trying to work out my feelings for Violet at the moment. That was for another night run, another ... well, another night.

There was a light wind on this side, blowing out of the Woods, strongly redolent of the Tillarny limes.

Was I nothing without the wireweed and the magic?

I paused at the Sun Gate, the water rushing softly under the bridge below me.

No.

I was the Fiellanese scholar to Morrowlea before, and—I chuckled aloud, startling myself a little—I was Mrs. Etaris' assistant clerk after. I was, it seemed, the Viscount St-Noire (albeit by accident of birth), and I was Mr. Dart's friend and Hal's, and a spite to all the smug conservatives who didn't want anything to change simply by being who I was.

I took a breath and ran through the Gate and across the threshold of shadow and deeper shadow into the Woods.

And if I were afraid of addiction—if I knew that my grandfather had been addicted to gambling, and that my father had been concerned enough to warn me as best he could long before I was of the age to begin seeking out such things—if I knew that I had always to be careful to stop when I drank or played at cards long before I wanted to, because I could guess—because I *knew*—that the wanting would not stop until it was disastrously too late—

—Well, I did know that, and I did *do* that, and I had the ruination of Roald Ragnor before me as a warning. He was blithe and merry and seemingly untroubled by any pricks of conscience or sense, but in two weeks I had yet to encounter him without a drink or a wager in hand, and sooner or later it would catch up with him.

At least if I had the Indrilline criminal family of Orio City after me it wasn't for gambling debts.

Chapter Twenty-Six
Mr. White has an Idea

INSIDE THE WOODS the road gleamed as if magical; and there were fireflies.

"Oh," I said, and decided that every one of my critics could be right if only I could see this sort of beauty from time to time, and I swore then and there that for the bees and the fireflies and the Tillarny limes I would be the Viscount St-Noire, crazy grandmother, unpleasant castle, mysterious curses, dragons, riddles, high Gothic melodrama, and all.

Round and around the curves I ran, fireflies twinkling beside me, above me, before me, behind me, road white and trees dark and so fragrant I could almost identify each as an individual by scent alone.

And then in amongst the houses, to the village green and the white inn and between them the well with its wellhead in the shape of a hive full of bees missing something to make it whole.

***

The fireflies, at first a few faint specks twinkling in the depths of the Woods, at length brighter, more numerous, and nearer. Each footfall on the old highway seemed to attract them, almost to create them; I half-imagined I could look behind me and see sparks rising from my feet and whirling away into fireflies, until my way shone dimly gold and all I could see to either side of me was a thickly clustered ribbon of light punctuated by the dark boles of the trees like sentinels.

In *Kissing the Moon* Fitzroy Angursell writes of how the Red Company stole the boat of the Sun and rowed it down the River of Stars, out of the Moon's country and all the way back into the mortal worlds.

The first time I read the poem I had stalled there wondering why the boat of the Sun had no sails and who rowed it ordinarily ('the Hours' was, I discovered, the scholarly consensus; for even the most notoriously banned poet in the Empire eventually gets studied by the Scholars), and I had nearly not noticed the beauty of the passage itself, until Violet read it out to me one summer's evening when we were supposed to be weeding.

I could not quite bring the words to mind.

Down the River of Stars—something something *the sky-road*

The Sun's road—something something

the Sea of Stars uncountable

Each of them named

And then something about

Our arms doing the work of the hours

Something about the movement of rowing, the wind from the places between the stars

And Jullanar of the Sea reaching her hand down

Dipping her hand down

Into the sky ...

I would have to borrow the Darts' copy and read it again, without the wireweed or the magic this time.

But now when I read it I would have, along with that ghost of a memory of Violet reading the poem while I pretended to dig up dandelions, now there would be this vision of the fireflies surrounding me in a river of stars uncounted, though perhaps the Lady of Summer knew each one's name.

We poured into the village, the river of fireflies and I, like a cataract of light, the heavy scent of the limes suffusing the air.

At the green I slowed to a walk, and then a slower walk as my feet touched the dew-sparkling grass. The fireflies, thick as festival lights, swirled around me, filled all the space of the green, the sky above us spangled brilliant as fireworks.

I halted at the well. The fireflies moved ceaselessly, flickering on and off, but so many of them they gave the impression of light reflecting off myriad glinting surfaces. At any moment I expected a Faerie ballroom to take shape out of light and shadow.

Figures did emerge.

My heart stopped a moment in shock, until I saw they had the barely-familiar faces of the villagers. They were confused and a little wary, coming out of houses and inn, some in their daytime clothes and some ready for bed.

They stopped in a loose circle around me, the fireflies illuminating them in strange patterns of shadow and speckled light. I nodded uncertainly at Mr. Horne and the innkeepers, who were closest to me. Mr. White smiled encouragingly; I wondered briefly why.

I opened the sack, withdrew my coat and put it on—now that

I was no longer running I was a little chilled—then cleared my throat. Stuffed the sack in my pocket, so all I held was the crock, smooth and cool and heavy in my hands. Cleared my throat again.

"I have come to answer the riddle, O dragon."

***

If for a moment the fireflies had seemed reflections rather than illuminations, for a moment the dragon seemed to be made of the spaces between things, rather than a body-in-itself. I watched as sparkling shadows turned into sparkling scales, and then coiled around the well-head as it had been coiled around the Dragon Stone there it was.

"Well?" it said.

My heart was thumping rather more than it had from running. *Be calm*, I said sternly to myself. I wanted the clear air of mortal danger: instead I had audience and fireflies and heavy scent and a riddle, and was thrown into the position I had last occupied at the final *viva voce* examinations at Morrowlea.

I had been waiting for my turn, hands shaking, while others presented their final papers, defended their theses, answered the questions of their tutors and occasional fellow students. I knew my final paper was rubbish, though I held to my thesis as being sound, and hoped mostly to redeem the incoherent mess I feared I had written. Our tutor had smiled when Violet defended her paper, then frowned when he looked at me.

I had not read Lark's paper, nor anyone's, before the examinations. I had been ill (so I thought), unable to concentrate on much of anything besides the running. Running I could channel the feverish energy, did not have to think, could let my thoughts jump as they willed until at last they settled into a semblance of calm focus. So I ran longer and longer loops, trying to exhaust the fear of the mysterious illness out of me, hiding from the knowledge the rest of my life was collapsing along with my health.

Wrote something of barely acceptable length, only coherent because Violet had forced me to give it to her to edit, the brilliant insight into Ariadne nev Lingarel's poem a mess of lines and allusions to other poets. It was still too bitter a thought to address my mind to how much I had failed the insight, the poem, my tutor.

But sitting there, waiting my turn, hands shaking, I had marshalled my thoughts as best I could to the arguments I knew were there, to the points I knew were sound, to the thesis I knew was correct, and new, and elevated what was considered only a minor masterpiece into one of the upper ranks of literature.

Or it could have, had I made the argument; and if I were right and the insight not merely a function of some strange deluded state of mind of someone in the later stages of wireweed addiction and magic loss.

I had not been put to the test of my knowledge of Classical Shaian poetry, nor to my ideas about Ariadne nev Lingarel, for before it was my turn it was Lark's, and all thoughts of poetry disappeared in a deluge of disbelief and betrayal.

And at the end of her smug and spectacular piece of rhetoric, when the tumultuous applause was dying down under the Chancellor's ironic eye, when Lark's tutor Dominus Marbone asked the traditional question of whether any of the students had a response—

I had stood up, hands shaking, knees (the shame!) trembling, voice barely sounding, and taken her speech apart point by point by point, as I had been taught to do by my tutor.

For that I had been stoned.

But also for that the senate of the university had awarded me First in the year.

I stepped forward, hands kept from trembling by the weight of the jade crock, knees unable to tremble because I was forcing them to walk, voice sounding far too loud because I was using my diaphragm to project it as clearly as I could.

"You gave me a riddle," I said.

Between the green and the white is the door.

Between the race and the runner is the lock.

Between the sun and the shadow is the key.

In the bright heart of the dark house

   is the dark heart of the bright house.

And therewithin, if the sap of the tree runs true,

   is the golden treasure of the dark woods.

Bring that to me ere the Sun and the Moon

   are at their furthest remove.

The way of the woods has many turns and few branches.

The branch of the woods has many turns and few ways.

The turn of the woods is the way of the branch,

   for good, young sir, or for ill.

"Well?" said the dragon.

I glanced at the villagers, who must have seen many strange things on a regular basis, given their mildly interested expressions; though perhaps that was a trick of the flickering light.

"The riddle," I began, and recited it.

I wish I knew more names of the villagers than simply Mr. Horne and the innkeepers Mr. and Mrs. White. At least I did know their names, and could see them, along with all their fellows who would soon—so I hoped—become familiar to me.

"Your answer?" said the dragon.

I took a breath, sneezed out of ancient habit, took another breath. "The answer is in two parts. First is the short one: a variation on the classic answer, which is 'myself'—in this case, 'myself with this honey crock'."

I held out my mother's jade crock for the dragon's inspection, and even more the villagers'. Lady willing, they would be the ones I would see day in and day out, whom I would be responsible to and for. I might even hope that one or two of them would let me bridge our stations and become friends. My grandmother the Marchioness might stay immured in her castle, but my mother hadn't, and neither would I.

"And that is your answer?"

"The first part," I said firmly. "The classic answer, and true as it goes. I was born on the 29th of February, between the White and the Green seasons of the year; I am the door, which opens to the future of the Woods. I am a runner, and the race is tomorrow, so this riddle—the lock—falls today, between the runner and his race; as you laid the riddle upon me after the announcement but before the competition.

"That which falls between the shadow and the sun is the body—mine again, key to the lock, the riddle. The bright heart of the dark woods is, of course, the honey of the bees of the Woods, which I woke by singing the song, *Heart of the Golden Trees*, which I was taught by mother, the dark lady of the woods whose name means 'black' in the old language. My mother died in the autumn— the dark heart of the bright house, when all the leaves are gold and the bees collect their honey from the autumn-blooming limes."

The dragon's eye was disquietingly ironic. Mr. White smiled encouragingly.

"My mother died and caused all the bees—and the villagers— to fall into stasis, and thus we come to the apostrophe, the turn, of the riddle: the way of the Woods has few branches—the line of the Noirells is narrow, without cousins or cadet branches. The path of the branch—well, I have few ways before me, and I choose this—"

"And is that your answer?" said the dragon intently.

"It is the first part," I said again, sure now—or as sure as I could be with my heart still pounding—that my second thought was correct.

"And so, the second?"

"Like all good riddles, this one has a metaphorical and a literal solution. The metaphorical I have told you. The literal I shall proceed now to demonstrate, if I may?"

"By all means," replied the dragon, with delicious irony.

I walked forward into the open space between head and tail so I could stand before the old well. Licked my lips, twiddled my ring nervously, sneezed again, and said:

"This is the old well, the heart of the village. It lies, as you can see, between the green—" I waved at the open commons behind me, "and the white." I bowed to the Whites, in front of their brightly white-washed inn. Mr. White grinned delightedly; Mrs. White was more solemn.

"The well, however, is dry." I touched the groove of the channel, the mouth of the spigot. "Courtesy of a friend of mine who is interested in regional names, I learned that the old names for these particular parts of a well in South Fiellan are the *runner*," I indicated the handle of the spigot, "and the *race*," and I touched the mouth.

"As you can see, they are in this instance blocked, or, as one might say, *locked*. It is nighttime, so the next part requires some assistance."

I pulled out the candle from my coat-pocket and performed the sole magical incantation I had so far learned. It was just as wonderful as the first time.

"Between the sun—" I held up my candle, "and the shadow is, of course, the body material, in this case revealing the *key* point, which is that something is not as it ought to be."

For just as with the jade crock, the shadows cast by the candle showed the carved patterns, here twisted out of coherence and beauty. I played the light over the well-head for a moment, then held up the crock so that my audience could see its pattern. A faint murmur rose from the watchers, except that the dragon was still but for the twitching end of its tail.

"Now we come to the centre of the riddle, which seemed obvious at first: the *bright heart of the dark house* and the *dark heart of the bright house*. The bright heart—the beehive in the cellars, I thought, in the house of Noirell; the dark heart, the curse that lies on the hosts of fair Melmúsion. Both true in their way; for the riddle has two answers. The literal one, though, is here in this well, where the water ought to run nearly honey-sweet and plentiful.

"*Drink of the fountain of Melmúsion*, say half-a-dozen poets, *and your heart will never grow entirely old*."

I looked at the fountain, the grimy bees, the blurred carvings, the stained dry spigot, the empty basin. I pulled out a clean handkerchief and carefully wiped off the grime until the stone—green and white jade as beautiful and rare as my mother's crock—began to shine, the gilded bees glitter like the fireflies. Cleaned out the channel of the water-race, and the handle of the runner, and finally set the crock and the candle down on the ground so I could use both hands to turn the whole top third of the well-head.

It creaked and groaned and for a moment I thought would not turn at all, but I was strong enough for the task, and eventually the whole portion moved into place. The dust caused me to sneeze for a considerable amount of time, but eventually I recovered, re-lit my candle, and played the light over the now-coherent pattern.

"The way of the woods has many turns and few branches: the road in, the old highway leading to a Border crossing, coiling and curving without cross-roads." I traced the great arc of a branch, the heart-shaped leaves, the starburst representations of Tillarny limes in full blossom. "The branch of the woods has many turns and few ways: you need only look at the trees around us to see that."

I took another breath. "The turn of the woods is the way of the branch—" and I set my hand to the runner, which, as could now be seen, formed the crown-canopy of the tree that the well-head was designed to resemble, and turned the handle, and waited breathlessly while only a cold dank air came out of the race, until at last there poured out the sweet cool water of the only accessible portion of fair Melmúsion, where the gods lived on ambrosia.

"And so, O dragon," I said at last, as the waster splashed over me, "here it is: the golden heart of the dark woods, drawn from the dark heart of the golden woods, the water that the bees of Melmúsion need as much as the nectar in the trees above us. And thus have I brought it to you ere the Sun and the Moon are at their furthest remove—which is to say, before the fullness of the Moon, which is later tonight if I am not much mistaken."

That I had succeeded I did not need the dragon to confirm, for the clockwork bees—now in their correct places—were being moved by the water flowing through the channels cut inside the well-head, and they now began to circle, gold and white and green, and for a moment glowed more brightly than the fireflies.

I blinked furiously. When at last my eyes cleared the dragon was gone.

"Come, lad," said Mr. White, slinging his arm across my shoulders. "You need a sip of my honey wine to warm you."

"Oh," I said, not sure whether to thank him or refuse or what.

He laughed. "It's all the better for a period under enchantment, I assure you."

Chapter Twenty-Seven
The Bandits have an Idea

IT WAS FIFTEEN miles by the Astandalan highway from the Water Gate at the edge of the Woods Noirell to the White Cross outside Dartington village.

The three-mile race was to start at noon. I left my grandmother's castle just after eight, at an easy lope that would get me to Dartington in just under three hours. That was rather more than my usual time, especially on a good road rather than cross-country, but I was carrying still carrying the jade crock and my coat, and I didn't want to over-extend myself before the race.

I was planning on *winning*.

I heard the town hall's bell distantly ringing ten when I passed the Green Dragon. Right on time, I thought happily, and cut behind the tavern to take the Greenway. It was a little faster to Dartington proper that way; and that way I did not have to pass the White Cross.

It was splendid running on the Greenway, the turf firm and dry and springy under my feet after the hard highway. The wind was behind me, fierce and exhilarating, the sky a piercing clear blue.

At the Dragon Pool I stopped to greet the Green Lady and ask her blessing. I figured it couldn't hurt—though the ruffians who used my distraction to capture me, alas, did.

***

They covered my head with rough sacking. It smelled strongly of dusty potatoes and magic, and I immediately started sneezing uncontrollably.

Eventually I recovered my breath. I found myself seated at the foot of a tree, bound about my chest. My wrists were tied together, but they'd left my hands free so I could do my best to cover my mouth and nose.

I wiped ineffectually at my face, wishing for one of the hand-kerchiefs in my pockets. I finally managed to blink my eyes clear.

Six ruffians—four men and two women—stood and squatted around me. All of them but one of the women were watching me in astonishment, several in disgust.

One of the men spat on the ground. "To think Ben said he fought like a true gentleman of the road."

"He did," growled another man, stalking closer. I squinted at him and decided he had been the bowman. "He took out Lonny in about three seconds."

"Huh," the first man said, scowling. "Gag him now?"

"Until the chief comes," Ben agreed, and despite my protests, so they did.

And then we all waited.

***

"We're sure it's the right man?" A large man, mainly muscle, stalked into my line of sight. His appearance, together with the suddenly-more-alert demeanour of the other ruffians, indicated that this was, at last, the chief.

Ben shrugged. "Fits the description."

"Ungag him," the chief ordered. Ben came over and fussed with the knot, which was painfully tight. I tried to hold myself still as he pinched the skin around the corners of my mouth. At length he managed to untie it, and the chief came over to stare broodingly down at me. "Could be, I suppose."

"He had a fancy red hat," someone else offered.

This suddenly registered. "You were trying to kill me on *purpose?*"

The chief spat on the ground. "We don't go round killing for fun, boyo."

"I am glad to know you have a code of professional conduct," I replied brightly. "May I ask *why* I have been so singled out? Or by whom?"

"No," said Ben, making a move as if to buffet me on the side of the head.

The chief held up his hand. "Let him be. He needs to be seen alive at one o'clock, or we don't get paid. As for you, be quiet or be entertaining or be gagged."

Ben grunted and went back to where he'd been squatting earlier. He did take out a knife and start sharpening it meaningfully in front of me. I tried to be pleased at having an adventure in the approved mode.

"Er," I said after giving Ben's whetstone its due appreciation, "since it appears we're going to be in each others' company for the next several hours, at least, let me introduce myself: I'm Jemis

Greenwing, the son of Jakory—"

I stopped at the way the chief lunged to his feet. He loomed threateningly over me. "Say that again."

I cleared my throat. "I'm Jemis Greenwing, the son of Jakory Greenwing."

There was a rumble from the other ruffians. I pressed my head against the tree trunk so I could see the chief's face. He didn't say anything, so after a moment I went on: "My father was an officer in the Seventh Army, the hero of Orkaty."

"That *bastard*," someone said in an ugly tone. If I could have moved into a fighting stance, I would have. I contented myself with glaring around the chief's legs.

"Wait," said the chief, standing back so he could regard me searchingly. "How can we be sure you're telling the truth?"

I couldn't help myself. I laughed. "Before this week, it had never occurred to me that anyone would ever want to pretend to be me. Do you meet many imposters? My grandmother gave the impression that there have been hosts, because apparently my life is a high Gothic melodrama as opposed to just a tragicomical one."

"Could be," said the chief ruffian, scowling. "What did Mad Jack take on every campaign?"

Perhaps the *bastard* in question was not my father? I coughed. "A book of haikus my mother gave him."

"He was my officer at Orkaty," the man said. "Our—employer—didn't tell us your name." He drew a knife from his belt and sliced through my bonds with three quick strikes. I tried not to flinch too obviously.

I massaged my wrists. "Thank you, sir. Did he happen to give you his?"

"Don't push it," the ruffian said, sheathing his dagger and offering me his hand.

I decided discretion was the better part of valour and nodded, though that didn't make my intense curiosity lower any. I stood, then backed away to make a formal bow, curlicues and heel-clicks included. My hat had disappeared in the capture. "Jemis Greenwing, at your service."

Well, there were still six of them.

The chief smiled with half his mouth and made a clumsy return bow. "You can call me Nibbler, and this is my gang. Now, lad, in memory of your father we're going to let you go, but there are those out there who wouldn't, eh?"

"And someone wants me dead."

It sounded totally incredible when I said it. But of course there *were* those who I presumed might want me dead: Lark for one, and the mysterious priests of the Dark Kings for two, and my uncle Vorel was still a contender for three.

By the Lady, I would be lucky to reach the Winterturn Assizes alive.

"Yes, and they're willing to pay." Nibbler jerked his chin at one of his gang. "No more questions. Moo, you take the lad back to the road."

I was still wondering if I'd heard his name correctly—nickname, surely—when he shoved me through a very narrow gap in the holly hedge and I found myself back at the Dragon Pool. The crock of honey and my hat were both on the ground, showing a certain want of tidiness on the part of Nibbler's gang.

With a wary glance around me—no one was coming in either direction, and I couldn't see anyone through the hedges, not even the retreating Moo—I picked up my hat and straightened the feather before putting it on. Then I picked up the crock of honey. While I was checking to make sure it hadn't been damaged, as astonishingly enough seemed to be the case, the wind carried the distant bells to me.

It was the half-hour chime, and I realized with a dreadful sinking feeling that there was no way at all that my little encounter with the ruffians had only taken twenty minutes.

***

If I go for a short run, an easy hour, it's a seven-mile circuit.

That's without having already run nearly ten miles carrying a crock of honey. But then again, it was only three and a half miles from the Dragon Pool to the Fair grounds.

I put out all other thoughts from my mind and concentrated on breathing.

How I loved running.

The world made sense when I ran. I made sense when I ran. Running, I needed to explain nothing, defend nothing, be nothing but what I was. My limbs obeyed me, my heart thudded as evenly as a Ghilousetten clock, my lungs drew breath and released it again without strain.

My thoughts lifted out of all concern for time. I vaulted the gate at the far end of the Greenway and swung onto the lane leading to the bridge. Across the bridge, wooden planks under my feet, and then I was back on the stone-paved road. Past the Old Arrow. Along the back lane to the tents clustered at one end of the Five-Acre Field that Master Dart gave over to the Harvest Fair each year.

There was a small wooden stand that was wheeled out from the granary every year for the race-course judges. The footraces began and ended in front of it, looping out along an ancient mile-long route around the pond.

Hal, Mr. Dart, and Roald Ragnor were standing in a cluster next to the stand. Hal saw me first, and cried, "Jemis! What happened?"

Everyone swung to stare at me. *Everyone* being my friends, the judges, and the spectators, which last appeared to contain most of the population of Ragnor Bella as well as that of Dartington.

"They've already started running," Mr. Dart said urgently, pointing off towards the right.

I thrust honey crock and coat at Hal, pushed through the crowd, and without any further thought, *ran*.

***

I caught up with the first straggler at the half-way mark.

The route was counter-clockwise around the Five-Acre Field, with the notable feature of a slow rise up to the judging stand as you made your way around the circuit. The spectators stood on both sides of the route. They appeared to be cheering, but I couldn't hear them over the sound of my own thoughts pounding out *faster ... faster ... faster* with each footfall.

I ran.

The Arguty steward's son always ran in the three-mile footrace, even though he always came last. He looked astonished when I passed him from behind.

I can run a mile in six and a half minutes. I can run three miles in nineteen.

The lagging cluster of runners had just passed the judging stand when I started passing them. Ahead of them were another clump, and then far ahead the clear leaders, six runners who were scattered all along the next half-mile arc of the course.

I ran.

I ran as if the dragon were chasing me. I ran as if I was outrunning an Indrilline assassin. I ran as if I would find myself at the end of the course.

I ran.

I passed the second cluster of runners at the halfway mark. Halfway through the race. Now there were just the six leaders.

I ran.

Third circuit. Three runners ahead of me.

I put my head down and *pushed*.

Half a mile left.

Two runners.

A quarter mile left.

One.

Ahead of me there was just Tad Finknottle, fastest man in the barony for five years in a row. He was running swiftly, steadily, apparently easily. I was gaining—ten yards between us—I put on as much of a sprint as I was still capable of—

That damned slow rise.

Chapter Twenty-Eight
The Baking Competition (Round One)

SOMEONE DUMPED A bucket of water over my head.

I spluttered, gasped, and made it back upright from where I had been bent over, hands on thighs, catching my breath. Hal and Mr. Dart were with me, a few yards away from the crowds, who were chattering madly. After a few more moments of heavy breathing, I managed to form words. My heart was still thudding painfully, and my lungs were burning.

"Water?"

Hal passed me a big wooden tankard. I gulped the first few mouthfuls, coughed and spluttered some more, and then at length felt sufficiently recovered to sip more decorously.

Ten yards or so over from where we stood, Tad Finknottle was surrounded by his own little cluster of friends. I looked away, to see that the main body of runners was only now crossing the finish line. The Honourable Rag was nowhere to be seen.

"Almost," I said, wishing I dared spit out the glob in my mouth. Hal wordlessly passed me another tankard.

Mr. Dart said, "You were behind him by three yards after a

five-minute delay."

I rolled my neck, shoulders, head. "I just didn't have enough left at the end." I sighed. "Domina Vlanotris—the cross-country games master—always said to reserve a bit."

"Where did you start running *from?*" Mr. Dart asked, passing me another tankard that someone gave him.

This one held frothy cool beer. I swallowed a few mouthfuls, wishing for more water. "This morning? Castle Noirell. But I—" I stopped, realizing there were far too many ears close by. "Never mind. Have you seen my uncle today?"

"He's been hanging off my brother and the Baron all morning."

I looked back at the stand. Sir Vorel was visible now between Master Dart and the Baron, who appeared to be arguing about something. No doubt whether I should be disqualified for joining the race late. I drank some more beer. Hal shifted the honey crock around in his arms.

"This is heavy," he said.

"Carved jade," I agreed. "Mr. White said that honey doesn't go off. If we warm the crystallized stuff up, it should be as good as ever."

"Mr. Greenwing!" Mrs. Etaris bustled up to me, bonnet askew and wisps of hair escaping from their pins. "Mr. Lingham, Mr. Dart. How was the race?"

"Second, I'm afraid," I said glumly, surprised to see her start to smile.

"That's *excellent*, Mr. Greenwing—oh my, yes indeed. Now, gentlemen, it's time—"

"For cake!" Hal laughed.

"And a few revelations," I murmured, but only Mr. Dart heard.

***

I told them about the ruffians while I started to cream the butter and sugar and Hal magically heated a small pot of milk so we could proof the yeast and a second of water in which we could warm up the honey. He had been responsible for acquiring the rest of the ingredients, which he had done in a haphazard kind of way. We had exactly the correct weight of sugar, a small cake of yeast, two and a half dozen eggs, and enough almonds to supply half the bakers.

We were the only men in the competition tent. Unlike the other cooking competitions, the cakes—always a highlight of the Fair—were made on the spot, at tables set up under a grand pavilion, then baked in the huge village bread oven. The village baker was always recused from the competition; the judges were the Squire, the Baron, and Old Mrs. Quimby, who had won the prize every time she had entered a cake until finally she had decided to permit others to have a chance.

"What do you mean, you were supposed to be seen alive at one o'clock?" Mr. Dart said. He was 'assisting' by holding our hats and coats. My shirt had more or less dried from the dowsing after the race. I was regretting my cravat's major disarray.

"Someone was setting up an alibi," Mrs. Etaris said thoughtfully. She was theoretically watching to make sure no one cheated. "Now ... what's happening at one o'clock?"

"This," said Hal.

"The horse pulls," said Mr. Dart.

"The archery contest," I said.

Mrs. Etaris raised her eyebrows. "There is also the luncheon given the dignitaries."

"I am so glad I'm here instead," Hal said, cracking the eggs into my bowl. "Beat those, Jemis, I'll start slivering the almonds. This is much more fun than being one of the judges."

"Wait till the judging commences," Mr. Dart said. "Speaking of, here they come."

Old Mrs. Quimby was in the lead. She was a small wizened gnome of a woman with iron-grey hair and iron-grey eyes, who always managed to shoehorn the fact that she remembered five Emperors into any conversation. This put her age somewhere on the north side of ninety-five, but that didn't seem to stop her any.

She planted herself in front of our table. Master Dart and the Baron stood on her either side. Master Dart was trying to keep a straight face and the Baron looked puzzled.

"But you're gentlemen," he said.

"I am trying to think," said Old Mrs. Quimby, "whether we have ever had two young men enter the baking competition before."

"They're *gentlemen*," said the Baron, a little more loudly.

"There was a fancy baker from Yellem who entered, oh, in the third year of Emperor Eritanyr's reign, but he never came back."

Mr. Dart was grinning at his brother, which wasn't helping. I decided my mixture was sufficiently fluffy, and turned to Hal. "Is the yeast ready?"

"Just about," he said, peering into the jug. "Here's the flour— how much did you want, again?"

"Two cups, please."

"Sifted or un?"

Old Mrs. Quimby tried to stick her finger into my batter. I

batted her hand away, hoping my expression looked mischievous rather than feral.

"Now let me think back through the five emperors ..."

"Here's the flour and the yeast mixture, Jemis."

Old Mrs. Quimby watched me beat everything together. She gave a critical sniff when I decided it was sufficiently mixed for our purposes. I glanced at Hal, who was blithely slivering almonds, at Mrs. Etaris, who was still trying to maintain a straight face, and at Mr. Dart, who wasn't even trying. I fished a clean cloth from Hal's basket of supplies and covered my batter with it.

"There we are," I said, smiling at Old Mrs. Quimby. "Do you need any help, Hal?"

"Just about done."

Old Mrs. Quimby said, "What kind of cake have you entered, young men?"

I gathered together our dirty utensils. "Bee Sting Cake from the Woods Noirell. It's one my mother used to make for special occasions ... Where did the crock of honey go, Hal?"

"It's under there." He pointed under the bench with his foot.

I picked up the crock and set it on the table. "And in case you were worried, it's *true* Noirell honey that we shall be using for it."

"Planning on drowning the cake, are you?" Old Mrs. Quimby said, cackling. "Carry on, young men. You're not entering a cake this year, Mrs. Etaris?"

"Not me," she said cheerfully. "I'm letting Mr. Greenwing have an open field."

"You *are* gentlemen, aren't you?" the Baron said.

Hal smiled brilliantly at him. "I'm the Imperial Duke of Fillering Pool, actually, and of course Jemis' proper title is the Viscount

St-Noire. Is that resting, Jemis? Shall we take a tour while the yeast does its work?"

The Baron was nodding, and then faltered. "The duke of—*duke*?"

Master Dart gave Mr. Dart a quelling glance that did nothing at all to stop his mirth. "Perry! Come, now, Baron, Mrs. Quimby's already on to Miss Kulfield's entry, and we don't want to be remiss, do we?"

"But a *duke*? And a *viscount*? Since when? Why are they making *cakes*?"

"Since his mother died, I imagine, and because they went to Morrowlea, I would suppose," Master Dart said, and tugged the Baron away.

***

We had a pleasant ten minutes or so wandering around looking at everyone else's baking efforts. I kept a close eye on both our batter and the crock of honey, until finally Hal said, "If it's worrying you that much, we can go back to our table."

"Yes," said Mr. Dart, "the people trying to kill you might decide to go after your cake instead."

"The thought has crossed my mind," I retorted, looking for Mrs. Etaris. My heart sank as I saw that she had been accosted by my uncle, her husband at his side as usual. "There's my uncle."

"Are you seriously worried about someone trying to spoil our entry?" Hal asked, looking at all the women—even the audience was almost all women—spread about the tent. They were definitely all keeping a close eye on us.

"There is some serious wagering going on ..." Mr. Dart said

softly. "Especially since you came second in the footrace …"

"I hope Mrs. Etaris feels we have done our portion for the Embroidery Circle."

Hal whooped. "I think you've amply repaid them for their cast-off kitchen utensils, Jemis. Stop fretting so and tell us about the riddle."

***

The only problem with this particular cake was that, being a yeasted cake, it required proofing times. After an hour we turned the batter into our cake pan, then had another half-hour to wait. Hal went over to the sink set up in a corner of the tent to wash up, becoming cornered by a group of young women as he did so.

"Does he need rescuing?" Mr. Dart asked dispassionately after a few minutes.

"I suppose he did tell everyone he was a duke …"

But neither of us moved from where we were leaning up against the table.

The Honourable Rag sauntered over. He examined our neatly arranged table with more interest than I'd have expected. "How do," he said, picking up the off-set spatula. "What's this for?"

"Spreading the pasty cream," I said.

He picked up the whisk. "And this?"

"Whisking the pastry cream."

"M'father's wandering around plaintively asking whether you're really a viscount."

"Mm."

He picked up the off-set spatula again. "What's this called?"

"An off-set spatula. Was there something you wanted?"

He waved the spatula in the air. I caught a faint whiff of ale. "Oh, depends. You giving odds?"

I took the spatula back. "I thought I was the subject of the bets?"

"Today, perhaps. There's more than one trail laid in the woods."

Mr. Dart, perhaps seeing that I was about to say something unconsidered—for I surely didn't have anything considerate to say—hastily said, "So, Roald, will you be following our Mr. Greenwing's example and enter your name next year?"

"Can't run; can't cook; what would you like?"

"Didn't you learn *anything* at Tara?"

He glanced at me, winked. "As if I'd let anyone know! Come, Mr. Dart, or we shall lose all our maidens to the visiting duke."

"It's part of the job," Mr. Dart replied, leaning back against the table so it took the weight of his stone arm.

"Better do mine, then," the Honourable Rag said, giving what I hoped was an exaggerated leer, and went off with loudly expressed and quickly-fulfilled intentions to kiss half-a-dozen Dartington girls to remind them of the attractions and minor harassments of home.

Chapter Twenty-Nine
Round Two

"THERE," SAID HAL, as the top layer settled gently onto the honeyed pastry cream with a delectable ooze.

I very carefully removed the cake knife and spatula. The top layer settled down another quarter-inch or so, did *not* tip over (as far too many early attempts at layered cakes had done), and a perfect, just absolutely perfect, amount of cream billowed out around the sides.

"That looks *splendid*," said Mr. Dart.

I went to set the utensils down, but there was no room left on our countertop. I lowered them to my sides instead, trying not to hit any item of clothing, and smiled foolishly at our cake.

"It does," said Hal after a moment, his voice judicial. "The gold leaf on the praline was a very good idea, if I do say so myself."

I went to punch him lightly on the shoulder, remembered in time I was holding a pastry-cream-coated cake knife, and desisted. "I think my mother would be proud."

"If you're *quite* done admiring your cake, Mr. Greenwing, may I have a peek?"

I laughed and turned so that Mrs. Etaris could approach the table. She was followed by the Honourable Rag, at just enough of a distance to pretend it was coincidence, not intention, that brought them along at the same time. Mrs. Etaris examined our cake for a long moment before letting out a long soundless whistle. "Well, gentlemen, I must say I am very impressed."

"You weren't expecting us to produce an edible cake?"

"That has not yet been proven," she retorted quickly, then caught my eye and laughed merrily. I reflected that this was the first time I'd really felt treated as an equal by the bookmistress, and inwardly rejoiced. Outwardly I produced another extravagant bow.

"Eh, watch that off-set spatula!" cried the Honourable Rag.

"Oh, were you listening earlier?" I said, feeling a little giddy. Too little sleep—Mr. White's superb honey wine—the long run— the ruffians—the race—and, most likely, the little bits of batter and praline and cream I had tasted to make sure the flavours worked.

The Honourable Rag examined our cake as assiduously as had Mrs. Etaris. I regarded it again: the gilded honey-coated almonds of the praline topping, the perfectly golden-brown crumb of each layer, the ivory pastry cream at just that exact height of bosomy glossiness to support the top layer without any hint of rubberiness.

"Well!" he said, and took off his gloves.

"What are you doing?" I asked, puzzled. His garnet ring—the match of mine—flashed a moment in the air, the simple flower still as much of a mystery as the magical properties of mine.

He reached out to the off-set spatula and running his finger down the edge to the collect the cream. "Not spoiling your cake, so stop fretting, Greenwing."

"I wasn't *fretting*," I muttered, daring him to try the same thing with the cake knife, but he merely turned away to greet his father with exaggerated affability.

The Baron was accompanied by Old Mrs. Quimby and Master Dart. All three of them looked astonished at our cake. I felt exceedingly smug. A glance at Hal suggested that he felt the same; somewhat to my surprise, nearly the same expression was on both Mrs. Etaris' and the Honourable Rag's faces. Mr. Dart nodded at Sir Hamish.

Old Mrs. Quimby somewhat unnecessarily elbowed her way past the Baron, planting her stick firmly in front of our table. The rest of us all backed away a few steps so that she could begin the judging, which she did by sucking on her teeth for a good minute. Master Dart, face suspiciously solemn, made a few notes in the Book of Judgment—an artifact dating back past Old Mrs. Quimby's memory, as she invariably mentioned at some point during the announcement of the finalists. The Baron merely stared, scowling. I confess his continued perturbation also made me feel somewhat smug.

Eventually Old Mrs. Quimby nodded. "You may bring it up to be tasted."

Master Dart gave her his arm, and the three judges made their way back up to the front of the tent.

"Did we make it through to the second round, then?" asked Hal, looking at the other competitors. A few were going up empty-handed and sad-demeanoured to look at the cakes that had made it through the round.

Most of the successful cakes were already at the front display table, where tradition had it they would be accessible to everyone after the judges had tasted them. As a result—and because Old Mrs.

Quimby was known to have a somewhat *salty* manner of expressing her opinions about the cakes—the sides of the pavilion had been rolled up and most of the combined populations of Dartington, Arguty, and Ragnor Bella, along with all the visitors, were crowding as close as possible. For a moment I thought I saw Nibbler the courteous highwayman amongst the throng, but he—if it was he—soon moved out of sight. Dominus Gleason elbowed his way to a prime position at the front, looking so obnoxiously smug I immediately tried to wipe my expression.

I had just turned to put the cake knife down when I smelled something burning.

I started immediately to sneeze.

"Oh, Jemis," said Hal. I twisted away from our cake, trying not to stab myself or anyone else with the knife, and saw that the burning was not from an early bonfire—nor from something left unattended in the village bread-oven—but was rather some canvas near the top of the tent.

I tried to catch my breath. "Tent!"

Mr. Dart raised his eyebrows. "I beg your pardon?"

I tried again. "Tent! Up there!" I pointed with the cake knife, but by then other people had also noticed.

No one cried 'fire'. A cloud had moved away from the sun, and with it cast a shadow sharp as a nightmare across the white canvas.

An endlessly long tail studded with spikes, its end flattening out into a shape like the ace of spades. Moving shadows across half the tent gave the impression of huge wings. And small at first, then enormous as it approached the canvas, the horn-crowned head.

Everyone stopped where they were as the little flame-licked patch of blackened canvas spread. The ashes started to drift down, and in the centre of the patch a hole appeared, brilliant in the sunlight. Then the shadow blocked out the sun, and into the relative dimness of the competition tent the dragon slid its jade-green nose.

At this point I heard the creaking of the tent's support structure under the creature's weight. Looked up to see the metal struts bending, bright-gold talons piercing the canvas around the peak pole. By the time I looked back down again the dragon was almost all the way through the rapidly-expanding hole, into an even-more-rapidly expanding space in the centre of the tent. The only person who hadn't moved was my uncle, who was staring at the dragon with an expression of absolute dread.

It came to me in a wrench of pity that dragons must have been a special fear of his. Everyone else was afraid, but he was petrified.

The dragon stepped down and began to draw its tail after it. It didn't have quite enough room, and moved over slightly. This brought my uncle into its direct line of sight.

The dragon blinked and started slowly to smile.

"Well, now," it said, "here's a pretty rabbit all ready and waiting."

Sir Vorel's face was white, his skin beaded with sweat. I could *feel* the fear flooding out of him. The dragon opened its mouth, obviously enjoying the prospect of such an easy target.

"Hey!" I said, and was briefly conscious of everyone else's shock.

The dragon snapped its head around. Sir Vorel crumpled.

"Hey!" I said again, hoping to keep its attention distracted. "What are you doing here? I answered your riddle!"

The dragon drew back its thin lips in what was not nearly so appreciative a smile. "So you did, young sir, and so I am a free dragon at last." It waved its head from side to side, blue tongue flickering out like a snake. All the people who had been crowding so close before to the display table were trying now to escape the tent, but the crush of people outside—how had they not noticed the dragon landing on the pavilion?—prevented them from leaving.

"And so you come here, why?"

It cocked its head at me. Something made a grinding noise. After a moment I realized the grinding was its talons digging through the mats laid on the grass to serve as a floor. Its voice came out as a low hiss. "I was summoned out of the Wide Dreaming to bear riddles to test the strength of the Woods in these lesser days. I was wooed with promises of the gold of the Woods. I was promised blood."

It arched its head so that its golden horns flared around it, all its spinal spikes rising up like a dog's hackles. Its eyes, so incongruously blue, so cold, so inhuman, were glittering like chips of broken glass. Its voice dropped down another note, into a deep, uncomfortable rumble that pulled me inexorably out of ordinary time into that world of mortal danger. I was conscious of nothing but the dragon, its eyes, the way it shifted its weight back to its powerful haunches, the coiling curve of its tail, some deep, deep vibration within its belly.

That fire came from somewhere.

It made a complicated movement that brought its wings back. It kept its eyes on me, trying to hold me, but with some faint awareness in my peripheral vision I saw how it was lifting its foot to pin my unmoving uncle to the ground.

"*I will take what I am owed,*" it whispered, in a whisper louder than any shout I had ever heard, and several things happened at the same time.

—Dominus Gleason and Hal both cried something in Old Shaian, though their voices jangled across each other and I could not decipher meaning—

—Mrs. Etaris reached towards her hip for a sword I had never seen her wear—

—The dragon opened its mouth—

—And I—snapped.

Chapter Thirty
I have One More Idea

WE HAD SPENT a good month on how to fight dragons in Self-Defense.

In the first lesson Dominus Lukel had discussed fighting one without armour, shield, lance, sword, or proper training. That class had been a roll-call of almost-famous heroes who had died facing definitely-famous dragons.

I had no armour, shield, lance, or sword, and as for proper training, well … Dominus Lukel didn't pretend he'd ever seen a dragon, much less fought one.

I did, however, have a cake knife.

And an off-set spatula.

I let out a wild yell of challenge and without further rational thought launched myself forward and into that clear sensible world of pure and perfect danger.

Deep in the throat of the dragon was a rising glow. Heat radiated before it, and I knew that fire was rising.

A dragon's weaknesses were the eye, the central underpart of the jaw, and the upper armpits.

Archers and lancers aimed for the upper armpits, and most often were the ones to come back victorious.

Knights who had lost their lances and their horses went for the jaw, and usually perished for their courage.

Superlative fools went for the eye, because it seemed like the easiest target, and regretted it very much when their arrows went out the back of the skull without hitting the brain, which in a dragon was set very deep towards the spine, far below the nasal hollows under the crown of spines.

I decided in the split second in which such decisions are made that I had no chance of reaching either armpit, that sticking a knife into a jaw full of dragonfire was a recipe for total disaster, and that really, everyone in Ragnor Bella was already in agreement that I was a fool, so I might as well aim to be a superlative one.

Also, I *did* know where the brain was.

I vaulted over our table and onto the one in front of us.

The dragon was moving with slow deliberation. It was unhurried, knew I was hardly a threat to be concerned with, not with fire rising in its throat. Not with a mouth full of hand-length razor-sharp teeth. Not with golden claws lifting over the huddled figure of my uncle to sweep round at me.

I threw the off-set spatula into its mouth, hitting the back of its throat with as much force as I could. The dragon swallowed automatically, confusion and anger warring for a brief moment as the spatula went down into whatever devil's brew of acid and fire was boiling in its stomachs.

The anatomy books had not been clear as to whether dragons had separate stomachs for fire and eating or if the digestive juices were so caustic they lit when exposed to air.

The dragon had lifted its head to swallow, giving me a split second again to decide between throat and eye. But I knew how hard it was to kill a dragon, that there was an asbestos palate-bone protecting the brain from the fires passing below, that the throat was bulging as those fires rose.

Another half-thought as I rolled off that table and under the grasping talons, dove in a running somersault over my uncle, launched myself up onto the table on the other side of the aisle. If I succeeded—*if I succeeded*—we could anatomize the dragon and find out.

The dragon had swallowed the spatula now and was turning, but it was turning slowly, its anger and its bulk making it sweep its tail out across the room, knocking over people, tables, and cakes with equal abandon. I heard the crashes as from a great distance. My mind was focused on the not-quite-blunt point of my cake knife and that single spot at the back of the eye socket where the optic nerves led straight down to the brain.

The dragon reared its head back. I waited, knees slightly bent, feet in the classic fencer's stance, stomach taut, left hand out for balance, right hand holding the cake knife at the ready.

This was almost as good as running.

The dragon launched itself forward in one all-out motion, mouth wide enough to swallow me whole—so long as I went in sideways, and so as it came the dragon twisted its head slightly to the side, so that instead of coming at me with its horns high above me, they were just to my left in a laddered semi-circle.

At some moment I could never have rationally analyzed I jumped up and sideways, grabbed one of the horns with my left hand, swung myself onto the bridge of its nose, and even as its teeth closed with an almighty crash where I had been standing I was using my momentum to plunge that cake knife all the way up to its hilt in—and *down*—through its eye.

Even as I shuddered at the cold jelly suddenly exploding all up my right hand and arm I was gripping the hilt more and more tightly, adding my left hand to force the knife through some barrier as the dragon flung its head wildly in the air. I gripped its snout with my knees as if I were riding a bucking horse, grimly determined to get the knife through its brain, and was only barely conscious of how much I was moving until with a finally tremendous jerk the I was flung hard into a rising incongruous sea of cinnamon and chocolate.

***

I sat up slowly, regretting it as the world spun around me. I closed my eyes and concentrated first on breathing, and secondly on massaging the feeling back into my hands. After a moment, I registered that something was dripping all down my face.

I had received a few head wounds, most courtesy of an over-enthusiastic Roald or Mr. Dart when we were boys, and my first coherent thought was that it must be a bad one to be streaming so much blood that my eyes were already all crusted over. I fumbled wearily in my pocket for a handkerchief and carefully wiped my eyes. Blinked numerous times to clear them, and finally stared at the brown and purple mess on the cotton in my hand.

"It's Mrs. Kulfield's Blackberry Chocolate Cake," said Mrs. Etaris, her voice soothingly normal.

I nodded without looking up. Touched my fingers to a wet patch above my ear. That was very red when I took it away, but

Mrs. Etaris went on, still very calmly, "And that is probably Miss Torrow's Sour Cherry and Hazelnut Torte."

I took a deep breath. "And the cinnamon?"

"I believe that would be Mrs. Jarnem's Quincy Apple Cake."

I took another deep breath, nodded a little too vigorously, crumpled the handkerchief up. "My uncle?"

"He appears to be unharmed."

I nodded again. Swallowed what seemed to be a mixture of honey cream and blood. "The dragon?"

"Oh, very certainly dead, Mr. Greenwing."

Her voice was *so* soothingly normal I looked automatically up to catch the merriment in her eyes. Her mirth was so contagious I smiled lopsidedly and raised my head to survey the scene before me.

My first thought was how totally *smashed* the baking pavilion was. Tables were flung hither and yon, many of them in splinters. I was sitting in the ruins of what had been the display table, cakes of all sort in all forms of disarray under and around me. Mrs. Etaris stood slightly to my right, beside the dragon's head.

I blinked again.

Mrs. Etaris was wearing the striped green dress she had been wearing that morning. She had somehow contrived not to be splashed by anything, and apart from her location—*right beside a dragon's head*—she looked almost—almost *damnably* ordinary. Yet she was calm, and matter-of-fact, and alone of all the people in my field of vision had been the one reaching for a weapon when the dragon arrived.

She had not had a sword at her belt, as presumably had become habit during her days as a student in the siege of Galderon. She was the bookmistress, the wife of the town constable, a prominent member of the Embroidery Circle.

She was patting the nose of the dragon.

I followed her motion up to the collapsed eye. The hilt of the cake knife was buried deep into the back of the eye socket, much farther in that I remembered being able to push it. "It was stuck on something," I said foolishly, staring at it. "There's such a small opening for the optic nerve—I thought I'd missed—"

"Dominus Lukel would be *very* proud," Hal said, coming up behind Mrs. Etaris. To my total astonishment he was still holding our cake. "We'll have to write to tell him that month he spent on dragon-slaying came in useful."

Mrs. Etaris smiled and stepped aside, revealing Mr. Dart hastening up behind Hal.

"Jemis! Are you a *complete* idiot?"

"Yes," I mumbled. "Is that our cake?"

"You got that knife all the way through the back of the skull."

"It was stuck. I had to make sure it got into the brain."

"Oh, you did that," Hal assured me, grinning.

"Lost your off-set spatula," said the Honourable Rag from right behind me. I jumped violently, finding myself somewhat unexpectedly on my feet. I reeled, was braced by Mrs. Etaris, and consequently smeared various cake components down her sleeve.

"Oh, no, I'm sorry, Mrs. Etaris."

"Dragon-slaying is somewhat notoriously messy, Mr. Greenwing. That is why it is usually done far from the haunts of men."

The lines sounded like something out of Fitzroy Angursell, but I couldn't place them. "Er, I didn't have time to draw it off."

"Young man!" came the high cackle of Old Mrs. Quimby.

"You have ruined *all the cakes!*"

"Except theirs," said the Honourable Rag. "It's very convenient."

Old Mrs. Quimby stalked towards me like an avenging goddess (albeit a somewhat decrepit one), one hand hanging off Master Dart's arm, other waving her stick in the air and nearly walloping first my uncle, then Dominus Gleason, and then the Baron, all of whom were making their way towards me.

My uncle's dumbfounded expression as he looked at the dragon was one I was sure I would cherish for the rest of my life. He halted a good ten feet away and started to sway. We all watched him without moving, to see whether he would faint or vomit or sound forth encomia or prophecies, but when he raised his shaking hand and pointed, it was not at the dragon, but behind me.

Chapter Thirty-One
The Honourable Rag has No Idea

THE BAKING PAVILION—or what remained of it by this stage of the proceedings—was quite close to the road. This meant that the coach-and-six that was thundering towards us was indeed thundering directly towards us.

The coach was black.

The harness was black.

The horses were black.

Whatever device might have been on the door was hidden by black crêpe.

It galloped towards us in a great rattle of of chains and couplings all accompanied by an unearthly two-tone groaning wail. The wail rose to a screech as the coachman hauled back on the reins, forcing the horses to sit nearly on their haunches to stop the carriage as it swung around to present its broad side at us.

The horses, snorted and panting, heaved themselves into a semblance of order, the coachman released his iron grip on their reins, and there was for a moment silence.

"If that is Lady Death," said Mr. Dart, "she needs to grease her axle."

Somewhere above us part of the pavilion structure fell down and landed on a bowl with a tinny ringing sound.

A footman jumped off the back of the carriage, hurried round to let down the steps, opened the door, and then stood beside it in rigid terror.

Apparently satisfied that our attention was sufficiently gathered away from the distractions of a recently-deceased dragon and a destroyed cake competition, my grandmother disembarked.

***

She had made an effort, I saw immediately: was dressed no longer in the filthy court gown of my earlier encounters, but in a different court gown of equal antiquity, sumptuousness, and incongruity. This one was made of stiff green silk with an overlay of ivory lace. It had what must have been steel-hooped corseting and a décolletage I found slightly uncomfortably low for my grandmother, especially as she emphasized the low cut with a necklace composed of three loops of emeralds interspersed with pearls.

She wore the whole parure, I realized after a moment: emerald tiara nestled into an elaborately curled hairdo, emerald earrings, rings on every finger. And she had changed her makeup: her lips were still brilliant red and her face white with that rice powder or arsenic, but she had chosen a slightly softer pink for her eyelids.

She still held the ebony walking stick.

She paused a moment at the bottom of her carriage steps, looking around the scene before her with those sharp brown eyes. She passed over both me and the dragon, paused briefly at Hal, continued on. After a moment she focused on the Baron, who was standing next to Master Dart and convulsively wringing his hands in a handkerchief. I felt a moment's pity for him; he hated anything to be unhygienic. Master Dart himself appeared nonplussed.

"Baron Ragnor," the Marchioness said. Her voice was stronger than it had been, easily piercing all the low buzz of whispers. "You look just as foolish as ever. Whatever have you been doing with yourself? This Fair is not as I recall."

The Baron kept wringing his hands, and added shaking his head wordlessly from side to side.

"We were surprised to be interrupted by a dragon," said Master Dart. "I'm not certain if you will remember me, Lady Noirell: I am Torquin Dart, Squire of Dartington. I was good friends with Jack Greenwing and your daughter the Lady Olive."

"I am here for my grandson," she announced, causing a fair stir among the crowd, who all turned to face me. I blinked and blushed as my grandmother stomped over, ignoring broken plates and broken cakes and broken furniture with equal aplomb. She stopped a couple of feet away to pull out her lorgnette and give me yet another piercing once-over. "I see my fears have been realized," she announced. "Your appearance is a *complete* disgrace."

Someone in the crowd of people hovering safely on the far side of the dragon giggled.

I felt my numbness start to dissipate under this barrage of un-expected criticism. My voice came out tartly. "I do apologize for not having realized I ought to have been dressed for a court ball this afternoon, Lady Noirell, but I'm afraid it seemed better to me this morning to dress appropriately for my day's activities. I did not intend to fight a dragon in the midst of these, but, well, as Mrs. Etaris mentioned just now, that's an untidy business and if I had been better organized no doubt I would have managed to do so somewhere less public."

The Marchioness stared at me, lips pursed tight, for a long, long moment. Then she cackled. "Come here, my boy, you have leave to kiss your grandmother. Fought a dragon, did you?"

Kissing my grandmother was not high on my list of objectives for the day, but I obediently crossed over the feet between us and gave her a light peck on the cheek, hoping as I did so that people didn't *really* use arsenic powder for make-up.

But even I knew that in the game of Poacher that was life, that invitation and that gesture was a Hand hardly to be beaten.

The Marchioness had lifted her lorgnette to survey the dragon. "Mmph," she said, or rather snorted. "You have successfully proven yourself to be the true heir to the Woods Noirell. Leave this carcass and this foolish embroilment of yourself with the lower classes. You have much to learn. Give me your arm to the carriage."

I was feeling somewhat stunned on numerous counts, but not so stunned that I was prepared to go meekly with *that* invitation. "I beg your pardon, Lady Noirell?"

"You may call me Grandmama," she said, with no softening whatsoever of her demeanour. "Do not be a fool: now that you are acknowledged as the Viscount St-Noire, you must learn what your duties are."

I took a breath. "While I do not deny that I have responsibilities as the—as the heir, you cannot mean for me to go with you this instant?"

"Of course. There is no time to lose. What could be more important?"

I bit back my first response, which was *Practically everything*— for that wasn't quite what I meant. I did think it very important

that the people, and indeed the bees, and presumably also the rest
of the natural habitat, of the Woods were properly cared for—and
I certainly had a great deal to learn about what it meant to be an
imperial viscount—but to leave *right then*?

"I can't leave everyone to clean up my mess," I protested, gesturing at the dragon. "We should invite Scholars of anatomy or
legendary creatures or—or—I don't even know—but there will
be Scholars who want to study the dragon, anyway. We ought to
inform them—and I have a friend visiting—and—" With a great
uprush of relief I remembered— "And I have work next week."

The Marchioness stared at me some more through her lorgnette. Hal came up to stand next me, as quietly and as meaningfully as he had when I stood up for my father against Lark, against the
whole studentry of Morrowlea, against the world. She examined
him, then made a visibly painful attempt at compromise. "Your
friend is the Duke of Fillering Pool? *He* is welcome to my house,
of course."

Hal bowed, bearing instantly fully ducal. I wondered what he
had done with the cake. "You do me honour, ma'am. Nevertheless, I have already been offered, and accepted, Jemis'—Lord St.
Noire's—offer of hospitality, which I trust he will extend through
to Winterturn."

"*His* hospitality! He has no property of his own."

"He has lodging in town, ma'am, which I find most comfortable." He smiled at her, still regally, but with the engaging air that
belonged to what I thought of as the *real* Hal. Except that Hal did
not seem to feel any contradiction between being Duke and being
Hal—

—How, I wondered suddenly, could he *possibly* think I was

more of a radical than he?

"As I am certain you will understand, Jemis needs a degree of basic education in both magic and what it means to have an imperial title in Rondé as it is now, after the Fall, which I am both perfectly suited and most willing to provide. You and your people have been under a curse for a number of years, and you need to rest, gather your resources, and prepare yourself for the higher-level teaching you are the only one able to provide."

I found my attention wandering back to the dragon. I was feeling rather shaky and wished there was somewhere to sit down, and possibly something to drink. I was pondering the rival benefits of beer versus coffee when I discovered Mrs. Etaris was again standing beside me.

"You were reaching for a sword," I blurted, though quietly. Distantly I watched Hal widening the circle of his charm to include the Baron and my uncle, who had finally recovered enough to greet the Marchioness.

Mrs. Etaris smiled, a little ruefully. "I was wondering if anyone noticed. It was foolish of me—it's not as if I've held a sword for many years."

"Was it your first dragon?"

She laughed. "Mr. Greenwing, have I told you how much I enjoy your sense of humour?"

I glanced sidelong at her. "I thought you believed me a cynic?"

Her face was still smiling, but her eyes, though sharp, were also kind. "The trials you have undergone to win the Woods—if I may be so alliterative—seem to have brought you more fully into yourself, Mr. Greenwing."

Hal was now explaining how he intended to pursue a full study of the Woods flora as his post-baccalaureate monograph ('while I wait for my ship to return from its expedition to the Far West'), and how fortunate he felt himself to have come in time to see the famous Tillarny limes in their autumn blossom.

I said to Mrs. Etaris, "You were the only one also moving to attack ..."

"And you were the one who slew the dragon," she replied. "*And* serendipitously—for I presume you were not anticipating this end to the competition?—completely spiked the gambling ring. Very well done indeed, Mr. Greenwing. I think—yes—I really think I must give you a raise. Consider your trial period over. Unless you would prefer to move to the Woods?"

I glanced sidelong at her again. She was smiling. I found my heart lifting. "And undo all Hal's good work? How could I?"

***

After borrowing yet more of Mr. Dart's clothes, we—Mr. Dart, Hal, and I—removed ourselves from the more raucous celebrations to a quiet distance from the bonfire lit in the centre of the fairgrounds. Just before I quite got down to the grass—for I felt sore all over, and was sure to be full of bruises on the morrow—I saw the Honourable Rag waving at me from near the ale barrel.

"I'd best go see what he wants," I muttered, and ambled over. I couldn't have gone much faster than that if the dragon had resuscitated itself and come chasing me, I was afraid. I felt nearly completely exhausted.

"We'll save you a piece of cake," Hal called from behind me. I waved my hand desultorily. I wasn't sure I'd care if I never saw another cake again.

The Honourable Rag offered me a tankard brimming full of ale. I accepted it with a murmur of thanks. He drew himself another, handling the common alehouse barrel and bung with ease, and then gestured me away from the lantern-lit table to a spot under the Fair Oak.

He checked that no one was using it for any purpose, covert or otherwise. The oak was a favoured spot at the Midsomer festival. I leaned against the bark and sipped the ale and thought about the insurmountable distance still remaining between me and bed.

"Well, Greenwing," said the Honourable Rag. "I owe you a cut of my winnings."

That was not what I'd expected him to say. "Oh?"

He shrugged, smirking a little the way he did so often now, pulled out a little purse visibly heavy. "Earned back all my debts and then some, backing you."

"To win or lose?"

"I'd've been a fool like the rest, either way, wouldn't I?" he said, chuckling.

I sipped my ale and made no move to take his purse. "Tell me, Roald, how do you know it wasn't my fault I was late for the three-mile race?"

I couldn't see his face well in the dim light. I could hear him chuckle though, a sound like his smirk—like silver-plated tin when you wished for, expected, *needed* silver.

"Do you really think I'm so stupid, Jemis?"

"No, I don't," I replied, anger rising at his light mockery, at the waste—at him being such a *drone*—

—Was struck suddenly by the memory of my mother explaining that the apparently useless drones had a fundamentally important role to play in the existence of the hive, and that this was so macrocosm and microcosm.

And three things connected, in a moment like the last hand at Poacher when the Emperor Card is laid down to reward or ruin all, and I said: "You backed me neither to win nor to lose, but somehow to contrive to demolish the competition entirely, didn't you? Were the highwaymen somewhere among the crowd to act if nothing else occurred? Come to think of it, I *saw* Nibbler, just before the fight started."

There was a pause. Singing rose up from near the bonfire, and the smell of sausages sizzling reminded me that I had expended an unusual amount of energy today, and would be courting trouble if I didn't get food and water inside me soon.

I could see the Honourable Rag's astonished and delighted grin from the light reflected on his teeth. Then he cast back his head and laughed uninhibitedly.

"*Good* boy."

Note

Bee Sting Cake *is the second book of Greenwing & Dart. Book Three,* Whiskeyjack, *finds Mr. Dart fending off enquiries about his inner life and Mr. Greenwing fending off accusations of murder.*

Please visit the author's website, www.victoriagoddard.ca, for the opportunity to join her newsletter, to be informed about new releases and to receive a free short story, "Stone Speaks to Stone," the true tale of what happend to Major Jakory Greenwing at Loe.

Made in the USA
San Bernardino, CA
14 February 2018